Rosie Talbot (she/her) belongs to the leafy wilds of Sussex, England, where she works as a bookseller. A lover of the spooky and macabre, Rosie writes stories that are like her hair: dark, twisted and certainly not straight. When not writing, she can be found obsessing about books on BookTok, or curled up with tea and cats, reading through her endless TBR. *Sixteen Souls*, her first novel, was an instant bestseller.

You can connect with Rosie at @merrowchild via TikTok, Instagram and X, or on her website www.rosietalbot.co.uk where you can sign up to her scintillating newsletter and gain access to free stories and artwork.

Praise for *Sixteen Souls*

"*Lockwood & Co.* meets *The Taking of Jake Livingstone* by way of York's most haunted landmarks, *Sixteen Souls* delivers fun and frights in equal measure. A fantastically spooky, thrilling adventure"
Kat Ellis, author of *Wicked Little Deeds*

"*Sixteen Souls* is the perfect mix of eerie and heart-warming. With vivid characters, fierce friendships and flawless twists, this book immediately pulled me in – I laughed, teared up and could not put it down. YA fantasy readers and ghost-story lovers, this is for you"
H.M. Long, author of *Hall of Smoke and Temple of No God*

"A captivating take of loss, friendship and love that had me gripped from first to last. I finished it with a smile on my lips and a tear in my eye"
Menna van Praag, author of *The Sisters Grimm*

"A gorgeously written debut that had me absolutely gripped. Rosie Talbot has created a deliciously creepy world with characters that you'll fall in love with"
Amy McCaw, author of *Mina and the Undead*

"I never have a problem screaming about books I genuinely love, and I love this book. The author's ability to evoke entire settings with minimal details is just amazing. The writing is rich; the characters sharply drawn. Welcome to the world, Charlie Frith – I can't wait to watch other readers fall in love with you. The only thing that made me scream louder than this book was finding out there will be a sequel"
K.D. Edwards, author of *The Tarot Sequence Series*

"Imagine a story that has all the character of York, then fill it with all the ghosts from there too … and whilst you're at it make it QUEER. Perfect if you like books like *Cemetery Boys*, *Ninth House*, *The Fell of Dark* and *The Taking of Jake Livingstone*"
Rory Michaelson, author of *Lesser Known Monsters*

"*Sixteen Souls* is a boundlessly clever, heartfelt queer take on the story of a sensitive young man who sees dead people. Talbot has crafted something chillingly delightful! Perfect for any ghoul-lover's shelf"
Adam Sass, award-winning author of *Surrender Your Sons* and *The 99 Boyfriends of Micah Summers*

"*Sixteen Souls* was ridiculously easy to fall in love with. Victorian ghosts, a delectable mystery, a luscious York setting, and an irresistible queer friendship and romance, *Sixteen Souls* is a perfect read for fans of Gaiman and Stroud. I wish I could read it for the first time again!"
Dawn Kurtagich, author of *The Dead House*

"*Sixteen Souls* transported me so entirely, I feel as if I have walked the streets of York and seen the ghosts myself. An outstanding debut, this thrilling adventure perfectly mixes spookiness with mystery, sadness with love, and is filled with gorgeous characters you won't want to say goodbye to"
Bex Hogan, author of *Isles of Storm and Sorrow* series

"A deliciously dark debut from Rosie Talbot. I dare you not to fall in love with Charlie and his ghosts in the heart of haunted York"
Cynthia Murphy, author of *Last One to Die* and *Win Lose Kill Die*

Please be aware that some of the material in this story contains themes or events of death/dying, gore and body horror, blood magic, violence, kidnapping, imprisonment and murder. For a full list of content warnings please visit **www.rosietalbot.co.uk**

WE THREE WITCHES

ROSIE TALBOT

■SCHOLASTIC

Published in the UK by Scholastic, 2025
Scholastic, Bosworth Avenue, Warwick, CV34 6UQ
Scholastic Ireland, 89E Lagan Road, Dublin Industrial Estate, Glasnevin, Dublin, D11 HP5F

SCHOLASTIC and associated logos are trademarks and/or
registered trademarks of Scholastic Inc.

Text, inside illustrations and author photograph © Rosie Talbot, 2025

The moral rights of the author have been asserted by them.

ISBN 978 0702 33341 5

A CIP catalogue record for this book is available from the British Library.

All rights reserved.
This book is sold subject to the condition that it shall not, by way of trade or otherwise,
be lent, hired out or otherwise circulated in any form of binding or cover other than
that in which it is published. No part of this publication may be reproduced, stored in a
retrieval system, or transmitted in any form or by any other means (electronic, mechanical,
photocopying, recording or otherwise), or used to train any artificial intelligence
technologies without prior written permission of Scholastic Limited. Subject to EU law,
Scholastic Limited expressly reserves this work from the text and data-mining exception.

Printed in the UK
Paper made from wood grown in sustainable forests and other controlled sources.

10 9 8 7 6 5 4 3 2 1

This is a work of fiction. Any resemblance to actual people,
events or locales is entirely coincidental.

The publisher does not have any control over and does not assume any
responsibility for any third-party websites or other platforms, or their content.

www.scholastic.co.uk

For safety or quality concerns:
UK: www.scholastic.co.uk/productinformation
EU: www.scholastic.ie/productinformation

For the dead.
Are you guys OK?

PROLOGUE

T̶H̶ESE VIOLEN̶T̶ DELIGH̶T̶S HAVE VIOLEN̶T̶ ENDS

I am the first to notice the breeze. It ripples at the candle flames and stirs goosebumps across my skin. The early July air is cloying at night but the thick brick walls of my pa's art studio contain a chill that not even the hottest summer can dispel. Although it is one of my favourite places, I'm unsettled. There is a strange reverberance in the air that makes me look from the knucklebones in my palm, and my last-minute reading, to the circular table we have set up beneath the peak of the high roof.

Usually, I work my divination in my clients' homes, but my current patron, Mrs Aldridge, seems nervous and asked to meet elsewhere. I couldn't very well invite her to our little flat above the garage for it is hardly impressive, and I couldn't impose on Mr Spicer – Pa's art dealer, Bea's father and an old family friend – but the studio Pa paints in has always had a certain magic, especially in candlelight.

Bea insisted on the candles, and that the coven come along this evening to help set up the space. She's strung dried herbs in bunches from the rafters to scent the air, and arranged witch bottles on the nearby sideboard for dramatic effect, as I do not need to tap into their stored essence to read the bones. She hums along to the Cavendish Three on the wireless as she lights the candles on the table.

"There," she announces, satisfied. "I think it's just the thing."

"It does look good," Bea's cousin Merle agrees. "No client will doubt that you are a real soothsayer."

"Of course not; Viola's prophecies are always spot on." Bea smiles at me. "No one reads the bones quite like her." There seems a sharp edge to her smile tonight. Perhaps it is only the light. The myriad candles she has laid out and lit cast a wrought, flickering glow over her face, and the faces of those staring down at us.

We are surrounded by witches: Circe, Medea, Pasiphae – the mother of the minotaur – Morgana Le Fay, Hecate and Grimhilde. My coven sisters all sat for the monumental paintings. I gave Circe my scowl and Edie posed for Medea. Bea sat for Morgana and Merle is immortalized as Hecate. Even my brother Theo got involved when he came home for the holidays, sitting for the figure of Poseidon cursing Pasiphae. The six giant panels are destined for the dining room of a luxury ocean liner. Pa has been working on them for the better part of two years and he plans to complete them within the next month.

I check the time: ten to nine in the evening. My client should be here any moment.

"Vi, can you ... feel that?" Edie frowns.

I hesitate, slipping the knucklebones into my pocket.

Feel what?

Suddenly, the scent of aromatic amber, cinnamon and saffron swallows me. Heat blisters a patch of air by the table. A nearby candle melts, sending a cascade of wax and flame down the cloth draped over the table. Several others follow in a gush of bubbling fuel and flame. Smoke billows up instantly, thick and dark.

The fire spreads quickly. In the time it takes for me to shout Edie's name, flames have jumped to the blue fabric backdrop and engulfed the canvas beside it. Years of Pa's work is destroyed in seconds. The fire is hungry for oil paint and varnish. The roar in my ears is overwhelming. I can't breathe. Smoke laced with poisonous gases from the paints and chemicals blackens the air. Edie has grabbed on to Bea, who is screaming in panic. We fall to all fours, hacking and coughing. My mind is a stunned, empty thing incapable of processing this nightmare.

The paintings are burning. *Are we burning?*

Merle's voice cuts through the cracking of the fire. I hear her scream, "Out!" and, "Follow me," but the rest is lost in the roar and groan of the blistering flames. The fire is everywhere. Smoke stings my eyes something fierce and when I try to clear them it just grinds the chemicals in. Someone grips my blouse. Edie. Through my tears I can see enough to know that we're close to the door and my heart thrums with relief. My head is spinning, body starved of vital air as the smoke infiltrates my lungs.

We've stopped and I don't understand why. Where is the door? A thumping noise sounds, rhythmic but weak. Bea is on her knees, one arm over her face, pounding on the wood.

It's closed. Why? Why is the door closed?

Forcing my limbs to obey, I drag myself from the floor and push my weight into the heavy oak. It won't budge. Edie says something but I can't hear her over the greedy growl of the fire and the pulse of blood in my ears. *Where is Merle? Did she get out?*

Reaching the door handle means standing in the thickest part of the smoke. Edie slumps beside Bea. They're both exhausted and gasping and I know I have to act or we three will die tonight.

Covering my nose and mouth with my sleeve, I scramble up, desperately searching for the handle. I can't see a thing and my lungs are burning. I find metal. It's cooler under my fingers and I think that is a good sign. Pull down, push forward, my muscles screaming, shoulder grinding painfully as it hits wood that might as well be solid stone for how little it yields. The door won't open. I yell for help and my aching chest fills with noxious smoke…

I'm falling.

Edie is above me, wreathed in flame.

Reaching up, I stroke my fingers down her cheek as the darkness closes in.

The day I died I rolled the bones for my fate.
I never saw death coming.

PART I
SOMA

The first bone of the set, the soma, represents the physical body and, by extension, the physical world.

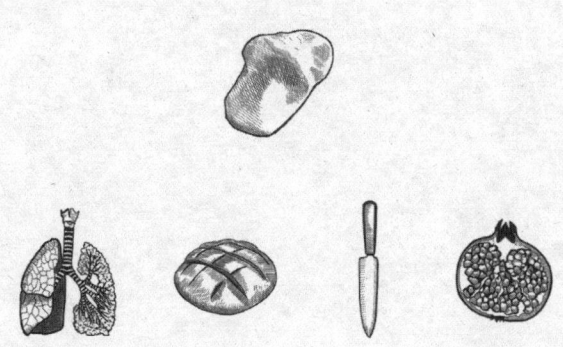

Lungs: the body/self-care/protection/health/inheritance/roots/prevention. Positive.
Bread: nourishment/hunger/physical need/sharing/to end a fast/generosity/respect/wellness. Negative.
Knife: death/injury/physical sickness/strife/war/cruelty/a task/purpose/power/honour/masculinity/precision/trust. Negative.
Pomegranate: life/fertility/pleasure/desire/reward/resurrection/femininity/sanctity/abundance/beauty/healing/health/childbirth. Positive.

I

THROWING THE BONES

I send out the invitations a week after the funeral, penned in black ink on cream card with a black-and-grey feather and a small sprig of rosemary tucked into each envelope. The rendezvous with my coven is at Betty's Tea Rooms on St Helen's Square. The newly opened cafe is very fashionable. Mirrors bounce light over fine sunbursts of wooden inlay, clean geometrics and etched glass. The cakes are small and pretty, scenting the air with rose and caramel.

Worry turns my stomach. They'll wonder why we're not meeting in the attic at Mr Spicer's, the birthplace of our little coven, but I need neutral ground in case this goes badly.

The day I died I saw what I wished to see, my arrogance clouding my judgement. I can't make that mistake twice. Let the girls think whatever they wish but I need them to listen to me.

"Miss Viola Sampire," I say to the server. "I have a reservation."

As I am shown to our table – well situated with a fine view of Davygate and St Helen's Church – I realize I'm the first to arrive.

It's unusual. Bea is always late, but Merle is on a schedule that runs a full half-hour ahead of everyone else. I expected her to be waiting, lips pursed beneath her severe brow, her choice of clothing shocking, or amusing, the establishment. There is nothing I can do but sit, smooth down my dress, pull my lips into a half-convincing smile, and wait.

There are – *were* – four of us in our little coven, a mismatch of girls drawn by the promise of power against a world that is determined not to give us any. It started with Bea: Beatrice Spicer, the daughter of Pa's art dealer and friend. Her father represents living artists like my pa, but also deals in more unusual esoteric items. Those that don't immediately find a buyer are kept in the attic, a large space that runs the breadth of their townhouse. Bea and I started playing there as children. We'd sneak up after lunch when the adults got to talking over coffee. It was not expressly forbidden, and so long as we didn't break anything, we had the run of the place.

Memories of our time in her attic among old parchment, herbs and candle wax are the happiest of my life. We explored the contents stored on the heavy bookshelves or in the dark wood cabinets and found historic divination sets, dowsing rods, empty glass bottles marked with red wax, and a library of old books with wonderful titles such as *Exploratory Theorems*, *Walking with Ghosts* and *The Witch in Fortune and Magic*.

Over the next few years we found an even greater distraction: ancient and arcane knowledge. Magic – or the promise of it, at least.

When Bea's slightly older cousin Merle came to live with her relatives and grew curious about the time we spent in the attic, our little coven was born. The quartet was complete when Edie, a friend of Bea's from school, was invited in two years later. I was jealous of her at first, guarded and sour that she'd infiltrated our trio, but she's too charming to come between anyone. Edie is a mouth full of poetry, fine hairs at the base of her neck, her laugh – close and eager. Our group naturally grew to encompass her, and soon I couldn't imagine our lives without her. I still can't.

I let the atmosphere of the tea rooms swallow me, ignoring the ache in my lungs. There are a number of nasty compounds in oil paint and turpentine that have seared my throat and weakened my voice. The doctors say I might never fully recover from the damage inflicted by the chemical-rich smoke.

It's been five weeks since the fire.

We should have buried her sooner, I think. But we had to wait for the investigation to determine a cause of death: asphyxiation from smoke inhalation from a fire caused by a spilled candle that caught on a tablecloth and spread faster than anyone imagined possible.

One girl dead. One brought back from the brink. Me. A building destroyed. My father's career in tatters. The report ruled it an accident.

After a fortnight in the hospital, I moved back to my family flat on Blossom Street to recover at home. Bea and Merle visited often but Edie came to see me every day. She held my hand and stroked my hair and coaxed me to take another sip of chicken broth when the only thing I wanted to do was sleep. She stayed all night most nights.

At the time I wondered why her unusually strict parents were letting her spend so long with me. They don't approve of our friendship. I once heard Mrs Turner refer to me as "an unnatural bohemian influence". After the fire, I was too grateful to look closely or ask too many questions. It was enough that she was there to drag me out of the hot flames of my nightmares.

That should have been the first clue.

Now, of course, I see far more clearly.

Glancing from under my lashes, I take note of the diners and servers at Betty's, searching for the people that only weeks ago were completely invisible to me.

I'm sure that, if the other diners could see her, they would think the grandeur of the tea rooms quite ruined by the poor dead girl trying to steal a lemon cake from the afternoon tea stand on the table beside mine. Naturally, she comes away empty-handed, her face bunching in displeasure.

"No treats for you today," I whisper, offering the child a friendly smile.

Her eyes go wide. She's a petite thing in a cotton nightgown and little slippers.

"Yes, I see you." I don't bother to whisper this time.

The ghost girl backs away. She runs, falling against another ghost at the doorway. A smart gentleman ghost wearing a black doublet with fine pewter buttons wrinkles his nose and ushers the child away before moving through the tea rooms with his companion, a woman in a pearl-studded hairnet and a high-necked ruff.

In the weeks since the fire it's become clear to me that spirits don't appear like storybook spectres: heavy with clanking chains, their luminescent skin peeling to reveal mouldering bones or grotesque features. And they're not wisps or disembodied voices or flickers of light at the corner of my vision. They look just like the living, so much so that unless they are wearing historical garb it is hard sometimes to know who is dead and who is not.

Several living people are looking at me, probably wondering why I reassured an empty patch of air. My cheeks flush a little but I catch myself. It's silly to worry what they think when I'm witness to proof of consciousness after death. I've always believed that earthbound souls exist, the countless books on magic that I've read attest to that. But to *see* them, to speak to them, to touch them and have them feel as solid to me as any living person? That is truly remarkable. I give the ladies at the adjacent table a soft smile.

I'm still debating my decision to speak to Bea and Merle today. Edie assured me that my new-found ability will be cause for celebration, with Merle digging out old texts to research my gift, and Bea asking a thousand questions and wanting to know what it is like. I had agreed, but now I'm not so sure.

Where are they?

The uncomfortable prickle of humiliation blooms up the back of my neck, creeping across my cheeks. What if the coven doesn't come when I need them most – when *Edie* needs them? Outside, Edie lurks in the shadow of the church. I asked her not to come inside. I need to do this alone.

I clear a space on my table and take out my set of knucklebones, so called for the long tradition of reading fortunes in animal bones. My precious set is unusual, made from the eight carpal bones in the human hand. Rolling them in my palm, they grind and clatter against each other like dice rattling at the gambler's table. No matter how long I handle them, they're always cool, even after being pressed beside my body in their velvet pouch.

"Will the coven meet me here?" My voice is barely a whisper as I toss the pieces high and close my eyes. The movement of the bones sears the softness behind my eyelids, scattering shifts of red as they fall. Sinking, I find the place where rituals bloom and thrive, a lake within my chest where each tumble sends out ripples of meaning.

"*The place where the spirits speak*," Merle once told me.

Except, I'm no longer sure that this feeling has anything to do with spirits. We believed the dead were the force guiding my castings but now I know that I don't need to be near a ghost for the bones to roll true. I'm starting to doubt the dead can influence nuggets of oiled and painted bone. A different magic guides the knucklebones, passive yet powerful. I feel it flex as pieces settle into a reading, all except the root bone. It clatters to the floor. I quickly retrieve it, then lean over the rest of the spread, half eager, half afraid.

The soma bone – the one representing the body – is showing the knife symbol. I hear the sound of someone crying, see paper crumpled in an angry hand. Negative. Nearby is the black mirror, the watery chalice and broken earth. All negative. The mind bone has fallen wide and rests on the edge of the table beside the soul bone that has settled on the tombstone symbol.

A knot throbs beneath my sternum.

They're not coming.

The message couldn't be plainer, but still I hesitate. Reading the bones is complex, a skill learned through experience and powered by intuition. Each symbol carries a wide variety of interpretations and the meaning is divined through the placement of the bones and the user's skill.

Whispers and glances come from the table next to me. I understand. The knucklebone set is a macabre thing to have out in public. It's not like me to feel self-conscious but I'm not welcome here any longer and I'll not sit like a sad sack waiting for friends who aren't coming.

Tucking the bones away, I rise. Gathering as much poise as I can muster, I stride out, leaving Betty's and its disappointments as a shadow at my back.

2

MISS SAMPIRE SEES ALL

As the door to Betty's closes behind me I'm faced with a busy intersection packed with the living and the dead alike. A group of men who look like they've stepped from a Bruegel peasant painting contrast with the modern crowd in trilbies and flat caps and long coats. I wonder if the two women in long skirts and aprons standing beside the boarded-up shop on the corner are scandalized by the length of hems today.

Summer is underway but the sky is leaden, threatening rain. Edie waves from the church. I wave back, preparing to cross the intersection. A hand touches my shoulder and I spin, surprised, as I scramble to assess the person behind me. Living or dead?

Living, one of the whispering ladies from upstairs. Perhaps in her mid-thirties, she has light skin and neat features. She looks tired. There is a heaviness to her eyes and little creases at her mouth.

"I'm sorry, I—" She's flustered. "Am I right in thinking that you are Miss Sampire, *the* Miss Sampire?" She holds a newspaper cutting out to me.

> **Miss Sampire Sees All:** unsurpassed in the ancient art of astragalomancy, she can divine your past, present and future. Ask any question and she will answer. Gives the best advice in Love, Business, Journeys, Sickness, Family affairs, etc. Finds lost items. Home appointments available.

I'm surprised. It's been a while since my little advertisements were in circulation. The clipping itself is creased and worn.

"You're younger than I expected," she says. I hear that a lot. The illustration that accompanies the advert is a fair likeness but it ages me.

"I'm seventeen."

"Goodness, just a girl." She eyes me warily. "I'm not usually into fortunes and I wouldn't go to just anyone, but you seem respectable."

Meaning I haven't decked myself out in silk scarves and long skirts and claimed a heritage that isn't my own to lure tourists into parting with their shillings. I leave the eccentric outfits to my mother who wafts around our house like a moth. Today I'm in a pale blue dress, a simple barrette in my curled and pinned hair, strands already frizzing in the muggy air.

My reputation is probably helped by the fact that my

father is a relatively well-known artist with a bright future, or at least he was before his studio burned to the ground. One of his portraits of me – the one I really hate – did well at the summer exhibition in London last year.

"I don't read the bones any more, I'm sorry." I try not to glance at the ghost girl from Betty's who has crept closer while we were speaking and is now crouching behind a lamppost.

"But inside, just now…" the woman goes on. "You might not remember me; we never met in person. I'm Mrs Aldridge."

No name should have the power to make my lungs tighten and my head spin, but hers does. How could I forget the client I was supposed to meet the night of the studio fire?

"My condolences," says Mrs Aldridge. "Such a senseless tragedy. I wish—"

I cut her off with a quick "Thank you", looking for a way to exit the conversation. Everyone knows about the accident. It was rather extensively covered in *The Herald*. "I'm afraid I'm late for an appointment."

"I won't delay you much longer, but seeing you today I must ask if you would reconsider. I'm still in need of your services. In fact, I don't think there's anyone else who can help."

Mrs Aldridge passes me her details written on a paper torn from her pocketbook. It's an address and a private number not a local call box. The silence between us grows strange.

I fold the paper neatly. "When should I call on you?"

"I'm in most mornings between nine and eleven." She offers her hand and I shake it. "You will call, won't you?"

Not eager, I decide. *Desperate.*

"Of course," I say, not yet knowing if I'm lying. A flicker of a nervous smile crosses her face, followed by a flash of pain that makes my heart ache. She scurries back into Betty's. A moment later the little ghost girl follows, giving me a wary glance.

"Did any of them bother you while I was inside?" I ask Edie when she joins me.

She shakes her head. "They don't pay me much attention unless I'm with you."

I'm amazed. How could anyone ignore her? In her wide-legged trousers and waistcoat, a fedora over her cropped waves, and men's shoes, Edie is a picture: the most striking person I've ever met. Her lips are painted red, brows neatly arched. On her lapel is the snake brooch I gave her for her eighteenth, and in the little pocket of her waistcoat is a monocle.

Slipping her arm through mine, we weave around families and shoppers, pausing to let an automobile trundle past as we cross towards the church. A few of the dead spot us and drift closer, curious. I've noticed that the older souls, those dolled up in historical fashions, are more likely to ignore the limitations of gravity than the souls that are more recently deceased. I wonder if that's because the dead are controlled by what they know of the world?

More questions.

Always questions.

We don't stop at St Helen's but cross Stonegate to Blake Street. I've no idea where we're going but I'm itching to throw the bones again and ask for direction.

Edie's grip on me tightens. "Don't be angry at them."

I shake my head, fighting the heat in my cheeks. "I'm not." She gives me a sly look. I sigh, slowing my pace. My lungs are sore. "Well, what am I to think?"

"That they're busy," says Edie. "Bea's opening night is coming up and she has constant rehearsal. Merle… Well, you know her. Her uncle bought her a particularly exciting book on Estonian folklore and she's not stopped reading long enough to open your invitation. Fixating on her research is her way of coping."

The only way Edie could know that is if… I can't believe she went to see them and did not tell me. Unlinking our arms, she takes my hand in hers like a sweetheart might, fingers curling into my palm. Something lifts in my chest. For a moment, I forget all my worries. Touching her is always a thrill. To do so on the street, in plain view, sets my heart racing – except, who will notice now but the dead?

They're still watching us and the attention makes me a little uneasy. I know Edie feels it too, the strange turning of heads as we pass, and whispers, like dry leaves dancing along cobbles. A few ghosts are following us: a girl with a basket of flowers, a man dressed in blue wool, a gentleman on a bike who I presume is alive until he passes right through a horse and cart coming in the opposite direction.

I'm not sure I shall ever get used to that.

"Look." Edie keeps her voice light. "Why don't we buy some peppermint creams on our way back to Blossom Street and spend the afternoon with *Nightwood*, just you and me."

My brother Theo brought a copy of the novel home on his last visit from Oxford. It caused a sensation in the house. Ma proclaimed it a masterpiece. Edie's parents steadfastly refused to let her read it, which seems reason enough to read it twice. An afternoon on the chaise in our front parlour sounds blissful.

But the way Edie looks at me, her eyes just a little sad, cuts deeper than I want to admit. There is so much we don't know about the fire, about me seeing the dead, about the afterlife and what awaits. The loss we've endured is a raw ache between us. This is hard for her. No, it's more than that. She's afraid. She doesn't want any of this to be real.

"We can't go back to how things were. You know that." My grip on her tightens, as if she might slip away at any moment. "They have to know. It's too important not to tell them that I can see ghosts. Think of what this could mean for our little coven. For you."

"I understand," Edie sighs. "And you're right. I want them to know too. It's just, when it's only the two of us I can pretend. Everywhere else, I don't really exist."

"I'm sorry." I long to make her smile again and to hear her laugh. She carries too much sorrow.

As we head north towards the theatre I catch my reflection in a shopfront. Alone. My form is distorted by light and glass, a ripple of sunshine hair and the floral print of my dress as we go by.

Like a lost soul, I think.

But against all the odds, I'm alive.

3

DEAR BEATRICE

A dead man stands in the oriel window that juts out over the arcade of the York Theatre Royal. It's a gutsy building: three storeys with turrets and a crocketed niche worn high like a crown. Brick, once pale, has long since darkened with age and soot, but it still seems proud, facing off against the elegant crescent on the opposite side of St Leonard's Place, where Edie and I stand on the pavement, looking up at the thin-faced ghost, his body cowed and shoulders hunched.

"Friend or foe?" I ask Edie.

"Too early to tell. Maybe we shouldn't go in."

"Nonsense. I'm not afraid."

A bicycle bell cuts the air. We flinch back from the curb as the messenger darts past, weaving around rumbling motors and a horse and cart that has stopped for the omnibus. When there's a reasonable gap, we cross St Leonard's Place. Nausea worms its way under my sternum to sink long fingers into my ribs. My lungs pull and I cough into my handkerchief. By the time we've crossed the street I have to lean against the arcade. I can't catch my breath.

Don't panic. Fear makes the tightness worse.

Edie guides me inside the York Royal, steering me away from the dust of the street. With no performance scheduled, there is little going on at this time and the foyer is empty. The doormen seem more interested in reading the paper until they hear me desperately hacking into my kerchief.

"Miss?" One of them comes over, leaving his colleague at the desk—

Oh. The second man isn't alive. I can see that he's another ghost: bristle-chinned and gaunt, dressed in a long yellowing smock with a cap over his hair. When I look over, the ghost from the oriel window stands at the bottom of the stairs. He's older than I thought, his face well lined. Like the ghost at the desk, he too is wearing a long linen smock and there are open sores on his bare legs.

I stand quickly, swaying a little. Edie is on one side and the doorman takes my other arm to steady me. "Can I get you some water, or a brew, perhaps? I've a kettle out back."

I decline the offer. "We're just here to see a friend. She's in the play."

'We?" The doorman's face flushes. "Sorry, I… Who was it you were coming to see?"

"Beatrice Delane." I use her stage name.

The smock-wearing ghosts shuffle closer, assessing me. I resist the urge to skitter away from them. It's too late. They know I can see them.

"The company's in rehearsal, miss. You can go through if you like but" – the doorman motions to the auditorium – "I'll warn you, Mr Mosley, the director, is in a temper."

"I'll take my chances."

Leaving the two smock men behind, we slip into the stalls. The house lights are up but the theatre itself smells of dust, the echo of warm bodies, and perfume. It's been a while since I've seen anything at the theatre but I remember the atmosphere. The space feels vast yet cosy, possessed by the strange magic of all playhouses, even the most dilapidated.

Onstage, the cherry-red curtains are drawn and a rehearsal is in full swing. Scenery painted with a glowing sun is being slowly hoisted behind the half-finished stage setting of a pediment and balcony. At the front of the stage, a striking dark-skinned man in an old-fashioned suit orates to the empty theatre, only to be shouted at from the pit by a florid-faced fellow with prominent front teeth.

Almost obscured in the wings is Bea. Lithe-limbed and statuesque, she wears her auburn hair very long, despite the fashion. It's been braided and pinned under a veil, her face framed by a few spiral curls. Her gown is a velvet kirtle with an apron and she looks suitably Shakespearean. She's always had that rare kind of splendour that makes her malleable, able to transform into whichever character is required of her. The first time I met her she told me we'd be friends forever because we're both named for the Bard's heroines: feisty and sharp-witted Beatrice and resourceful, changeable Viola.

As for me, I am all golden hair paired with a plum mouth, long lashes and a scowl. Sweetness turned sour. I have always struggled to be anything except what I am: a desperate, dangerous thing with secrets wound around my heart.

The look on Bea's face when she sees me in the auditorium is one of pleasant surprise.

"Who are *you*?" snaps Mr Mosley as I approach the stage.

"A friend of Bea's."

"I shall take five," says Bea brightly. "If you don't mind. Just while you go through the reblocking with Andreas and Millie."

Sitting on the edge of the stage, she reaches out. I give her my hand and she slides into my arms in a ruffle of velvet and curls. Quickly, I let her go, lest Edie get the wrong idea. Smoothing her costume, Bea walks a little into the stalls where we might have better privacy.

I can sense that Edie wants to say something but she holds her tongue. I watch her watch Bea with a pained expression on her face and my heart hurts at the sight. Guilt makes what I am about to do so much harder.

Bea turns on me before I can speak. "It's high time you came to see one of my rehearsals, after all you are one of my greatest friends and a tremendous support—"

"Did you receive my invitation?" I cut in.

"Invitation?"

"For tea at Betty's today." I pause, hoping for recognition that doesn't come.

"I'm terribly sorry, darling, I didn't see an invitation. It's been so frantic that I've hardly been home." Bea laughs lightly and it's the fake laugh that she puts on for producers and journalists. "Sometimes it feels like I live at this theatre."

"Well, I … waited for you."

At my tone, her smile slips. "We can't all simply drop our lives to have tea, Vi. Opening performance is a few days away and there will be some very important studio people in attendance."

When Bea is pleased with you, she makes you feel like the centre of her whole world. A smile from her is a blessing. A frown is condemnation. Now, her expression is flat, giving me nothing. I hate that a part of me aches to make it better.

"It wasn't just tea. I have something important to tell you." I try to ignore how rotten and uncertain of myself Bea can sometimes make me feel. "It's about Edie."

Bea's gaze flashes with something like regret. "You shouldn't have missed her funeral. She was our best friend and you weren't even there to say goodbye. It looked strange. Merle and I made excuses for you, but—"

"Tell her," says Edie.

We'd planned to go. Edie, especially, needed to say goodbye to the life that was once hers. In the end, she couldn't face seeing her friends and family carrying the pain of her loss, and I couldn't leave her alone. So, I stayed home with her, curled up on the chaise, stroking her hair and we talked about anything and everything to distract us.

"Tell her," Edie repeats, a little pull in her voice and I feel like a coward.

I dragged Edie here demanding that we reveal the truth today, but now that I'm standing in front of Bea, my fears rise up to meet me. She and Edie kept the true nature of their relationship hidden, but on Edie's seventeenth birthday we all slept in the attic after a night of celebration and spell craft. I woke in the middle of the night and I saw Bea kiss Edie in the firelight.

I saw Edie kiss her back.

It is no secret that Edie loves women the way my brother loves men. It might not be spoken of in polite company but it is nothing to be ashamed of. But I didn't know that of Bea, and I never suspected there might be something between them.

Will Bea be angry that I have kept Edie to myself for weeks? Or worse, will she hate me for being able to see and speak to Edie when she cannot? We're all close, the best of friends, but what Edie and Bea shared goes deeper still. There is a nasty knot in my chest whenever I think about it because Edie and I don't keep secrets from one another.

Frustrated tears bubble close to the surface. I bite them back and admit, "I'm talking to Edie."

Rather than facing Bea and her stunned silence, I look at Edie. She's a little taller than me. Her eyes are green-grey. She has a tiny scar on her top lip and light freckles on her nose. She looks so alive.

But she's not.

I gather the strength to speak again. "I didn't go to her

funeral because for me, Edie isn't gone. She's still here. She's a ghost."

Bea's mouth gapes as she shakes her head, eyes shining. "Why would you say something like that?"

Does Bea not believe me? She must. That souls walk among us is no new revelation for a witch. We have read plenty of manuscripts on the subject in our little attic: seances and spiritualism, mediumship and summoning.

"Because it's true!" I'm desperate for her to understand. "I started seeing spirits after the fire. Edie was with me in hospital, and at home. She's right beside us now."

Bea looks to the spot I indicate, her gaze sliding right through Edie, and the pained, needful expression on her face is part-grief and part-longing. It does something horrible to my stomach.

Bea shakes her head. "It can't be. Edie's dead... And you ... *you're* not supposed to be able to see her."

The entire cast and crew have stopped to watch Bea cry. It's not a pretty stage cry but ugly sobs, her face turning blotchy and eyes swelling. For some reason I remember her expression the night Edie died: hair plaited and coiled on her head like some Viking warrior woman, eyes wide with fear as her fingers slipped from mine. The smoke was too thick and she moved too fast. I lost her and I lost my way.

"Vi, I don't think we're welcome here." Edie's voice is ripe with worry.

It takes me a second to realize she's not referring to Bea, but looking at the back of the auditorium.

Behind us are four ghosts. The first is the man from the oriel window. The second is the other smock man from the lobby. The third is just a boy, younger than the others, his eyes shadowed, his expression a glower. The last is perhaps in his late twenties, but his time on earth wasn't kind and his cheeks are riddled with smallpox scars. Fearful or friendly, none of the spirits I've encountered before exude what I feel from these smocked figures as they advance down the stalls towards me: brutal anger.

Get out, I think. *We need to get out.* I stumble, but Edie catches me and we spin towards the stage, searching for another exit. I grope in my pocket for my knucklebones but what defence are they against spirits?

"Go," Edie urges.

My lungs tighten again. No, not now. *Not now.* The only way out is through the stage door, behind the scenes and into the bowels of the theatre.

With all eyes on me, I run.

4

FLESH AND BLOOD

The sharp stink of turpentine and paint greets us along with surprised faces, dark fabric and ladders stacked everywhere so that I have to weave in and out to get through the fuss. Voices curse as we dart around disused pieces of set to find the exit is blocked with lumber, men and tools.

A second door leads to a corridor and a stairwell for the actors. I ignore the stairs and twist into the warren of corridors, searching for another exit, or a place to hide. The air smells of nothing in particular, the magic of the theatre fading to plain whitewashed walls and brick.

There's someone ahead. I stop. Edie bumps into me with a little gasp.

"Who in the world is *that*?" I whisper.

A gaunt actress with waxy skin and sore eyes lingers at the end of the corridor. Her costume is a nun's garb with a plain, voluminous habit missing the wimple. I am confused because I do not remember there being a nun in *Romeo and Juliet*. There isn't much light but what there is glints wetly off her scalp. My hand flies to my mouth in horror. Someone has slashed off her hair and done a rather rough job of it, catching her skin and leaving bloodied tufts. It is all make-up and artifice but the sight of her makes me shiver.

"Excuse me," I call. "Do you know the way out?"

"Vi." There's a warning in Edie's tone and I know, even before the woman starts to cry, that in my panic I've mistaken the dead for the living.

She's a ghost.

"The Grey Lady, do you think?" I whisper. Bea told me the story of a young nun said to haunt the York Royal. If she appears to actors on opening night, the show is fated to be a success. She's supposed to be benevolent.

Edie grips my arm. "I don't see how a glimpse of *her* could be good luck for anyone."

"Help me. Please." The nun's voice is a song, made for chanting liturgy and prayers. It strikes me how young she is, only a handful of years older than us. She's cradling her belly. I see its roundness and remember her legend and with it her terrible fate: bricked up alive in the walls of the convent that once stood here for breaking her vow of celibacy with a visiting noble.

My blood fizzes with anger. What happened to her lover? Nothing, I'll wager. He was rich and entitled and, most importantly, a man. He took what he wanted and left her to the consequences. It is too often women who carry the burden of men's sins.

"What can we do?" I ask, daring to get closer.

"They're here." Edie taps my arm and I swivel to see the smock men clustered in the corridor behind us. Between the glowers of the men and the whimpers of a lone, heartbroken nun, I know who to take a chance on.

I close the distance. "Please don't let them hurt us."

The Grey Lady towers over me and I am not slight for a girl. Her pain is terrible and for a moment I'm overwhelmed. Her palm slides to cup my chin: a soft, loving gesture. Without thinking, I move my hand over the nun's, feeling the warmth of her flesh. She is *real* to me. Whatever world this woman and Edie and the smock men are a part of, I am part of it too and it feels more concrete than the solid theatre walls around me.

"I have waited so long for a seer like you." The nun's voice is eager.

Edie shouts a warning and I'm torn from the Grey Lady's grip. A snarl in my ear and sour breath on my face: a smock man muttering, his anger quickened into something ripe and deadly as he hauls me away from the nun. They're all around us – three, four, no, seven of them. Edie screams my name, elbowing through the masses towards me. I reach for her and grasp stained linen as I'm swallowed by whispers layered into an insidious hum that raises the hair on my neck and makes my nausea surge.

"Blood and bone and flesh and blood and bone and flesh."

The Grey Lady comes to my defence, face twisted into

a snarl, pushing the smock men off me. Her teeth are bared and there's a dangerous glint in her eyes as her fingers slide through my sleeve to latch tightly on to my arm. She begins to pull me down the corridor and the fluttering of fear in my heart becomes a roar. The shortest smock man twists her wrist to break her hold on me. I cry out in pain as the Grey Lady's nails bite into my skin and tear. As she lets me go, a smock wearing ghost bundles me backwards into Edie.

"It is *your* blood Agnes hungers for," he snaps, pivoting to put himself between us and the nun. "We're trying to help you."

There is a flash of desperation in her face followed by sickening anger. She's no longer the sad, helpless woman she was. Instead, she has a predator's focus. The ghosts I'd feared only moments ago hold her back. My lungs rattle in my chest, pinching with pain as Edie and I slip away, heading for the front of the theatre. Behind us, the smock men cluster, blockading the Grey Lady. She snarls and the sound of her anger nips at our heels.

I blink.

She's suddenly just ahead of us, teeth bared and hands clawed. One of the smock men shouts a warning. How did she move from one place to another in little more than a heartbeat? I need a defensive theorem that I can shape and execute quickly. My thoughts riddle through incantations, discarding them like the useless chaff they are. Spells to talk to angels, to call on spirits and demand answers, to help flowers grow, to sour nightmares.

"You can't have her, do you hear me?" Edie steps in front of me, shielding her body with mine as the Grey Lady advances. "Run, Vi!"

I won't leave Edie, not now, not ever. A charm comes to mind, one of Bea's glamours to hide pimples. It's such a little spell. It doesn't so much hide as distract, but if I blend it with the glyphs for vanishing and concealment it's possible I can spin an enchantment strong enough that we could disappear for a short moment, long enough to get away.

But I have no blade for the blood offering. For something like this, there must be blood.

The Grey Lady slashes at Edie. The air in front of us puckers with distortion and the lanky smock man appears between us and the advancing nun.

We run, searching for another exit, but all we find are dressing rooms and screams in the air that I can't seem to breathe. The Grey Lady's wails echo after us. It's a dead end; we must have missed the back door – if there is one. I wrench open the last door in the corridor and we tumble into a dressing room that smells of stage make-up and the softness of bodies. There are chairs, two dressing tables spread with wigs on stands, brushes and face paints. I scramble through the belongings, gasping in triumph as my fingers find an open manicure set. I snatch the scissors.

"She'll be here any moment," gasps Edie. "We need a way out and you can't walk through walls."

There is a large, upright wardrobe with a few costumes hanging in it. Sweeping them aside I climb in, pulling Edie with me. The door snaps shut, plunging us into darkness. The fur trim on a long robe tickles the back of my neck. When I swipe it away, the wardrobe creaks. I go still, not daring to move too quickly in case I give our hiding place away.

"What is the plan exactly?" hisses Edie and I suddenly realize how close she is to me. My heart leaps and I feel my face flush, glad for the darkness. Why am I blushing? We've shared beds before, fallen asleep tangled together with her nose pressed to the nape of my neck but here, right now, I want so desperately to touch her cheek and kiss her mouth.

It is not me she loves.

I fumble in my coat for the small witch bottle I made from an old pill bottle. Behind dark amber glass, five iron pins are bound in red ribbon and snared with a thorny section of rose stem. A rodent's skull painted with a glyph that enhances the agency of the contents is also tucked inside and sealed with wax.

"A spell to disappear," I say, my voice hushed and breathy.

"A witch bottle won't do," Edie hisses in return. "You need active magic."

There's a warning in her voice. Active power is hungry and consuming, and the only source I have to offer is myself. Self-syphoning will weaken me; the body has only so much to give before sickness and decline is the result. Mr Spicer has always cautioned against relying on it, but I have little choice. Edie knows it, and so do I. It's why I stole the scissors.

"Just this once," I promise her. Opening them, I dig the sharp point of one blade into the flesh of my thumb until the heat of blood blooms on my skin. I gasp, less in pain and more in surprise.

"Even if you self-syphon, an abscondium theorem only works against the living." There's a new animation to Edie's tone, the one that always emerges when she's talking theoretical mathemagics. "You are hiding from the dead."

She's right and I curse myself.

"Unless," she adds, "you integrate the glyph for soul in the opening sequence."

She shifts until she's pressed close into my back, arms around me. My nose is almost to the wood of the wardrobe door as her fingers smooth over the back of my hand, closing around it, her upright thumb against mine.

"Ready?" she huffs in my ear, and a delicious tingle chases over my skin.

Focus.

If I make a mistake or we miscalculate, there will be unintended side effects – temporary blindness – or perhaps I might cancel out my new ability to see the dead. No more Edie. The thought is too painful to contemplate, but I do not want to be torn apart by a flesh-hungry nun.

"I'm ready," I whisper back.

We move together, her hand gently guiding mine as I press my bloody thumb to the hard wood and trace the opening glyph of the glamour. It's a short, sharp theorem; a primary glyph balanced by a simple magical equation. A temporary flit of misdirection at the centre extends it into a more specific command – *souls, pay me no heed*.

A pinch of pain that has nothing to do with my lungs sears my lower chest. It feels like an invisible person is sinking their fingers into my torso to draw out something vital. A self-syphon ties my blood into a working and gives the magic access to my own soul, using it as fuel. It's uncomfortable, but not agonizing, which means the spell is working.

Using my free hand, I pinch the air past my face and draw it back over my eyes as Edie helps me add the final glyph. The piecemeal theorem takes hold, magic snapping into place and settling to a low heat in my thumb.

I can smell Edie's perfume – peony, freesia and amber. The day of the fire we stopped off in town and tried a sample in Woolworth and the phantom scent still clings to her like cobwebs. Her hand is clutching mine, her body pressed firmly at my back, other hand snaked around my waist. Spinning slowly in her arms, I find the collar of her shirt, then her chin and cheek under the pads of my fingers. Her palms slide to the small of my back, fingers curling. I hold on. Without her, I think I might drift away entirely.

I whimper, hating myself for the weakness. Edie squeezes me tighter, her cheek against my temple. For a blissful moment I let myself be still with her. I'm safe. She's safe. We're just hiding in a wardrobe as a lark.

A door clatters open and voices chime into the dressing room. The actors? Before I can do anything the wardrobe is wrenched open. I blink in the sudden light at the young woman with mousy hair and a button nose – Millicent. She looks right through me, seeming to consider the items in the wardrobe. Behind her, the Grey Lady floats through the door, her eyes pinpointed with menace and hunger.

A flood of raw panic. My heart thunders and I think that I can feel Edie's heart too. A second passes. Another. Reaching into the wardrobe, Millicent grabs one of the coats and drags it out, pulling it through Edie, who winces and shudders at the intrusion. Then, the wardrobe door is shut in our faces. I hold my breath, waiting for the nun's hands to breach the wood and grab me. But they don't come.

There's more noise in the dressing room and Edie and I both tense, painfully alert. Are those different voices? Yes – men this time and muffled as if they're whispering.

"Not in here," says a voice. "I'm certain she's death-touched."

"If you're right, this changes everything," says a second. He sounds close, his words crisp and clear. "Meryem needs to know."

I will what energy I can into my makeshift theorem, begging our tentative abscondium glamour to keep working. There's the sound of shuffling feet and some more conversation that I can't make out because whoever the men are, they've lowered their voices again.

The power of my spell burns out like a candle, suddenly extinguished. The pain in my lower chest lifts, the glyphs shatter and someone beyond the door says, "Aha!"

The wardrobe door opens. Unbalanced, I tumble out with a yelp, my momentum carrying me from Edie's hold into another's. I blink at the sudden light and look up at the young man whose arms I've ungraciously fallen into.

5

OUR LITTLE DREAMER

The man has cool brown skin, tight dark curls cut short and his strong jawline is shaven. I register that he's rather handsome in a dishevelled, roguish kind of way. He's in some kind of simple historical costume of a linen shirt, waistcoat and breeches with a yellow cravat at his neck.

Goodness, his eyes are silver. However did he manage that?

"Put me down, please," I say firmly.

He does, though he continues looking at me, rubbing his arm where my elbow jabbed him when I fell. I can't fault his shock at finding a girl with wild hair and a wilder expression in a wardrobe, but does he have to stare at me with such a direct expression? And where is the fellow he was talking to?

Edie steps out of the wardrobe after me, eyeing the young man warily.

"What were you doing in there?" he asks.

I try to think of something to say that won't sound ridiculous. "I found things a little overwhelming and I needed space to think. This seemed as good a place as any."

"A wardrobe. Wasn't it dark, Miss…?"

He's fishing for a name but I won't give him one. "I like the dark," I admit instead. As I always do when I'm annoyed, I've dropped the softness of my father's Yorkshire accent to mimic my mother's sharper London tones. "It's safer."

The man raises his brows. "There are monsters in the dark, devils and men who might do you harm."

"Well, if you hold a lantern in the blackness, then not only do the monsters know *exactly* where you are but you yourself are blinded and at a disadvantage. Best to stand in the dark, let your eyes adjust, and slip through unseen."

Edie snorts a derisive laugh. The actor blinks, annoyed, and I realize that he can hear her. That is no costume he's wearing. The waistcoat, breeches and eighteenth-century style jacket must be what he wore in life. And those silver eyes – of course he can't be alive.

"Do not be alarmed," he says. "I'm friendly and I can show you the way out."

I narrow my eyes, defiant. "What makes you think I want to leave?"

"You blazed backstage like the wild hunt itself was after you. Either your audition got out of hand or you're being pursued by someone unsavoury. And you're bleeding."

Everyone looks at my thumb and the red streaking my

fingers and blotched on my clothes. In the dark, I must have cut deeper than I intended.

"Do you feel faint?" He's looking at me like I'm about to keel over.

"Sir, I'm a woman. It would be rather inconvenient if I collapsed at the sight of blood, don't you think?"

As the ghost guides us through the maze of corridors to the actors' entrance and delivers us safely on to the street, there's no sign of the Grey Lady or anyone else. He makes casual conversation, telling us that he's new to York but is enjoying the city immensely.

"Your eyes?" I ask, unable to contain my interest.

"A secret for a name. Surely that is an acceptable trade."

I glance at Edie. She shrugs. "I'm Edie. This is Viola."

"And I am Tempest – Tempest Lawson."

"Charmed," I say. "Now tell us about your eyes."

He smirks. "Very well. Silver eyes are the mark of a mirrored soul."

Mirrored soul? I've never heard of such a thing. I've read books that reference communicating with spirits, even how to trap dangerous ghosts, and many spells feature mirrors, but the only magical mirror I know of is a soul glass or ghost mirror, obsidian surfaces that can be used to charm and beguile the dead into reading fortunes for the living.

"I have questions," I say.

"And I look forward to answering them, but not today." He bows to us politely, trying to hide a smile. "I have an appointment I must keep, but I'm sure I'll be seeing you both again soon."

And just like that, he's gone.

"I don't trust him," Edie announces, breaking the long silence that's taken us from the theatre most of the way home. I'm tense and afraid, jumping at loud sounds and flinching when any ghosts get too close. I've never had cause to fear them before but now I know the truth: there are souls walking the streets who wish to do me harm. And they can do it with ease. They can touch me, so what is to stop them coming after me? Nervously, I glance back over my shoulder but there is no sign of the Grey Lady.

"I would like to know more about what a mirrored soul is," I say, thinking out loud. If I am to survive the attentions of the dead, I need to know everything there is to know about ghosts and spirits. "We should check the attic library. I'm sure Merle will have heard of the term, seeing as she's read every book up there twice over."

Edie's mouth pinches. "And if she reacts to your news as badly as Bea did?"

I don't want to think about that. I won't pretend that Bea's response doesn't sting, but it's only one wound among many. Merle isn't softer than her cousin, but she's certainly more pragmatic, and she doesn't have an ... *attachment* to Edie the way that Bea does. I am certain she will take it differently and Bea will come round.

The bustle of Blossom Street embraces us: big red buses,

brewery lorries, the horse drays unloading up the road, children clustered outside Almgills sharing newly bought sweets. I try to relax a little as we pass Hargreaves' fish and poultry shop, all busy this time of day. Several nuns from Bar Convent approach, their long black robes flapping as they walk.

"Viola, Edie!" Ambrose Petty, the jovial big-bellied landlord of the Lion and Lamb waves from the door of his pub, as he did every day before his death. "Thank you for speaking to my wife about Phillip. It's frustrating to be witness to his bad dealings and not be able to do a thing about it. Thanks to you, she's thrown him out and threatened to call the police if he doesn't return what he stole."

His good-for-nothing nephew, Phillip, a childhood bully of mine, has been pilfering from the pub takings since Mr Petty's death and his poor wife was getting more and more flustered that her weekly figures weren't adding up. Mr Petty was at his wits' end until I became what I am and was able to help him. He was one of the first ghosts, aside from Edie, that I met and spoke to, and it feels good to have made a difference to the comfort of his afterlife.

Mr Petty seems to notice how pale I am. "You quite well, lass? You're looking a might peaky."

"Nothing that rest won't cure," I reassure him with a wave.

He's satisfied and calls a blessing after us. The truth is, I am eager to retreat to the sanctuary of home, lock the doors and hide behind the simple wards I've set up there.

My family flat is small and, being above the garage, often smells of motor oil and gasoline, which bothers no one except Theo and he is rarely here. My elder brother raised himself well and is now making his mark on the pretty boys of Oxford under the pretence of studying Classics. I miss him desperately.

We usually have gas and electric light, but since the studio fire Pa has no income and so we are relying on candles, oil lamps and coal. I hang my coat in the long hall. The walls leading up to the main flat are heavy with paintings, mostly Pa's, but many others came as gifts from his friends. A still life – lemons on a cheery tablecloth – is missing and I hope they did not have to sell it as they did the piano.

"Ma?" I call.

She's waiting for me in the lounge, sitting primly on the sofa beside a lean man in his mid-twenties with straw-blonde hair, small eyes and a soft chin. He smells of pomade and cigarettes and has grown a moustache since I last saw him. A mistake. I do not think it suits his face shape. He stands when he sees me, expression irritatingly eager.

"Mr Saunders." My tone could chill the Arctic. "What a surprise. You will forgive me if I don't stay. I am, regretfully, bleeding."

I hold up my bloody hand.

Ma rises abruptly. "Viola, what on earth—"

"It just needs cleaning." We have ointment and bandages in the kitchen. Before anyone can protest I sweep out and along the corridor. My thumb isn't my only wound. My breaths are short, my lungs are tight and my arm aches from where the ghostly Grey Lady gripped on tightly.

I have turned down Mr Saunders' interest twice since last summer. I do not think that being so enamoured with a portrait at the Royal Academy exhibition as to not only purchase it, but to then track down the sitter to propose marriage, is the romantic gesture that my ma believes it is. Not only do I loathe that portrait – it makes me look entirely too sweet and placid – but I am certain that Mr Saunders is smitten with an ideal that doesn't exist. He doesn't know me well enough to love me, but I know his type: a collector of occult artefacts, and I have no intention of being collected like one of the esoteric curiosities he purchases from Mr Spicer from time to time.

My thumb is straightforward enough to rinse under the sink, but my arm is another matter. Pulling off my lacy cardigan, I fully expose the injury: four nasty scratches where the nun's nails dug deep into my skin. They sting and are still oozing, the flesh around them already starting to bruise.

"It isn't as bad as it looks," I lie when Edie hisses in sympathy.

She watches as I clumsily try to tend to the wounds one-handed and I know that she's itching to do a better job of it but can't. "I cannot even hold the bandage steady for you," she grumbles. "Everything slips through my fingers."

Everything except me. She can touch *me*. The thought threatens to bring heat to my cheeks and speeds my pulse. She is so beautiful.

I look up to see Mr Saunders in the doorway. A wealthy businessman's son, his perfectly tailored and spotless afternoon suit is made from quality linen. He looks so placid and eager to please that I almost take pity on him. It isn't my intention to be cruel but he simply refuses to take my, "No, I will not marry you," as an answer and that irks me.

"It is good to see you well, Miss Sampire. Especially after that dreadful fire—" He cuts off when he sees my arm, his usually even-tempered face suddenly shadowed and serious. "Who did this to you?"

Mr Saunders comes forward and, before I can protest, draws a charm mark on my arm. I sense a flare of power drawn from the flat hip-flask-sized witch bottle in his suit pocket and then the pain from the scratch dulls and disappears; the bleeding stops.

"Magic can't heal," he explains as if I'm a complete amateur. "Your body must do the work itself, but I can at least lessen your pain and disinfect the wound."

I shrug out of his grip, trying to temper my anger. "I didn't ask you to."

He blinks. "No, but—"

"Mr Saunders, you worked a theorem on me without asking." I glower at him, enjoying the rising fluster in his expression.

"I wish you would call me Henry." His lips tighten. "You know how much I care for you."

"If you care so much, then you would ask permission before you make decisions on my behalf, especially pertaining to my own body."

"I only meant to help."

I am not in the mood to deal with him. My bones feel watery and my head is spinning thanks to the active magic I used today. I need to rest, but Saunders lingers.

"Rupert Spicer asked me to assist him with a local matter," he explains, even though I did not ask. "I've taken a house near the cathedral for a month and I hope that we might see more of one another while I am here. I understand that later today your mother will be going to London for a few weeks. I have promised to keep an eye on you while she is away."

"Oh, I bet you did," mutters Edie under her breath.

"What local matter?" I ask, curious.

Mr Saunders raises his brow. "Nothing for you to be concerned about."

Typical. The men let us girls dally around with magic but never tell us their serious business. Grumbling internally, I am distracted long enough that Saunders is at the kitchen door and putting on his hat before the other part of what he said registers in my mind. Ma is going south *today*?

"Miss Sampire, perhaps you would like to have lunch with me on Friday?" asks Mr Saunders.

Ma answers for me. "Oh, she would be delighted, sir. Thank you for your kindness."

Mr Saunders tips his trilby, gives me a hopeful smile and departs, but I am too distracted by the suitcase beside the door to care. It doesn't look as if Ma is taking many things to London. I suppose the artists she'll be posing for don't expect her to wear much, or they'll drape her with old bed sheets and strands of silk to make her into some goddess or saint.

She hasn't worked for anyone but my father in years and, as a married woman, it's considered rather unseemly that she does. If it wasn't for the fire, she wouldn't have to leave. Pa wouldn't have lost the paintings he'd been working on for the better part of two years. It was his greatest commission and when it burned, so did his career.

I have no one else to blame for our situation. I may not have caused the fire but we were at the studio because of my ambition to earn a living reading the bones.

When our visitor is gone, I ask, "How long are you away?"

"A month at least," Ma replies. "Unless you go to lunch with Mr Saunders and accept his proposal. Once you are engaged I am sure he will take very good care of us all."

The worst thing is that she is right; Mr Saunders has said so himself. It would not matter if Pa never painted again; we would all be taken care of.

Our little dreamer, Ma used to call me with loving pride, until I grew into a young woman with few practical skills other than the ability to perform arcane rituals and embarrass her at parties. Tolerably bright with a pretty face, nothing is really expected of me but to keep myself pleasantly occupied until a man like Saunders decides that he is in love with me. If my mother is to be believed, becoming a surplus woman, perpetually single and unwed, is the worst possible fate.

It is my greatest ambition.

There is nothing wrong with being married, only I rather think most girls put little thought into the reality of it. Instead, they let themselves fall in love with the idea of being in love.

The real facts of marriage are far less certain and the facts of life are positively off-putting. I've seen the horrible truth of marriage, thanks to my parents. The way I see it, a wife becomes the property and caretaker of her husband from the moment they are wed, and the man may behave as badly as he wishes with little repercussion, while she is under constant social scrutiny.

I want no part in it. I do not love Mr Saunders. I am not even attracted to him and never have been, not to any man.

"Well, if you won't accept him, then you'll have to get a job," says Ma. "If only your typing was better, you might get a place at one of the firms in town."

I flop on to the chaise. "I don't want to be a typist."

Before the fire, I'd planned on becoming a celebrated diviner, exploring the esoteric arts and pushing the boundaries of magical knowledge into the age of modern scepticism. I would earn myself a living and share a house with Edie, who would write prize-winning novels. Her experimental style and frankness would be condemned in some circles but celebrated by those who matter. Bea would inherit her father's business dealing artworks and rare collectables and Merle could run it, because she has good business sense, while Bea pursued her acting career.

Now, that can only ever be a dream.

"I don't want a husband," I add firmly. "Not ever."

"Well, suit yourself." Ma pins on her hat. "But they are useful for some things, like keeping a roof over our heads. Make certain your father eats while I am away, you know how he gets." She searches through some correspondence in the bureau, tucking a letter into her pocket. She is right about Pa. He gets up most days to simply fall into a bottle. "And either find work or *please* make an effort with Mr Saunders." I must make a face because she scowls back at me. "Or any other eligible, wealthy men who show interest in you. I am not fussy."

I follow her downstairs to bid her farewell, trying not to grumble. I could chase after Mr Saunders right this instant, accept his hand in marriage and then Ma wouldn't have to go to London at all. Perhaps I should. It is my fault that we are in this predicament.

"Make the best of yourself, Viola," are Ma's last words to me before she kisses both my cheeks and hurries off to catch her train south.

I must check on Pa. I find him upstairs in bed, fully clothed, snoring softly and stinking of drink. He's a fine-boned man, birdlike and delicate, with watery eyes sunken back into his skull so that he always looks a little melancholic. It is a suitable countenance for an artist. Ma has removed his boots at least. I pull the quilt over him and return to the front room where Edie is waiting.

"Edie, would you think me callous if I took up Mrs Aldridge's offer to read the bones for her? I can't stand the idea of working in a factory, or as a typist, or—"

"I don't mind," she says quickly. "I always assumed you'd go back to it when you felt ready. I don't think Bea or Merle expect you to stop either, not when you are so talented. It is this new gift I fear."

When I go to bed, Edie wraps her arms around me and starts to sing softly under her breath. She can't sing for toffee, we both know that, but her trying for my sake soothes me. I settle against her warmth. Pressed together with no sense of how her body will be slipping through the coverlet rather than moving with it, I can pretend she's still alive.

"Sleep," she whispers in my ear. "I'll be here when you wake."

I close my eyes and fall into fire.

Lurching upright into Edie's arms, I gasp stuffy summer air and force off the nightmare.

"Again?" asks Edie as I shake against her. Nodding, I push my sweaty hair off my face and try to steady my breathing, hyper-aware of how close Edie's mouth is to mine and it feels like the threads of my control are unravelling right before me.

No, I cannot think of that. It's better to face my nightmares. I dream of the studio blaze almost every night. The aromatic scent in the air before the candle melted and fell wafts over me and I'm left with a strong sense that it wasn't an accident. It's not the first time I've felt like this, but it's the first time I've woken with the realization that feeling might not be a part of the nightmare.

The candle fell when no one was near it.

The door wouldn't open.

Edie, Bea and I were discovered just five paces from escape, having succumbed to the smoke at the door. Bea was barely alive. Edie and I were dead but I was revived shortly after. I've read Merle's account in the investigative report. As she escaped the studio the door slammed behind her and jammed shut, and although she pulled and hammered on it she couldn't get it to budge. It took a team of firefighters to open it, but they were adamant it was not locked.

"Edie." I turn to her. "What do you remember of the night we died?"

She shakes her head, looking away. We haven't talked about what happened in detail. It's too painful for us both.

"I hate to ask." I swivel until I'm sitting in a tailor's seat beside her and pull her hand into my lap, threading my fingers with hers. "It's important. Please."

"Did you remember something new?" Her voice is a whisper.

I don't want to tell her my suspicions and lead her memories. When I don't go on, she sighs deeply and closes her eyes. Her lids flutter slightly. Cute little creases form across her brow.

"Heat. The smoke was blindingly thick. We crawled, heading for the door but it was closed and…" She trails off, swallows once and opens her eyes. "We hammered and shouted for help. You stood up to try the handle, right into the darkest part of the smoke and then you collapsed. I caught you. You were breathing and then you weren't, and I knew we were both going to die. I knew it." She blinks and looks at me as if seeing me for the first time. "I felt you let go and I couldn't let that happen – I had to save you somehow – and then I … died."

This is what it is like to drown, I think as I look at the expression on Edie's face as she speaks. The panic and agony, the way she whispered that last part because it was almost too raw to speak out loud and suddenly I have her in my arms, forehead to hers and I want to get even closer but I don't dare. Everything with her is too fragile.

I absorb what she has confirmed for me: the door wasn't locked and there is nothing on the outside that should have stopped us from escaping. Unless—

Reluctantly, I let Edie go and, opening the silk purse on my bedside, I throw the bones and ask the one question I've never thought to ask before.

Was the studio fire truly an accident?

PART 2
MIND

The second bone is the mind bone and focuses on the inner working of thought, knowledge and self-awareness.

Sprouting Seed: youth/inexperience/growth/potential/
new beginnings/communication/vulnerability/
cleanliness/improvization. Positive.
Scroll: seeking knowledge/a scholar/learning/
intellect/diligence/wisdom/patience/escapism/
potency/agency/permanence. Negative.
Scales: law/justice/truth/an advisor/a mediator/neutrality/
balance/restoration/evidence/consequence/harmony. Positive.
Rope: ties/unions/partnerships/marriage/opportunities/
old ideas or feelings/limitations/demise/failure/
exhaustion/imprisonment/secrets. Negative.

6

WAKING tHE BONES

There is a peculiar calm that comes over me when I throw the bones, no matter how pertinent and vital the question.

Traditionally knucklebones are crafted from goat or sheep bones and are far larger than the eight delicate nuggets of yellow cream in my palm. My set is human, made from the small bones that sit just above the wrist. I suppose they are not "knucklebones", but that is what they were called when Mr Spicer purchased them for me in Greece. Supposedly, they are already over a century old and were taken from the corpse of a condemned man. The coven presented them to me in a raucous attic ceremony in which Bea insisted on us wearing long, old-fashioned cloaks and chanting until Edie got the giggles.

She isn't full of mirth as I roll the bones in my palm now. I've come to know the set so well they feel like an extension of my senses. I retreat into a place of steady calm, feeling the thrum of phantasmic residua as I whisper my question and toss them high. The light is low, but I can sense each piece as it rises and falls like a pebble into the watery chambers of my heart.

When they have settled, I hover my hand over them, searching for their answer in the arrangement that they have landed in. Each bone has a core indicator – soma, mind, heart, soul, world, root, time, self – that must be noted first. Small as they are, each is hand-painted with four tiny images and there are layers of possible meanings for each. It is up to me to interpret them correctly. I once described the sensation to Edie as like hearing music, with each possible meaning a chime in my mind, but that feels like a paltry explanation for what I truly experience.

The resonance is deep, calling to the residua in my own bones. A passive magic, I need not fear draining my life to use it, but to read correctly I must be familiar with myself as much as with the bones.

All eight have scattered wide with the last, smallest bone – the self-bone – at the dead centre of the spread. Its tiny painted eye stares directly up at me. The others are in an even distribution around it: lungs, scales, quill, witch bottle, walled garden, hive, flames. A blade of shock shivers up my spine as I hover my hand over each, feeling radiant heat, and smelling acrid smoke blended with a faint trace of wine and saffron.

The night we died, I rolled the bones to determine the outcome of the session with Mrs Aldridge. It was a practice roll to attune my senses before she arrived. The bones scattered and coalesced into a clear meaning: change, opportunity, new gifts. Death lurked there too, I realize now, but I didn't see it because I wasn't open to it as an interpretation.

I won't repeat that mistake. There is always more than one level of meaning to the bones. I must put my ego and expectations aside and read true. But no matter how many ways I think through the answer in front of me, the result is always the same. After the shock comes overwhelming horror that threatens to choke a sob from me.

"Edie, it wasn't an accident." The words are hard to say.

She's trembling. "What do you mean?"

"The fire wasn't an accident. Someone meant us harm."

Stricken silence and I wish I could take it back, make it all not true just to soothe the devastation and misery in her eyes.

"But no one was near the candle when it spilled," she says. "It has to be an accident."

My hands are shaking as I gather the set to throw again, this time asking, "The night of the fire, was the door of the studio jammed on purpose?"

I feel wood under my palms, taste copper, and feel a brief hook like sensation under my ribs. The bones answer, *Yes*. But there are more negative symbols in the mix: the veiled figure, the bread and the half-drawn curtain. The answer is more complex than a simple affirmative. The veiled figure could symbolize an enemy, perhaps whoever trapped us in the studio.

Only one of us got out.

"Did Merle lock or jam the door?"

Edie gasps, but doesn't interrupt. Merle was the only one

of us who got out. She could have done something to block the door on purpose. She wouldn't. No coven member would deliberately hurt another, but I have to ask to cover every possibility. Thankfully the bones roll a clear negative this time. I sigh with relief and so does Edie.

We sit with that a moment, Edie's hand finding mine and holding on tightly. Someone killed her. Someone murdered her and tried to kill me and Bea. Merle was lucky to escape before the door jammed or she might have perished too. I expect to feel sadness but I've had my fill of mourning. Instead, ragged rage sears me so sharply that I spring out of bed and start to pace.

"Who would want to hurt you?" I ask.

Edie just shakes her head. "I'm not important enough to have enemies."

With a trembling heart, I put the question to the bones. As it is not a simple yes or no answer it requires all my focus. The veiled figure comes up again, the hive symbol beside it pressed against the image of the curtain on the time bone along with broken earth, magpie in flight, quill, scroll and the seedling. This answer is wrapped up in a brief vision of the nape of Edie's neck, the drumbeat of dancing feet on wood and iron nails and bones rattling in a witch bottle.

The symbols are complex and a little confused, which means there are layers to the events one question cannot decipher. The curtain might mean a secret not yet revealed or something hidden in the past. That the symbol lies so close to the hive, which primarily represents a group, makes me wonder about the meaning of the broken-earth symbol – perhaps a shattering, division and strife.

Does it refer to the frictions of our little coven or is it speaking of a different community with a grievance against us? I cannot think who it might mean in that case. The magpie indicates communication, unless paired with the seedling, which it is. That is a clear indicator of a birth, or rebirth. I am sure that the scroll here means a quest for knowledge and agency. The quill could be creativity and talent, but also falsehood and illusion.

"What do you see?" Edie asks after my silence stretches too long.

"I don't think you were the target, at least not you alone. Someone has a secret," I say. "One that they will apparently kill to keep. They seek knowledge, perhaps held by a community at odds with itself."

"But why are we a threat to them?" asks Edie.

I pose her question to the bones. Pain spikes behind my eyes. I have a headache coming. I am too tired for this and the answer confuses me. Once again, I'm reminded how astragalomancy is much more of an art than a science. "We … aren't." All the symbols have come up as negative. *I'm* missing something, asking the wrong questions or simply failing to grasp the correct interpretation.

"It's been weeks since the fire but—" Edie sniffs, her emotions threatening to overspill. "What if they're still after us?"

It's a vital question. I ask the bones: *Is our coven in danger?*

Flashes of red velvet against the inside of my eyelids, distant voices raised in an argument that I can't understand and the carved balustrades of a theatre. Could it be the York Royal? When I look at the bones, the flame icon is close to the scroll, indicating something well planned is falling apart.

"Their plan didn't work out," I say. "Things have changed. I think the theatre is involved but I'm not sure how."

Edie's breath hitches. The air is too hot in here. Sweat pricks my skin and sticks my nightgown to my back. My temples drum, headache deepening, but we still need to ask the most important question of all.

"Who did it?" asks Edie, as if she can read my mind. "Who killed me?"

The bones clatter as I roll them in my palm, hesitant yet eager. I cannot fathom who wants to do us such harm and kill one of us, or the entire coven. Who would hate us that much?

When I finally throw the bones, I inhale the smell of smoke, see melting wax and hear a door slam shut. My breath catches, lungs screaming in sudden tightness. The pain trips me up. I gasp and curse, knowing I need my atomizer. It is beside my chipped sink and takes a moment to set up and longer still until my breathing becomes less ragged.

It is several minutes until I am able to read the spread that the bones have made on the coverlet, and the answer makes me sway and lurch. Edie slides an arm around me and I find comfort in her. She is the foundation of my very world and I almost lost her.

"It is someone close to us," I manage to whisper. My lungs stick and hitch with each breath. "Either someone we know, or someone who physically lives close to here. I cannot be sure, but I … I can roll again."

"Not now." Edie's tone is firm. "You're in too much pain and you are exhausted."

Frustration threatens to become tears because I know Edie's right. There are so many other questions we need to ask but I can do very little right now. After self-syphoning active magic today and then rolling the bones for so many questions, my body and mind are done.

"We will need to warn Bea and Merle," says Edie. "Whoever killed me might decide to strike again."

7

DEATH-TOUCHED

Later that morning, I haul open my front door to find a dangerous man glowering on my doorstep. Phillip, Mr Petty's nephew, has always been a bad sort. When we were children, he'd wait outside Almgills or Mr Peckitt's sweet shop on Micklegate and demand a sugar tax to let us past, forcing us to give him a sherbet fountain or some Barratt's fruit salads. He's grown into a brute of a man, a bully and a thief with little regard for others.

I am under no illusions as to why he's here today.

"You bitch," he hisses in my face.

He's a stocky, solid lad, Theo's age, broad-cheeked and strong-jawed, with movie-star looks and a criminal's heart. He favours a bowler hat, though he's never worked a day in an office, and his clothing is something of a performance – dapper, but dishevelled.

I push past him, livid that he would come to my home and make a scene.

The Forsselius Garage is already open, pumps scenting the air with petrol and motor oil. The kindly gent who tends them is outside in his familiar fawn overalls, an unlit pipe between his teeth. He might intervene for me and I don't wish to get him in trouble. Phillip isn't the forgiving sort.

Edie and I stride away towards Micklegate Bar, and I button my summer coat as I go. It will soon be too warm to wear it but the morning air is still fresh. A Victorian gentleman, a ghost I have seen striding along Blossom most mornings, tips his hat at me as we pass. I give him a friendly nod though my stomach clenches at the sight of him. I hate that the Grey Lady has made me afraid of every spirit I don't know well.

"What do you think you're playing at, eh?" Phillip follows me, needing to say his piece. "You're a liar and a fraud taking advantage of a widow in mourning, swindling her out of money and tarnishing my good name—"

"Good name?" I snap, whirling around to face him.

"Don't, Vi," warns Edie. "He's got a temper on him."

He does, but so do I. Besides, there is nothing Phillip can do to me with so many people hurrying past and the morning traffic heavy on the road.

I clench my fists. "I've tarnished *nothing*. You do not have a good name to squander and I haven't swindled anyone. Unlike you, I've not taken a penny from your aunt. You ought to know that your uncle is watching your every move and he's disappointed in the man that you've become."

As if my words have summoned him, Mr Petty appears on the pavement beside us, a pedestrian passing right through his body. It's enough to startle me, and Phillip takes the flash of apprehension on my face to mean that his intimidation tactics are working.

He sneers, taking a step towards me. "This is part of some con. You want me to pay you off, is that it? I know your family needs brass, what with your old man's studio going up in a blaze—".

"I don't want anything from you," I retort. People are paying attention now, heads swivelling at the swell and pitch of my voice.

"If you say one more thing against me, I'll—"

"You'll what?" I challenge. Men like Phillip always expect women to back down. I won't give him the satisfaction. "Steal my sweeties? I'm not a child any more."

From the dark flash in Phillip's eyes I know he means me worse harm. I should be quaking and, beneath my simmering anger, I am. But I see hot rage, indignant that he should so blatantly accuse me of defrauding someone when he's the thief and liar.

"Please just apologize and tell him what he wants to hear," says Edie.

I can't. That is the keen difference between Edie and myself. For all her wit and intellect, independence and sureness, she is, at heart, gentle. She knows how to pick her battles, whereas I, like Bea, cannot retract my stinger. I am too stubborn. Phillip grabs my arm roughly, right where the ghostly nun's nails bit into my skin, and I wince in pain.

"Oi, what's going on?" a voice calls up the street. The gentleman in fawn overalls and a couple of other mechanics from the garage are striding our way. Phillip lets me go, but if looks could kill, I'd be dead.

Then it occurs to me that whoever is trying to hurt our coven is *someone close to us*. Phillip is not a friend, but I have known him my entire life and he lives in close proximity. Could he have blocked the door of the studio?

It's possible, but what would be his motive? It was only *after* I started seeing the dead that I placed myself in opposition to him. Before then, I'd see him around but we never spoke, and I certainly did nothing to harm or upset him.

"Watch yourself, Viola," he sneers. "People who get in my way always regret it."

He strides away as the mechanics come to my defence, fussing over me until he is safely out of sight. But I cannot shake the feeling that we haven't seen the last of Phillip Petty.

There are eyes on us as we arrive at Spicer House, a grand townhouse built from light stone on the corner of Micklegate and St Martin's Lane with arched windows bracketed by decorative columns and tall chimneys. Only a ten-minute walk from my home on Blossom, it stands proud beside the little patch of green that is the St Martin's Churchyard, and is my favourite place in the world. Today, though, my skin pricks and the eerie sensation makes me certain, somehow, that someone is watching us.

"Do you feel that?" I whisper to Edie after we've rung for entry.

She nods, expression tense as she glances around. My first thought is that Phillip has followed us. Then I think of Tempest Lawson from the theatre and wonder if we'll run into him again soon. I hope so, for I want to know more about his silver eyes.

Irma, the housekeeper, lets us in with a welcoming smile, and asks after my health. She's been with the Spicers for a long time and I suspect she knows most of the family secrets. She takes my coat and hangs it up in the hall. Before the door closes I scan the street, looking for something or someone out of place, but find nothing.

The Spicer abode is an art gallery on the ground floor with the family's private living quarters on the floors above. It's an elegant space. The gallery is divided by paint colour: deep olive green for old world paintings, and chalk white walls for the more contemporary artists. Few know that there are other showrooms towards the back of the house painted blood red, where a specialist occult collection is displayed.

We wander through the contemporary gallery, a rather lovely front room stripped of most of its furniture and hung with paintings and prints. There are some wonderful pastoral woodcuts by Robert Leslie Howey hanging here and a painting of a fishing village by Rowland Suddaby that is to my taste, having a freshness of both palate and brushwork.

The protective wards are strong here and I feel myself relax a little now we are safe behind them. They are anchored by four large witch bottles hidden in each corner behind the wall panelling or under the floorboards. Their effect is subtle, but successful: potential customers in these front rooms are put immediately at ease and are far more open to persuasion. It is a salesman's dream and Mr Rupert Spicer is excellent at what he does.

A jolt of uncomfortable recognition strikes me as I lock gazes with a pair of familiar eyes: a three-quarter length portrait of me sitting with my hands clasped in my lap. With his fine command of light and form, there is something of William Orpen in Pa's style, but while the critics might dismiss Orpen as unfashionable, they love my pa. If only he could paint again, he might salvage something of his career.

I'd forgotten this portrait still hangs here, waiting for a buyer. I prefer it to the one Pa sent to London for the exhibition, but I still do not like it for similar reasons. Why he made me appear so inert, I'll never understand. There's no fight in my eyes, no ambition or want or desire. Mr Spicer called the portrait "a beautiful mystery" when he first saw it and I know my pa is exceptionally proud of it, but it makes my skin crawl.

Edie and I venture to the back of the gallery and sweep aside a heavy velvet curtain to enter a part of the building fewer customers get to see. Only practitioners of the esoteric arts are invited past the curtain to view the items in the red rooms.

The lighting here is lower, the shutters and curtains closed, to lend the space an atmosphere of reverence and mystery.

The spells are subtler too but just as potent. Less concerned about influencing customers, they are ripe with protective theorems against thievery, corruption and rogue magic. Here are cursed reliquaries, enchanted silverware, charmed mirrors and witch bottles, though most of the bottles are kept locked away in Mr Spicer's office adjacent to the red rooms.

The office door is already ajar as I raise my knuckles to the wood. Before I can knock, a female voice floats out. "My father and I will only trap them if they become a danger, Rupert. Not a moment before. Uncorrupted souls can't hurt the living."

Edie gives me a curious look and I press a finger to my lips. She nods, almost imperceptibly.

"There is now a death-touched in the city," Mr Spicer replies. "What of her safety?"

My heart races. Death-touched? The term is familiar, having been mentioned in passing in a book I read a few months ago on syphoning glyphs, and I am sure Tempest said it when Edie and I were hiding in the cupboard at the theatre yesterday. Were they talking about me? Shifting my weight, I glance back at Edie who is eavesdropping at my side.

"At least tidy up the necromic cycles. Please, Rachel. If she falls into one—"

"They are already trapped. I won't bottle innocent ghosts. You must warn her of the danger. Guide her yourself, as you always have," replies the woman.

"I know you're keeping souls back."

In the long pause that follows the silence bristles, buzzing with restrained anger. I want to see inside the office and see who Mr Spicer is talking to, but I daren't move or the creaky floorboard to my left will give me away.

"I have buyers lined up," Mr Spicer's voice comes again, tinged with desperation. "An entire shipment of bottles for Lord Darlington went missing. I need replacements as quickly as possible. I can offer you an excellent return."

"I don't doubt it," replies Rachel. "But I have a code of morality and empathy."

"Your father—" Mr Spicer hisses.

"Has his principles, the same as I," she adds. "We are scientists, first and foremost, and are working for more than just personal gain."

"Yet without selling souls to me you would have nothing to fund your research."

"I refuse, Rupert. You will not convince me, or my father, to break our code."

"Please, the other soul catchers I've been relying on have either disappeared or shut down their operations. I'm in a pinch here. Lord Darlington is an excellent customer; he buys only the best bottled souls, theorems and magical artefacts, and he is very well connected. Pleasing him is good for business. I will pay you handsomely if you can replace his shipment by next week."

"I can replace the shipment," says Rachel. "But I won't trap innocent ghosts to do it. I can start with Mary. Whoever stole her bottle from you released her, I suspect by accident, and she's been corrupted."

"Is she a shade?"

"Potentially. I have yet to get close enough to be sure. But I do know that she's been hunting her own kind, which means I must bottle her again. Lord Darlington will just have to be patient for more than that. How did you lose an entire shipment anyway? Are you sure it's not the same thief?"

"No, Mary's bottle went missing from my safe weeks ago. This delivery of six bottles, worth a fortune, was taken in transit. I'm looking into it."

They say their goodbyes and the office door opens. I snap my attention to a cabinet housing two saintly reliquaries and a bone rosary, but keep an eye on the woman as she passes. Perhaps in her early thirties, she's wearing slacks and a shirt with a smart jacket, worn open. On her nose are spectacles in a curious half-moon design, which are both distinctive and out of place.

At Edie, she pauses and *whispers* something into her ear. Shocked, my mouth drops open.

She can see the dead.

I stand there like a fool and the woman leaves with a long, meaningful look in my direction. I want to chase after her and demand to know everything that she can tell me about ghosts.

"Viola, my dear!" Rupert Spicer strides from his office with open arms. He has a friendly face made friendlier by a neat beard and rather wild hair, which suits him very well. Ma always says that it's appropriate to look eccentric in artistic circles so long as your taste is perfect, and Mr Spicer's taste is very fine, though it tends towards the dark and strange. There is a reason his business thrives selling esoteric items, magical manuscripts, theorems, spells and witch bottles to the occult community. The art gallery is mostly a front, though he has done well for my father over the years.

Mr Spicer embraces me as if I am fragile. "I am immensely cheered to see you. Bea told me you were recovering but when I saw you in hospital you looked very sick. How are you feeling?"

"I'm well," I lie, hugging him back.

Mr Spicer holds me at arm's length and frowns playfully. "You can't trick me, Viola. You've been running about these rooms since you were little. I know you too well."

I sigh. "Sometimes I still struggle to find my breath and I get the most terrible headaches, but if I am careful I can get on."

The conversation I just overheard runs through my mind but I can't make head nor tail of it. Who was that woman? I am almost certain that "death-touched" refers to those who can see spirits, like me. But what is a necromic cycle? Or a soul catcher? I'm desperate to know more and the questions burn on my tongue but I cannot ask without making it obvious that I was eavesdropping.

Mr Spicer smiles, eyes crinkling. "A little miracle indeed. You are not the kind to give up, tenacious to the end, but you mustn't overdo it. It's important to know when to let something rest." He squeezes my shoulder affectionately. "And how is your father?"

My face must say it all because his smile slips.

"I do have some good news. I've had recent interest in the remaining portrait of you."

"Please tell me that interest isn't from Henry Saunders."

"At least he is consistent."

I bristle, irritated, but we *need* the painting to sell. My parents' savings are gone. Father has already lost the studio and we are now struggling to pay our rent.

"Will he really buy it?" I ask.

"I rather think he will. He is most enamoured with you." He squeezes my shoulder. "Has he proposed again?"

"No, but he invited me to lunch. Is it true that he intends to remain in the city for a few weeks?"

"Yes, we have business together. I expect he will want to see a lot of you while he is here." Mr Spicer smiles knowingly. "If you will forgive me, my dear, I have client appointments and a small crisis to mediate. Unless … there is something else you wish to discuss?"

His expression is expectant. I hesitate, unsure of what to say. He knows of my new ability, I am certain of it. Bea didn't want to believe me when I told her, but after the shock wore off she will surely have told her father. From what I overheard of his conversation with the woman he called Rachel, he does know and so will be able to answer some of my questions. But it feels important to discuss it with my coven sisters first. Besides, we have more pressing concerns than me seeing the dead and I am certainly not willing to discuss the fire with Mr Spicer until we have evidence to back up my readings.

"No, nothing," I reply finally.

"The girls are upstairs." Mr Spicer bids me farewell and retreats to his office. Edie has vanished and my heart gives a flutter of worry before I wind my way through the rooms to the central stairwell and see her on the landing.

"What did Rachel say to you?" I whisper when I reach her.

Edie bites her lip, worried. "She told me to leave."

"Leave?"

"Spicer House is not a safe place for souls. That's what she said."

"Nonsense," I reply. This house has always been our sanctuary. I do not see why that should change.

8

WE WITCHES THREE

I've climbed these stairs so many times that, unthinking, I account for the uneven tread and avoid where the wood squeaks. Although she doesn't stir the air or make a sound, I can sense Edie behind me, as if I am always attuned to her: a part of me seeking out a part of her.

My knucklebone set is safe in the purse strung across my shoulder. I long to clatter them in my palm, to feel their closeness and the promise of reassuring guidance.

The attic itself is a sizable room stretching across the entire house, the roofline of old tile supported by great ancient beams. Antique rugs are layered over well-worn floorboards. Aside from the circle of space in front of the fire where we have four armchairs, a table and space to practise our craft, the room is filled to the rafters with bookcases and cabinets stuffed with esoteric delights, unsold curiosities and handmade witch bottles. Beeswax scents the air along with motherwort, linden and rose with a hint of lemon balm and hawthorn touched by smoke.

Home, I think. *My true home.*

A pang of guilt rushes me at the thought that my own family don't know me half as well as my coven sisters and Rupert Spicer do. As much as I love my ma, pa and brother, I belong here.

Dust dances in the morning light. The shutters are open and a pinch of warm air refreshes the otherwise stuffy atmosphere. Merle and Bea are sitting in the high-backed chairs beside the fireplace, talking. Or rather, Bea is talking.

"Andreas is such a generous actor when he relaxes into the role and very handsome – oh, don't look at me like that. I have my sights set higher, *if* I can secure a better role—" She turns at the sound of the door opening, eyes growing wide. "Vi?" Bea crosses the room to pull me into her arms. "You frightened me yesterday. Why did you run? What happened?"

"I'm sorry," I reply. "Spirits were chasing me."

"Spirits?" Bea breaks the embrace, holding me at arm's length to peer into my face. "You mean ghosts at the theatre and … you really can see Edie?"

"I'm sorry. I shouldn't have sprung it upon you like that and I shouldn't have kept it a secret for so many weeks, not from you." Over her shoulder I make eye contact with Merle. "Either of you."

"It's true, then?" Merle is dramatic in a long dark wrapper from another century with a high lace collar and billowing sleeves, her hair done up in gleaming curls. Her arms enclose my other side and her perfume is the comforting smell of paper and ink and the dust of old secrets. Mousy-faced, she has none of Bea's beauty or elegance, but holds a stoic grace of her own. She is so wonderfully good-looking, solid and real beside Bea's ethereality.

I'm slung between my friends, holding the cousins tight with relief. My secret is out and they forgive me for keeping Edie to myself. Edie has taken up her usual seat by the fire and I think my heart will break again. I step back from my coven sisters. "We have a lot to tell you."

"She's really here?" Poor Bea looks as if someone has struck her. "Right now?"

I've never seen her this nervous. Her emotions are so close to the surface she could overspill at any moment. My heart softens for her because I know what passed between her and Edie. Their kiss is burned into my mind; one memory of Edie I wish to forget.

"She's here," I confirm, gesturing to where Edie is sitting, and I describe what she's wearing, so that they know she isn't marred by signs of her death and is utterly herself.

Merle laughs with fresh tears in her eyes. "She always did love the serpent brooch that you gave her."

"I wish you could see her too," I whisper to them, but to Bea especially, meaning it as an apology.

"Perhaps we can." Merle dashes over to one of the tall cabinets and riffles through a drawer to retrieve a hand mirror the size of her palm set in a metal frame. Like many that have passed through the Spicers' collections, this mirror is not glass but a black, polished stone, used for many magical purposes.

I immediately think of Tempest yesterday and his comment about being a mirrored soul, something else I must seek to understand, and soon.

It's only when we're sitting around the fireplace, each in our preferred armchair, that I notice how plain an object the obsidian mirror is, with no sigils or runes carved into its surface or backing. Merle repositions it to reflect the fireplace and the armchairs opposite her where Edie and I are seated, and then I realize that Edie is visible in the glassy surface, which should be impossible. One of the first things we established after her death was her lack of reflection.

"There you are," Merle breathes, her smile wavering as her eyes threaten tears. "Hello, darling Edie."

Bea leans forward and snatches the mirror. Merle helps her angle it correctly and when the reflection catches, Bea's face goes stony, almost angry. "Oh, Edie," she whispers. "It should have been me. It should have been *me*."

"Tell Bea I'm sorry that I left her," says Edie softly.

Bea blinks and trembles, pushing Merle away in her surprise. "I can hear you. I can hear her; h-how is that possible?"

"I expect it was built into the theorem that powers the mirror," says Merle. "Though I've yet to fully understand the mechanism. I can't hear her, so we must have to be touching the obsidian mirror for it to work, and it must be angled correctly."

Bea reaches for Edie, eyes going wide as their fingertips brush in the reflection but they pass through one another. It breaks my heart. I can't bear to see the pain on Bea's face so I look away.

"Vi, we need to warn them," says Edie. "Ask Merle to touch the mirror again, please."

I do, and Merle reaches over to grasp the handle just below where Bea is holding it. Edie makes eye contact with me and I nod very gently to let her know that I'm ready.

"I read the bones," I swallow, my throat tight and chest aching. "We asked about the fire, the door and the night Edie died. It was no accident. Someone did this to us, to Edie. They want the coven dead."

"Maybe it's a fanatic set against the spiritualist movement." Bea is seated in her armchair like it is a throne. "Akin to a modern-day witch burning."

We all shudder.

"But then how did they hear about us?" asks Merle. "It's not like we go around advertising our services."

I flush crimson. *I* did. I advertised my divination skills in local newspapers and my reputation was growing within occult circles and among unfulfilled housewives. It is possible that someone with intense beliefs targeted us because of me. But it seems rather far-fetched, like something that might happen in a detective novel, and not real life at all.

"Well, fanatic or not, setting a fire was a risk," says Edie. "There were no guarantees it would kill any of us so they might have stayed nearby to make sure they were successful."

Taking out my knucklebone set, I clear books and teacups off the little table between the armchairs. My head is pounding, but I have to try for a reading. Edie makes a disgruntled, disapproving noise. I ignore her and throw the answer to a whispered question. "Was the killer present at the studio at the time of the fire?"

My palms are sweating. It's been weeks since I read in front of the full coven. Something that always came so naturally to me is now a struggle, marred by my self-doubt and my lingering headache. Still, my mind lists the potential meanings of the symbols on display, assessing the proximity of certain bones to the others and slowly I smell the aromatic saffron and wine scent again. A bead of sweat rolls between my shoulder blades. I close my eyes to the flicker of images waiting there – fine silks with delicate beading, Bea's long red hair, Merle pulling at the door handle, a bloody hand tracing a glyph into a wooden surface…

An answer emerges. "They were there."

Bea covers her mouth with a gasp.

"We need the names of everyone who came to help," says Edie.

Merle shakes her head. "I don't know who the men were, locals who heard my shouts, but the woman was Vi's client that evening. I can't remember her name."

"Mrs Aldridge," I say. "Is there any way she could have jammed the door without you noticing?"

Merle is quiet for a little while. "I don't think so, no."

"Unless—" We all look at Bea. "What if magic was used to seal the door?"

"It took three grown men to pry it open," says Merle. "A theorem could deter someone from opening it, but to physically jam the hinges so completely? I simply don't see how that could be done with a theorem."

"What if they were self-syphoning?" I ask, rubbing my thumb.

"It's very risky," says Edie. "But if they were prepared to pay the price, then yes."

Bea raises her brow. "Maybe Mrs Aldridge is an occultist."

"Even if she is, why would she want any of us dead?" asks Merle.

"I don't know." Edie chews on her bottom lip. "But someone does."

"Mrs Aldridge didn't want me to come to her house for her reading," I say, thinking out loud. "She insisted on visiting me. I didn't think much of it at the time, but now…"

No one speaks into the following silence. Bea looks like she has just been stung by an insect: tense and uncomfortable.

"We ought to go back to Pa's studio," I say. "To check for magical residua in case any theorems were used. If there are any, we might recognize their style and signature and find the culprit that way."

It makes my skin crawl just to think of going back there. As far as I know, none of us have been to the studio since that fateful evening. I hear that it is near enough a ruin. It will break my heart, but we have to check.

Bea swallows. "I'll go."

"Not alone." Edie shakes her head.

"*You* shouldn't go back at all. Nor you, Vi," Bea insists. "You both died there! I have some time before my rehearsal. I'll have Father drive me down and then drop me off at the theatre. I won't tell him anything he doesn't need to know, not until we have some answers."

"Very well, and we will call on Mrs Aldridge," I say.

Edie clears her throat. "Once you are a little more rested."

"Then it's decided," says Merle.

I gather up the knucklebones and store them safely in their little pouch. Getting up, I sit beside Edie and take her hand, aware of Bea and Merle's eyes on us. "We three witches pledge to find out who did this to you, and take revenge."

"Always out for blood, aren't you?" says Bea with a wicked grin. "A girl after my own heart."

Out for blood. Yes, I am. I will not stop until I find out who did this and when I do, I will kill them.

9

IN THE ORANGERY

According to the address she gave me, Mrs Aldridge resides in a proud semi-detached Victorian on St Peter's Grove with a fine rose garden and clipped box hedging at the front. Merle has accompanied me, serious and sombre in a long black dress with suede gloves and a dainty hat with a veil. It ought to look ridiculous, especially in the heat of summer, but it suits her. Edie is attired, as she has been since her death, in her waistcoat and fedora, no matter how sticky the day is. The temperature doesn't seem to affect her in death.

I had to rest most of yesterday, soothed by a cool cloth to the head and Merle's herbal teas. In the end, she used a small charm on me to help my lungs recover and settle my headache. I slept all afternoon, waking to Bea's return and the news that she uncovered no remnants of spell work, glyphs or residua at Pa's studio.

I don't know if that is a relief, or a setback. Perhaps it is both.

Now that Bea can use the obsidian mirror to see and hear Edie, they have a lot to catch up on. I'm sure that Edie wishes Bea could see and touch her instead of me. A hollow, empty feeling threatens to drown me. I have selfish blood. I won't apologize for wanting but I have made it difficult between us, my own secret burning a hole in my chest.

This morning, Bea was called to the theatre for a rehearsal. We travelled with her as far as the Royal and then went on past Gillygate and up through Bootham to the Aldridges' house. Again, I feel the strange sensation of being watched. Mrs Aldridge's front garden is long and well enclosed by hedging and healthy roses. If anyone is spying on us, it must be from the house itself but the windows catch the glare from the sunshine and it is impossible to see beyond their gleaming surface. It's not yet ten in the morning but I am sweating in my cotton dress, having chosen longer sleeves to cover the scratches left by the Grey Lady.

I have to knock twice before a plain young woman only a few years our senior opens the door. Dressed in the simple gown and apron of a domestic, she's slender-framed and demure, eyes never straying higher than my lips as I introduce us. I feel like I've met her before. There's something familiar in her open oval features but I cannot place her at all.

"Miss Viola Sampire, Miss Merle Spicer and Miss—" I remember Edie is dead and not to be introduced, and stumble inelegantly over my words. "To see Mrs Aldridge."

I feel utterly grim – my stomach a quiver of snakes, and my palms damp – but that's irrelevant. Projecting confidence is half the job, so I tease my lips into a tight smile and don't let it waver. Finally, the maid meets my eyes, then Merle's.

"Viola Sampire?" She seems stunned, poor thing, and I wonder if we've interrupted her in the middle of some vital task.

"We are expected." I raise my brow a little and she seems to come to, stepping aside for us to enter.

The house is as fine inside as it is out, an artful blend of newer pieces tastefully combined with antiques. At first glance I see nothing that hints at Mrs Aldridge being an occultist but I suppose most practitioners don't advertise their interest in the esoteric mysteries to every guest that enters their home. The maid mumbles something and we follow her down the hall, past a formal front room and the stairs. As we do, I hear the echo of a child crying and look up to a ghost staring at me from the first-floor banisters. To my shock I realize it's the little girl from Betty's, still in her plain nightgown. What on earth is she doing here? Her face is grey and gaunt. I don't remember her looking so … sick.

"Hello there," I call, trying to sound cheerful when the very sight of her churns my stomach. "Won't you come down?"

She jumps and scurries away like a frightened mouse.

"A ghost?" whispers Merle, who has the obsidian mirror in her purse but is yet to take it out as it isn't exactly inconspicuous.

"A child." My hands shake. The girl's presence is unsettling.

"One I've seen before. She seems particularly attached to Mrs Aldridge, but she won't talk to me and she is afraid."

"Let me talk to her," says Edie, climbing the stairs. Edie's never been fond of children, but she's awfully good with them, having many young cousins and several nieces and nephews. If anyone can calm the little girl, it's her.

I realize then that the maid is staring at us with open shock.

"Are you all right, miss? Only..." She gestures to the stairs. "There's no one there."

"I am quite well, thank you."

Still, she hesitates. "Perhaps you should come back another day. The master of the house is not—"

"We are expected," I repeat firmly.

Still, she hesitates until Merle tips her head and makes a quizzical humming sound. "We've met, have we not?"

"Oh, I don't think—" mumbles the domestic, looking startled.

"Yes, yes, you worked for my uncle last year cleaning the galleries. What was your name again?"

"It's Lottie, Miss Spicer." Lottie dips a curtsy. "It is good to see you both again."

Of course! I remember now. A quiet, unremarkable woman who did her work well, she was there for a few months and then moved on.

Lottie escorts us to the back of the house where Mrs Aldridge is working in a glorious wrought-iron orangery filled with hothouse flowers, orchids and dwarf trees in pots – lemon, lime and other citrus. The earthy wealth of humid air mixes with the green of fresh leaves and exotic flowers. I'm sure the committee establishing a botanical garden in York would be thrilled to get their hands on any of the plants in here. Although verdant, it is not rambling and overgrown but neat and clean. Even the workbenches housing the seedlings in trays are clear of dirt.

"Welcome, thank you so much for coming." Mrs Aldridge greets us cordially but there is a slight waver in her voice. "Some tea, Lottie," the lady of the house asks the maid. "Served in here, please."

"Yes, ma'am." Lottie bobs a wobbly curtsy and flees.

"I think we unsettled her a little," I admit.

"Oh, she's tougher than she seems," says Mrs Aldridge. "I don't know what I'd do without her." She puts down the pruning shears and shakes my hand. "Thank you for calling. I admit, I wasn't sure if you would after—" She lapses into an awkward silence.

I fill it with an introduction. "This is Merle Spicer, my associate."

"I hope it is all right that I'm here." Merle beams. "You have a beautiful home."

"Th-thank you." Mrs Aldridge's hands are shaking. She's clearly nervous.

"And you can be assured of my complete discretion, of course," adds Merle with another smile. "We've met, briefly, though I don't expect you recall."

Mrs Aldridge's gaze flicks to me. "The fire?"

"Yes." Merle's smile becomes sad. "I wanted to thank you.

If it weren't for you summoning help that night, two more lives might have been lost. You saved my cousin and my friend with your quick thinking."

"I did only what anyone would do. I am so terribly sorry for the loss of your friend."

"Thank you. I have been meaning to ask." Merle catches my eye and despite the swelling pressure in my chest and the dread in my veins stirred by the memories of that night, I have to stop myself smiling because Merle is being so utterly herself. I should have known she'd ask Mrs Aldridge the difficult questions as soon as she entered the house.

"The night of the fire," says Merle, "do you remember anyone hanging around or lingering where they shouldn't?"

Mrs Aldridge is already shaking her head. "I couldn't say. I am not from that part of town so I do not know who belongs there and who doesn't. The papers said it was an accident?"

She turns it into a question and I know that I must give her something. "The bones have indicated otherwise."

Her eyes flare wide and she clutches at her heavy art deco necklace. A believer, then. If she was sceptical of my abilities as a diviner, she might appear less convinced.

We're invited to sit at a round table with a view towards an ordered cottage garden in full August bloom. Merle leads some opening chit-chat, asking about the plants and how to tend to them properly, easing Mrs Aldridge's nerves with a subject she enjoys until she is more relaxed.

I am suddenly very curious as to why Mrs Aldridge has invited me here, especially as she insists she knows nothing about the fire. Most of my work is divining love matches, but she's married and doesn't seem the type to have an affair. Does she suspect her husband of infidelity? Perhaps she has lost something precious. I've found plenty of lost items using the bones as guidance, even once catching a thief.

A thought occurs to me and I call myself all kinds of a fool. The bones give me the power to see what others cannot and know what is hidden. Word of my skills was spreading, both through my advertisements but also as satisfied clients told others about my discretion and accuracy. The culprit might be someone trying to stop this meeting from happening.

"Have you told anyone about this meeting?" I ask, interrupting the flow of Mrs Aldridge and Merle's conversation.

"Goodness, no," says Mrs Aldridge, then stammers over her words. "Not that I'm ashamed, but my husband is a man of science." She covers her mouth and the tense little laugh that escapes. "Albert would not approve of your being here but I must try everything I can to find the truth."

I know exactly how she feels. "On the day of the fire, who knew you were coming to see me for a reading?"

"No one ... only Lottie, but she is very discreet."

Merle and I exchange a glance. Ah, yes, because domestic servants never gossip. If Lottie had told someone who was anti-witchcraft, they could very well be behind it all. But who could that possibly be? Occultism isn't a hidden practice, but nor is it something that most average people put much stock in. Mr Spicer has as many clients who collect occult items for their historical value as for their genuine magical properties. And if there was such a thing as an extreme anti-witchcraft group, would they truly target a small coven of four young witches when Mr Spicer and his associates work far more complex theorems than we can dream of?

Somehow, I don't think so.

"How does it work?" Mrs Aldridge folds her hands into her lap, expectant.

Time to earn my keep. Taking the bones from their silk pouch, I let her see them.

"Are those human?" she asks.

"Most certainly. Bone, especially human bone, is a great conduit and storehouse of magical residua." I proudly pick up the smallest of all the bones painted with an eye, ear and mouth. "This is the self. It represents you in relation to the questions you ask. The other bones are called the soma, meaning body, the mind, heart, soul, world, root and time. Each has four images. You ask the questions. It's my job to interpret the answers through my connection to the spirits."

That last part is unproven but it sounds impressive.

As I speak, I find myself settling back into the familiarity of the reading. The bones are cold to my touch and I can feel them humming against my skin, eager to get to work.

Edie returns and stands by the tidy potting table opposite where we're sitting. "The child either can't or won't talk but she was insistent I see the sick boy upstairs. She is very concerned about him. His name is Christopher."

A sick boy? He must be Mrs Aldridge's son. Perhaps that's

why I heard a child crying when I rolled the bones yesterday.

Mrs Aldridge hesitates, chewing on her lip, her eyes filling with sadness. For a moment she seems like she might cry. "I-I do not know where to start."

"Is it about your son, Christopher?" I ask.

She is surprised. "How could you possibly—" Her lower lip quivers. "We've seen countless doctors and no one can diagnose him, let alone offer a cure. He improves at times, only to suddenly relapse worse than before. We're incredibly grateful to Lottie; without her care he might not have lasted this past month." Taking out a handkerchief, she dabs gently at her eyes. "But he is in decline and unless we discover what ails him, he will die."

Mrs Aldridge has nothing to do with the fire. That much is clear. She is simply a distressed mother trying to find a cure for her sick child. The weight of her hope settles on my shoulders.

Closing my eyes, I clink the bones against one another, feeling them connect and retreat. Holding the question in my mind, I ask, "What is making Christopher Aldridge sick?" and I throw the bones high, opening my eyes just in time to see them arc down and land on the tablecloth with several soft thumps. Two of the bones hit each other and scatter in opposite directions. That is significant. A crossroads.

I reach for the little flickers of image, scent and sound that the bones gift me: sickness, a red palm, a twisted and angry face, a bloody handprint on wallpaper, a crying boy vomiting up his meal. My body pricks with distress and my skin feels tight. I sway in my seat, sensing hunger and anger and a great, terrible need.

Gently, I touch the soma bone, which primarily represents that which is physical. The body. It shows a tiny image of a loaf of bread. The stink of sickness floods my nose and I almost gag. My stomach cramps. I have never felt so empty.

"Nourishment, or a severe lack of it," I say. Could it be that simple? "Does Christopher have any issues with food?"

"He struggles to eat," Mrs Aldridge replies. "Lottie has him on a special diet and we've seen some improvement, until we don't."

I sigh deeply, frustrated to be struggling, and scan the rest of the spread. I need to help this child. The stark clarity of it is shocking after so much self-doubt. His problem *is* about nourishment. I roll for the different food groups – for wheat, dairy, eggs, nuts – but they come up negative. It couldn't be that simple or the doctors would have found the trigger and eliminated it from his diet.

"Ask her about the ghost girl," suggests Edie. "Something's not right about that child."

I believe her. Despite her love of the occult, Edie doesn't get gut feelings the way I do. She's strangely practical and she only speaks when she has something necessary to contribute.

"Did you ever have a daughter?" I ask Mrs Aldridge.

My client frowns. "No, Christopher is our one and only child. Why do you ask?"

I hesitate, not wanting to upset her, but the simplest way to find out more is to ask.

"I see the spirit of a little blonde girl of about eight or nine." I deliberately keep it vague and do not mention that this aspect has nothing to do with bones and divination and everything to do with a haunting. "She seems concerned for Christopher. Do you know of a child like that, a friend who passed away, perhaps?"

Mrs Aldridge thinks for a long moment, then shakes her head. "No, I'm sorry."

The heavy atmosphere is broken by the maid, Lottie, who enters the hothouse with a tray of piping tea, cups and saucers. It seems absurd to drink hot tea in such temperatures but a cup will calm my nerves.

There's a crash – porcelain on saucer sharply jarring. "Do be careful, Lottie," Mrs Aldridge scolds. "I apologize; she's not normally this clumsy."

Saying nothing, Lottie hurries to serve Merle and then myself. Her hand trembles as she sets my cup and saucer in front of me. I smile at her, but she won't meet my eyes. Taking a second, smaller teapot, Lottie serves Mrs Aldridge, dips a wobbly curtsy and scurries off. There is milk and sugar, or lemon, the wonderful scent of bergamot wafting in the steam from my cup. Tea is one of the joys of life. I raise it to my lips.

In a heartbeat the ghost girl appears beside me, eyes wide with alarm. Edie lets out a cry of surprise when, quick as anything, the child viciously grabs my right arm and shakes it. Hot tea splashes over my knees. Pain scalds my thighs. Gasping, I wrench my arm from the girl's grip. The cup strikes the tiles and shatters, sending porcelain spinning across the floor.

Edie grabs for the girl, hauling her away from me, and the dead child snarls and scratches like a cat in a trap. Cursing, Edie snatches her hand back – the girl has bitten it – and then the child is gone, sprinting away through the wall of the orangery and into the garden.

"Little viper," Edie hisses and runs after her.

I'm too stunned to even apologize for the loss of the cup. Mrs Aldridge calls for Lottie to bring a broom and flutters over me, concerned. My legs sting but I'm more put out that one of my favourite dresses is stained.

When Mrs Aldridge's back is turned, Merle mouths, *What happened?* at me and I give a little shake of my head. Not here. I know spirits can touch me and certainly hurt me, the Grey Lady proved as much, but to be so suddenly and roughly mishandled by a child ghost concerns me. I am shaking with the realization that my ability comes with great dangers, but then so does all magic.

Lottie is full of apologies, even though she did nothing wrong. She uses a damp cloth to soothe my burn and clean my dress. A door slams somewhere. There are footsteps in the hallway and an older man with a ruddy face appears at the hothouse door.

Mrs Aldridge stands bolt upright, looking guilty. "Albert, I wasn't expecting you home."

"Is this her?" the man snaps. He's a gruff, fleshy sort, with greying hair and a thick moustache. "Winifred, I explicitly forbade you from engaging in this nonsense."

"Darling, Miss Sampire and her friend are only trying to help."

"Help?" Mr Aldridge sneers. "Our son is dying and you consult *witches* for an answer?"

"Talented witches," Merle points out, though I wish she wouldn't, but now she's on a roll and there is no stopping her from speaking her mind. "Who expect to be paid."

I put my head in my hands.

"I'm not giving you a penny!" Mr Aldridge roars. "Out!"

Mrs Aldridge is blazing red with embarrassment and stands to walk us to the door but her husband plants himself fully in her way and ushers us towards the exit like we are vermin. My chest is tight and my anger pounds with indignation over the insult as we step out into the heat of the day.

"Mr Aldridge, if I could just—" As the door is slammed in our faces I catch a last glance at my client and the desperation and humiliation in her expression.

"Bastard," mutters Merle.

Edie meets us at the front gate. She had no luck catching up to the ghost child. I feel restless and uneasy. I've already upset a rabid nun with a taste for flesh. Now a young dead girl is out to get me. I am not safe any more. Not on the streets of this city and perhaps not even in my own home as my enemies can walk through walls.

And poor Christopher. If I cannot divine what ails him, he may very well die. I cannot let that happen. What's more, between Bea's trip to Pa's old studio and our visit here, we're no closer to finding out who is trying to kill us, or why. With no answers, we're easy targets.

They could strike again at any moment and we are not ready.

10

TRAPPED

Merle stops in at the York Royal to watch Bea's performance. Fear ripples through me at the memory of the Grey Lady stalking me backstage with her greedy eyes and bloody scalp. I cannot risk returning to the theatre and so I elect to walk home, even if the exercise does make me wheeze.

To my surprise and delight, Edie decides to accompany me rather than visit Bea. We walk in amiable silence as far as the museum gardens. I'm certain she is worrying about the little girl and poor Christopher as much as I am. The day is fine but it's overly hot in the sun. The ghost of a lady in long white skirts with a lapdog under her arm scolds me for not carrying a parasol to preserve my complexion. Edie laughs because it is now the fashion to tan. On the other side of the gardens we cross the river at Lendal Bridge.

My heart races as it always does this close to the water. I remember the first time I saw the Ouse after the fire. It never gets any easier, except perhaps at night when the river is full of stars and I can hear jazz on the wind, a ghostly spool of music winding into the night. This late in the morning the broken sunlight dancing along the river's surface does little to detract from the grasping hands reaching from the waters. There are thousands of souls in the Ouse, trapped by the river. Or I presume they are. I've never seen one pull themselves on to the bank and I do not mean to get close enough to discover more. They are sinister and melancholic and I intend to keep my distance.

With the bridge at our backs, we turn on to quieter streets. It gives us more opportunity to talk openly without worrying about the living giving me strange glances. The dead are everywhere in all manner of garb: soap sellers, flower peddlers, children with dirty faces and toothy smiles playing in and out of the yards. There seem to be more Roman soldiers around today, their armour glinting in the sunlight. My stomach clenches in apprehension. A ghostly tanner is at work to our right, seemingly unconscious of our presence but something about him warns me to keep my distance.

I hate that I am so afraid. Surely most of these spirits mean me no harm but I can't forget the Grey Lady's hungry eyes.

We take a narrow road that is little wider than some of the passageways riddling the oldest part of the city. A pricking shoots up my spine and across my skull, warning me that something is wrong here. Gripping Edie tightly, I look behind us, sure I'm to find the vicious grimace of the nun from the Royal in my face and hear her voice singing her prayers as she stalks me. There is nothing there and yet I *feel* a presence.

Ahead, a figure steps from a doorway so suddenly that I run right into him. The sun is out but his face is shrouded in shadow from the tall buildings either side so that I can't immediately make out his features. Is it a soul come to harm me? It takes me a second longer than it should to recognize the bowler hat and realize it's Phillip Petty.

We're not far from Blossom Street. Was he waiting for us? I try to side-step and go around him but he moves to block my path.

"You're a problem, Viola." His voice is low and dangerous.

I jut my chin. "I'm delighted to hear it."

"My aunt kicked me out because of you."

"You stole from her. It is no surprise your family wants nothing to do with you."

"If you tell him such things, he will beat you," Edie warns. "*Please*, Vi, do not be a fool. You have such a temper on you."

She's right. For her sake I turn on my heels and walk back up Barker Lane. It will take longer to get home along Toft Green, but so be it. Phillip follows, gunning for a fight. My lungs pinch and my legs ache but I pick up the pace. Edie hurries along with me.

"Oi." Phillip grabs my shoulder, pushing me through a gateway into a long, narrow yard off the gardens behind Micklegate.

"You don't want to mess with me," I warn, shoving him

away and standing straighter. "I read the truth in the bones. I see the dead. I'm a psychic and a witch."

There it is: his own fear wrought on his face. I feel a flare of satisfaction. For all he pretends not to believe in the occult, he does. And he is afraid. I take out the witch bottle I tucked into my purse beside the pouch that houses my knucklebones. Phillip takes a step back, as if expecting a grenade. Little does he know I can't hurt him with it, not immediately. "If you ever touch me or anyone I care about, I will curse your manhood to slowly wither."

He blinks. "Is that a *threat*?"

I furrow my brows in mock pity. "Oh dear, try to keep up. Of course I'm threatening you. Now, be a dear and go away."

There's a dangerous crackling atmosphere around Phillip, the promise of violence. Perhaps I have pushed him too far this time. Again, I go to walk away, being careful not to put my back to him. He sidles out to block my escape and there is nowhere to go but deeper into the yard. No way out, unless I bang on the back doors of the houses here and someone takes pity on me.

Phillip makes eye contact with someone over my shoulder and it's only then I realize my mistake. He isn't alone. Behind me is a ratty-looking young man with a mean face. Phillip is close now, so close I can smell the funk of his hair pomade and fresh sweat. He looks at me with a hard, nasty gaze and I feel another zing of fear strike my spine.

"They used to stone witches, didn't they?" he says to his friend.

"Oh, aye." The rat-faced goon picks up a loose brick from the side of the yard.

I'm starting to understand that the bully of a boy I knew has grown into someone treacherous and unpredictable and, like the hot-headed fool I am, I've given him plenty of reason to target me.

"Run!" snaps Edie.

"None of that." Phillip's thick arm slides around my neck and he pulls me into a corner of the yard, Rat Face following. There's sweat on my back. Edie screams and launches herself at the men but her blows have no impact. I could scream, but I can see by the glint in Phillip's eyes that he's waiting for an excuse to sock me in the stomach.

Playing on his fears might be my only chance. I begin to chant low under my breath, the words a nonsense mixture of Latin and random sounds that come out as a strange and unsettling language. Recognizing my plan, Edie reaches through Phillip and Rat Face to mess up my hair and drag her fingers down my face, contorting the skin as I start to twitch and snap my teeth.

Phillip quickly lets me go, and he and Rat Face take a very generous step away. Rolling my head on my neck, I sway, dropping my shoulders, bending my knees and tilting my head as I moan. As worried as she is, Edie cracks a smile. I must look ridiculous, but that is better than the alternative.

With a great shout, I lunge forward, startling Rat Face so much that he drops the brick and trips over. I throw the witch bottle at them. It shatters, spilling a bird skull, iron filings and bundles of herbs. Phillip shrieks and jumps. Seeing an opening, I dart through the gap between them and sprint out of the yard.

My shoes slap the cobbles sending jolts of discomfort up my legs. My lungs constrict and I gasp, slowing after only a few seconds of running. *Not now. Please not now.* My breathing is laboured, each chestful a rattle. I cannot keep up this pace, especially not in this heat, but with terror searing my heart I push on. I just have to get to Micklegate. It is always busy, even in the baking heat or pouring rain. There, someone will surely be able to help me.

Footsteps and threats echo behind us. They're coming. My muscles scream but I have to keep moving. I want Edie's hand in mine as reassurance. I'm barely an arm's reach from Micklegate and possible safety when I realize she isn't with me.

"Edie?" I try to say, but my lungs don't have the air and the sound comes out strangled. I pivot on the corner. Phillip and Rat Face are charging towards me, and between us is Edie, unmoving in the passageway, her eyes ripe with panic.

I try to shout her name and a fit of coughing erupts from my lungs. Panic flares in my blood, hot and sharp.

"I can't move," she cries.

I step back into the alley, ignoring her shout of protest.

"Go, Vi. They cannot hurt me."

But whatever has her trapped might do her harm. I won't abandon her. Not ever.

Reaching for her hand, I feel a strange pressure in the air

and then I'm through it, finding her fingers in mine. I pull and she slips forward but then stops, her body locking as if there is an invisible plate of glass in her way that she cannot traverse.

The men rush through Edie and reach me, eyes glowering, cries of victory on their lips. Rat Face grabs me, tearing my hand from Edie's as Phillip smothers my mouth with his meaty arm to stop me screaming. They drag me back down the alleyway, past where Edie stands. She throws her arms around me and holds on tightly.

God, it hurts. She's pulling me one way and Phillip is trying to wrench me another. I hear Rat Face making a fuss about how, "She's fucking floating and that shit ain't natural."

"Darned witches," Phillip grumbles, winning out over Edie who sobs my name as I'm dragged back up Barker Lane.

There isn't enough air in the world to fill me. I can't breathe as it is, let alone with this oaf's hand over my face. My veins are fire. I want the power to tear Phillip and his friend to pieces. *Fight harder*, screams my mind, but my body has nothing more to give. My chest is too tight. I am going down, my shoulder jarring painfully against the pavement.

Rough hands at my neck. Wet spittle on my cheek as Phillip hisses in my ear, "I protect my enterprises and *you* are a meddler."

Anger replaces my panic. Edie's wails echo in my ears. Her distress is a blade through my heart and I remember her wreathed in flames, obscured by smoke, as the world went dark. It's happening again: her voice cries my name as everything grows hazy.

A sharp pain blooms through my cheek bone. Something cracks in my elbow. Hands pull at my clothes and the cross-body purse I wear. A fresh terror surges through me. Will they rob me too? Violate me? Firm hands close on my throat and I hear a seam rip and a stranger's shout before all I know is darkness.

PART 3
HEART

The third bone is the heart bone and represents feelings and intuition as well as emotional needs.

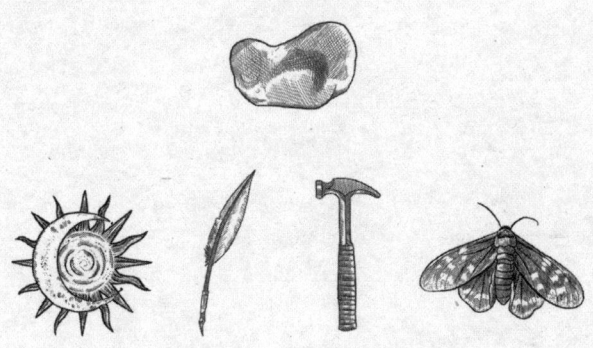

Sun and Moon: duality/neutrality/overcoming obstacles/leadership/authority/cycles and repetition/travel/non-binary identities/tranquillity. Neutral.
Quill: creativity/talent/empathy/kindness/a message or letter/the act of writing or drawing/falsehood/illusion. Positive.
Hammer: strength/precision/craft/skill/productivity/blacksmithing/building/the act of destruction/violence/aggression. Negative.
Moth: loneliness/sadness/the night/hope/new beginnings/change/transformation/growth/inner wisdom/intuition/insects. Neutral.

II

AWAY FROM PRYING EYES

A sudden warmth blooms through my chest and the knots in my lungs unravel, as if someone has pulled on one end of a very tight bow and my ribs have come apart. Air floods my airways, the darkness recedes, and I look up into a face I recognize.

With a flare of elation, I realize it's the woman Mr Spicer was talking to about the death-touched. Is her name Rachel? I'm relieved to see her again. The throb in my cheek bone is deliciously painful and I taste copper in my mouth.

"Are you well?" she asks, tucking a witch bottle into her pocket.

I nod, although I'm stunned and aching. Rachel stands, clearly confident I'll live, before she makes off along the road shouting at a fast-retreating Phillip. His accomplice, the rat-faced man, is slumped against the brick wall to my left, awake and terrified, his eyes almost all whites. He's grunting like a beast but doesn't get up. Scuttling away from him, I get to my feet, wincing at the scrapes on my palms.

"Edie?" I gasp, hurrying to her.

She's still a few paces away, her hand to the air. "I'm trapped! It's some kind of theorem that stops me from moving out of this small circle. I think it's her doing it." Edie points to Rachel, who is on her way back, having lost Phillip. "She was hidden behind a high-level abscondium theorem, threw both men off you without even touching them, and used a separate incantation to help you breathe."

Passing us, Rachel walks over to Rat Face, who grunts and strains to get away from her. He can't seem to speak, as if his lips have been sealed shut.

More magic.

"If you or your friend go after this girl again" – Rachel points to me – "I will lock your body and steal your voice so that the only things you can move are your eyes and I will leave you like that for the rest of your life. Do you understand?"

Rat Face nods, his expression pleading. With a sigh, Rachel's elegant hands shape a glyph in the air before touching her thumb to the young man's forehead. Immediately his mouth falls open and he reaches for his throat, as if checking his head is still on his shoulders, then he's up and running as fast as he can round the corner.

I attempt to not openly gape in amazement, or envy. Rachel's power and mastery of complex theorems is impressive. Not only did she balance multiple theorems at once, but she had Rat Face trapped in invisible chains and his tongue stilled. Such magic *is* possible, with the right syphons, but it is way outside the abilities of our coven. My cheeks redden in embarrassment. She must have self-syphoned to work such theorems, meaning she used some of her own health and life to save a complete stranger. It's a bold and impressive show of strength.

Does it mean I can trust her?

I look at Rachel, *really* look at her. The little half-moon glasses suit her well, as does the steel in her eyes. I've never in my life seen a person so noticeably clean. Not in a moneyed way, she is merely neat and considered with her hair pinned back from her face on one side and curled. Her striped sporty jumper is lightweight and short-sleeved, and like Edie she favours wide-legged trousers.

"Thank you. Phillip might have killed me." I shudder. "And you just… I-I've never experienced magic like that. What theorems did you use?"

As I speak, a sliver of confused interest flits across Rachel's features, then settles. "Several of my own devising. You were lucky I was here."

"Why *are* you here?" I ask, then flush pink because that sounded a little sharp and very ungrateful. "I only mean that my friend Edie is stuck inside … well, I don't know. A spirit sink?"

I recall the term from a battered copy of a book called *Unstable Spirits* that I read a little of before Mr Spicer had it rebound for sale. It detailed the use of magical theorems to trap ghosts and force them into answering questions about the world. A little unnecessary. Most of the ghosts I've encountered have been perfectly talkative.

"Nothing so permanent," says Rachel.

"It had better not be!" exclaims Edie. "Once a ghost disappears inside a sink, there's no retrieving them."

I tremble, imagining Edie being stuck forever. Bile rises in the back of my throat. "You *can* get her out, can't you?"

"Of course." Rachel twists her fingers and a battered satchel bag appears in a nearby doorway. An impressive and casual show of power. She must have a stockpile of witch bottles in that bag of hers, but I didn't see her draw on the stored essence inside them.

"It's a ghost trap," Rachel goes on. I blink at her like a fool, struggling to remember the difference between a ghost trap and a spirit sink. I wish I'd spent less time focused on various forms of divination and read more widely like my coven sisters. Perhaps then I wouldn't feel so eclipsed by this woman and her experience.

She's not the first practitioner I've met. Many visitors to Mr Spicer's house are occultists, but we rarely get to see them work a theorem that's anything more than a little glamour or charm designed to amuse and entertain. The greatest working that house has seen was when Mr Saunders and a friend of his from university – a Mr Harrow – helped Mr Spicer set the wards. Our coven was not permitted to be present, left only to admire their handiwork after it was complete.

"I can dissolve the trap and free your friend," Rachel reassures me as she begins to search through her bag, setting an empty witch bottle on the cobbles.

But why set a ghost trap here? I cast my memory back to the overheard argument between Rachel and Mr Spicer – something about a shipment going missing and how she has an ethical code she refuses to break for his convenience.

He called her a soul catcher. She called herself a scientist.

"Because you don't take innocent souls?" I say, watching her reaction carefully.

"Correct. I only catch ghosts that are a danger to their own kind and shades that are corrupted by magic and therefore a danger to the living." Rachel pulls a stick of what looks like red wax from her bag. "I'm attempting to trap a dangerous soul that has been feeding on other spirits in York. This roadway is a favourite haunt of hers."

"Ghosts can *feed* on each other?" I ask, the shock of that revelation eclipsing the ten other questions that sprung to mind as she spoke.

"Oh, yes. The dead have few rules, but not syphoning phantasmic essence from another deceased soul is one of them, though there are plenty that do. The emperor up at the Minster is notorious for it as a form of punishment."

"Who makes the rules?" asks Edie warily.

Rachel laughs at that, a dry mirth that makes me think there is more to whatever she might say in response. "No one authority, I suppose. Emperor Septimus Severus likes to style himself in charge of the city's ghosts, alongside several other ancient spirits who call themselves the Old Souls."

Ghosts are organized? They have a society of a kind, they communicate, help and harm each other. It makes sense.

"The emperor breaks his own rules?" I say, frowning in confusion.

"Like any successful politician," says Rachel. "I advise avoiding their attentions. They have some strange ideas about death-touched. They will hurt you if they can."

Something warm settles in my chest and I realize that she is the first to confirm my suspicions. Now I have a name for what I am and what I can do. Death-touched.

"How do you handle them?" I ask.

"I pay them no attention. They avoid me because I have grounds to trap and bottle them, and as I'm not death-touched like you, they can't hurt me."

That brings me up short. She's not death-touched? I'm disappointed. "But you *can* see ghosts?"

"Only with the help of these." Rachel taps her half-moon spectacles. "Most occultists and soul catchers use an obsidian mirror to see the dead but they're rather unwieldy and terribly inconvenient. I developed the lenses instead. They also allow the wearer to see hidden magic, essential in my line of work. What kind of occultism do you practise?" she asks before I can spring another question on her.

"I read bones."

Rachel's brow goes up. "An osteomage."

"Astragalomancy, to be precise."

"How charming. Are you any good at it?"

"She's *very* good," Edie snaps from her spot in the ghost trap. "Show her your knucklebones."

It is then that two terrible things happen simultaneously. Rachel swivels suddenly, like an animal sensing a predator approaching. As she does, my hands search for my purse and the soft silk bag that is always tucked inside, but do not find it.

I look around the road in a panic. My bag might have fallen off when Phillip and his friend tore me down but I know in my gut that it isn't true. I recall the sensation of hands pulling my clothing, the pressure on my body, and the sound of fabric tearing.

My purse is gone and with it my knucklebone set. Phillip has stolen them.

12

KILLER INSTINCT

There is a moment beyond the white wave of panic at the loss of the bones that is strangely calm. Regret pools deep in my heart alongside irritation and self-loathing. How could I be so careless? They're our one means of decoding the truth about the fire and Edie's death. Not to mention my hopes of earning a living to support my family. Now they're in the hands of a violent bully and it won't be easy to retrieve them.

Before I can think of a plan to get them back, Rachel snaps, "She's coming! Quickly, get against the wall."

"Who's coming?" I ask.

"The soul I'm here to catch." Shoving her bag aside with her foot, Rachel gestures to the recessed doorway, meaning for me to step inside. "We need to hide."

"But Edie—"

Rachel shakes her head. "There's no time. She'll have to be bait."

"Bait?" gasps Edie at the same time that I say, "Absolutely not."

There's a change in the air from muggy warmth to electrical static that sends a nasty prickle over my skin. As the day wears on, the air has grown heavier and now I scent rain. A storm is brewing above us and the clean sky is tinged a deep, burnished blue.

"I'm sorry, but this is the fastest way to capture Mary, the ghost I've been hunting, and also get Edie out of the trap." Rachel's whispering now.

A dewy glow has bloomed over her forehead and her cheeks are flushed pink with excitement. She enjoys the pursuit, I realize. But it is no big game animal we're taking down. It is a ghost who consumes souls, and my darling Edie is immobilized and in her path.

"No," I say. "Dissolve the trap, now."

Rachel gives Edie a worried glance. "I *can't*. Not in time."

"Then hunt this Mary a different day."

"I've been tracking her for *weeks*. The trap is set. You're the ones who stumbled into it and ruined—"

"I'll do it," says Edie, looking over her shoulder as a breeze gusts down the roadway, sending a crumpled newspaper fluttering. The air is a blissful breath of cool on my hot skin.

"Edie—" I start, but she cuts me off.

"What choice do I have?" Her chin is set and her gaze determined. She likes to sound brave, but we don't know what is about to happen. What if this ghost tries to feed on her?

Rachel drags me back into the doorway. "Don't move or

speak until I give permission," she orders. "No matter what happens. She'll only show interest in Edie if you're not on the menu. Souls like her hunger for death-touched blood above anything."

Rachel doesn't wait for my answer before reaching into her pocket and crouching to draw a quick glyph on to the brick at our feet with chalk. Her theorem is unfamiliar and in an unfamiliar alphabet, but I sense a change around us as magic blushes the air, ensnaring us in tendrils of power.

Are we invisible now?

My attention moves to the alleyway as a ghost comes into sight. For a horrifying moment she reminds me of the nun from York Royal in that she is slender and dressed in black and moves as though gravity has no hold on her. But I see as she approaches that she is far older in her face, her stringy hair greying under a dirty linen coif. There is something unsettling about her – neck too long, eyes bulging and overly prominent, gnarled hands with long sharp nails that look a lot like claws.

As she spots Edie her mouth splits into a wicked grin. Edie's gaze is fixed on the alcove where Rachel and I are hiding but I know neither of them can see us. I can tell that Edie is pretending not to be afraid, even though she's shaking. I hate the idea that she might feel abandoned and that she's facing this monster alone. Why did I let this happen?

"Hello, pretty," says Mary, sidling closer to Edie. "Got yourself caught, have you?"

Mary grins wider, inhumanly wide. This close her skin is grey and sagging on her bones, like melted wax.

"I'm stuck," Edie says, affecting a pleasant, relaxed smile. "Will you pull me out? It would be very kind of you."

She reaches for Mary and cocks her head, giving the ghost a sweet little smile. My stomach turns over. Although I know it to be a ploy, and an unsubtle one at that, I cannot help the flare of protective fear in my stomach. The notion of Mary laying a single one of those crusty clawed fingers on Edie makes me want to destroy her.

"Nice try, catcher," Mary calls, not taking her eyes from Edie.

Beside me, Rachel tenses.

"As tempting as your little snack is, I think I'll leave her here." Mary leans as close as she dares to Edie without being caught in the trap. "I've found far more nourishing morsels to satisfy my hunger."

Suddenly, I know what I must do. Mary isn't going to step into the ghost trap, and Rachel is right, she is too dangerous to roam the streets. Breaking through the theorem cloaking me, I dash the five short strides towards the ghost trap and, before Mary even realizes I'm there, I shove her inside. Edie sees me coming and prepares, swinging her arm so that as Mary tumbles forward, her clenched fist connects with Mary's jaw. There is an almighty crack, Edie yelps in pain but Mary goes down, stuck fast by the ghost trap. She howls in anger and thrashes.

Rachel is beside me in a flash, the empty witch bottle in her hand. I don't know what she means to do with it. Mary has Edie by the ankle now and she's ... changing: grey-skinned limbs stretching too long, her body distending as she looms over Edie. Her expression is grotesque in its cruel anger.

"Your wretched trap can't hold me for long," she spits.

"Stop her!" I cry to Rachel, who is already chanting a theorem. I can feel the effect, like I need to sneeze but can't.

All of a sudden, Mary stops and looks to Rachel, anger contorting to shock and then horror. "You bitch, you bloody bitch—"

Mary's curses falter as her face fractures, fragments lifting from her form, creating deep fissures. There's no blood. She comes apart as if she's made of husk and dry dust. Her mouth opens in a wordless scream, teeth streaming from her skull as they splinter and all the parts of her lift into the air like a gruesome trail of smoke. The coil of particles breach the ghost trap and are sucked into the witch bottle in Rachel's hands.

Edie huffs a breath of relief but the magic doesn't end. I know the moment it wraps around her because she freezes, expression flickering with discomfort.

"No, not her!" But my protest means nothing as my best friend is taken next, her body breaking up as she reaches for me, fear in her eyes. Her pretty face is the last part of her to fragment, fissures riddling her smooth skin, cracking her eyes, and severing her pink lips. Someone is sobbing and, I realize, as the last of Edie disappears into the bottle, that it is me.

Stoppering it with a cork, Rachel grimaces an apology as she hands the bottle to me. "I had no choice. I'm sorry. The theorem transfers every perished soul within the trap. I had to contain Mary, which means taking your sweetheart too."

The glass is slightly warm to the touch and inside, within a swirling maelstrom, I see the flash of an eye, a mouth, a clawed hand. "What is she doing to Edie in there?" Oh God, I think that I am going to vomit.

"Nothing. Their loops won't intersect. At least, I very much hope not." Rachel pulls a stick of blood-red wax from her pocket. "The theorem that keeps souls contained mimics a necromic cycle, enhancing their phantasmic energy."

"Wh-what's a necromic cycle?"

Rachel hesitates, as if surprised I do not already know. "Most of the dead you see look somewhat normal, that is to say, they do not go around with the marks of their death on them. They are likely free souls, able to roam where they please. Some are perhaps tethered to a place or person, and a little more limited in their movements, but if you ever see a ghost who is static or confined to one small area and who shows signs of the way they died, then you must not get close to them."

"Why?" I whisper, stomach churning with nausea.

"They are consumed by their deaths and unable to break loose from their memories. Their phantasmic essence turns inwards and repeats their last moments. I have heard that death-touched are vulnerable to them. Get too close and you will be sucked into the loop and suffer their fate. But, mimicking this structure with magics allows a soul catcher like myself to safely contain ghosts and enhance their essence for use."

"Edie is ... trapped in her own death?" I ask, horror-struck. "Please, you have to get her out—"

"I can't here, not without freeing Mary too. I need a controlled environment." Rachel snaps her fingers and a small flame appears at the end of her thumb. She uses it to melt the stick of red wax, sealing the cork into the bottle. A drop splatters my palm and the hot sting helps me push past my panic to reconnect with myself.

There is a sharp sound and a hairline crack spiders through the side of the bottle. I gasp in surprise. Rachel curses.

"I've never used one bottle for two souls before," she admits. "It's not stable. We have to act quickly."

With the bottle sealed, it takes her another few moments to erase all signs of the ghost trap and invisibility theorem, pocketing her chalk and wax. The glass bottle containing Edie and Mary fits into the leather satchel. "Come along; the sooner we get to the lab the faster we can free your friend."

When she shoulders her bag and heads towards Micklegate, I follow, heart in my mouth, and I swear I hear her mutter under her breath, "And we'll see what you're *really* made of."

13

BENEATH THE CRYPT

In the stories, graveyards are always haunted but there are no souls in sight as Rachel and I hurry through the wrought-iron gates of York Cemetery. Plump clouds pillow over the sun and the storm breaks, fat drops of warm rain shivering from the sky. Neither of us is carrying an umbrella but after the heat of the past couple of weeks the rain is a relief.

My nerves are singing. Every second that Edie is in that bottle is a second too long. Ahead, an elegant Neo-classical building watches over the cemetery. When we reach it, Rachel moves off the path and on to the grass between the graves. The rain makes it slippery underfoot. The delicious, fresh scent of wet summer greenery envelops us as she leads me around the side of the chapel to a door at the back. It opens at her touch and we head inside a dark crypt under the main building.

There are no electric lights and we grub through the gloom. Up ahead is a wall of tombs, some carved with epitaphs, but many are featureless. Rachel does something, I'm not certain what, but there's a grating noise and a stack of tombs swings inwards to reveal stairs going deeper into the earth.

"What's down there?" I fight to keep the nervous tremor from my voice. No one knows I'm here. If something were to happen to me…

No, I cannot think like that. I may not yet know if I can trust Rachel, but I am at her mercy because she has Edie trapped in a bottle and I already know that there is nothing I would not do to get her back. Rachel is known to Mr Spicer and she saved me from Phillip and his goon. I do not think she means me or Edie any harm.

"It's the lab I share with my father," says Rachel, gesturing for me to go first. "I have wards set up. It's safe."

There's a warm glow emanating up the stairwell but I take the steps cautiously as there isn't a banister, and emerge into an expansive low-ceilinged chamber. Gas lights flicker from sconces along the walls, casting shadows and making it look like a gothic novel come to life.

"Father?" Rachel strides past me and dumps her satchel on the huge oak table in the centre of the space.

There's no sign of anyone else here, although the lamps are lit. It is as damp and airless as a cave, except the walls are stone blocks with some areas of smooth tile. It is blessedly cool after the muggy heat outside. With the bookshelves and cabinets stuffed with curiosities, alembic beakers, scientific equipment and occult items, it feels rather like an underground Frankenstein's laboratory. Without the corpses. Or so I hope.

To the right of the entrance is a kitchen of sorts: a large, deep stone sink and sideboard stacked with enamel plates. There's a kettle and paraffin burner and a frying pan hanging on a hook beside a small, curious door of unpainted metal with a heavy handle and a series of rubber tubes attached. Each tube runs to a witch bottle set up on wire stands nearby.

Rachel stretches the kinks out of her neck. "Hold this, please."

She gives me the bottle that Edie and Mary are trapped in. The weight of it feels wrong, far too light to contain two souls. Inside is a turmoil of grasping hands and sharp nails, and Edie's freckle-dusted cheek. The hairline crack is definitely deeper, one small pressure away from shattering.

My stomach flips with nerves again and I look away, drawn to the visible magic etched into the stone above the doorway and chalked into the flagstones beneath our feet: all wards and protections. Additional power shines over the metal door in the wall. I stare at the magical theorem etched into its surface, trying to reverse engineer it, with little luck. There are simply too many unfamiliar glyphs, but I recognize the symbols for "soul" and "life" and "preserve", and one part of the equation is clearly related to the redistribution of energy.

Rachel pulls what looks like an old-fashioned zoetrope from a cupboard – a hollow circular structure on a tall base, like a cake on a stand. There are slits cut out of the metal sides, allowing the viewer a glimpse at the illustrations that animate when it spins. Theo and I played with one at our grandparents' house when we were children. Except here there are no drawings of running horses, monkeys playing the cymbals or seals bouncing a beach ball. Instead, the space where the illustration strip goes is a collage of broken mirror shards.

Rachel sets the zoetrope on the table and I motion to the bottom part of the stand, which gleams polished black. "Is that obsidian?"

"Black tourmaline." Rachel starts to snip off sections of copper wire as long as her forearm. "It has equally powerful phantasmic properties and is far more grounding."

She works fast, twisting several lengths together, she knots them through the top of an old circular birdcage, threading them back and forth through the metal frame. At the bottom she wires the ends into metal clips, which she then attaches all around the zoetrope. Opening the spelled metal door, Rachel takes out a witch bottle from the shelving beyond and places it on the table. Made of clear glass and sealed with red wax, the inside isn't packed with etched bone, crystals and oils as I expect, but with a swirl of hazy fragments. I catch sight of a bright-red military uniform, a gold button, a blue human eye.

"That is no witch bottle," I whisper.

It contains a soul. A ghost.

In that moment, I realize my mistake. Phantasmic essence is the basis for all magic. It is the most fundamental mathemagical principle, represented in alchemy by the sun. All theorems require a syphon as fuel, often referred to as the "soul source", called so because to self-syphon is to use one's own soul. It makes sense then that ghosts contain the richest source of phantasmic essence after the living human soul. It is no great leap of understanding to realize that they can be syphoned into magical workings in place of the practitioner's own life.

Rachel is a *soul catcher*. I witnessed her spelling two ghosts into a bottle that, at first glance, looks like a basic witch bottle, but is not. A new understanding rings into my mind: to work complex theorems Rachel doesn't rely on witch bottles or self-syphoning. She is burning *souls*.

And she isn't the only one. Inside the safe in Mr Spicer's office, among his important papers and other valuables, is a changing collection of glass bottles that I assumed were particularly potent or prized witch bottles. Before now, I'd never questioned why some such items are always under lock in his office, whereas others are out on display in the red rooms.

I have been a fool.

Mr Spicer always warned us not to self-syphon except in emergencies and to rely only on witch bottles. Bea asked once if there was an alternative, and he changed the subject so effortlessly that I am only now realizing that is what he did. I shiver, feeling stunned and a little numb.

Rachel speaks my name, jolting me from my thoughts. "You've gone rather pale."

"Mr Spicer deals in ghosts, in souls, correct?" I half ask, half state.

"Yes." Rachel frowns, clearly puzzled. Of course she assumes I already know all about Mr Spicer's dealings.

"When you syphon from the souls that you bottle, how long do they last?" I ask, determined now to find out as much as I can.

"It depends on the theorems they're fuelling. Master theorems require more power, but the design of these bottles enhances each ghost's essence, stretching it as far as possible."

"And once their phantasmic essence is used up, they die?"

"They're already dead," Rachel replies simply.

Even without a physical body Edie is the most essential aspects of herself: her humour and wit, her kindness, her love of literature. She isn't an echo of a person, she is a person, the person she was when she was alive.

"But they're not," I say. "Not really."

"Don't look at me like that." Rachel steps closer, staring directly into my face as if she needs me to understand. "I don't trap ghosts like Edie, but those like Mary who are dangerous to death-touched like you and to other spirits, or in very rare cases, to the living. Not that Spicer respects that." She shrugs. "It's a thriving market and he has to compete, but I won't compromise."

"You've met other death-touched, then?" I ask, hopeful that she can teach me more about my new abilities.

"No, you're my first. There are very few of you." She drops her gaze back to the apparatus on the table. "I would like to discuss it in detail, but right now we must divide Mary and Edie before the bottle shatters under the pressure of two competing death loops." Rachel passes me a jam jar of dark viscose liquid and a fine paint brush. "Do you know auxiliary glyphs?"

"I'm reasonably confident in Cyrillic, the Quentenian cycle and alchemic symbology."

"Quentenian is best. We need a containment theorem around the outside of the apparatus, but leave this final panel empty or your sweetheart won't be able to escape."

That is the second time she has referred to Edie as my sweetheart. My girl, not just my friend. I should deny it, but even as my cheeks flush with heat, I don't correct her.

"Where you'd normally indicate your intended syphon, mark this glyphic." Rachel draws it out for me on the corner of a notebook. It reminds me of the golden ratio wrapped around a sideways T with an additional curve that ends in a simple equation I don't recognize.

I do as Rachel instructs, hoping I don't make any mistakes.

"How does this work?" I dare myself to ask.

"We will release the souls as the zoetrope is spinning," says Rachel. "The mirrors will distract them, mimicking the status inside the bottle. The theorem should contain them, except for one small door through which Edie can escape while Mary is confined in the birdcage up top, only to be reabsorbed into the bottle once Edie is free.

"How do we make sure Edie's the one who gets out?" I ask.

"That is on you," says Rachel. "You two clearly mean a lot to each other."

"Yes, I—" The words catch in my throat. Edie has always been a brick: steadfast and reliable. She is the one person I can truly rely on even among the sisterhood of our coven.

The bottle shakes violently, rattling its copper stand.

"If it breaks, we're not prepared. It was never meant to hold two ghosts at once but it … it's far more unstable than I ever predicted." Rachel looks nervous as she thinks something through. "One last precaution, just in case." Cutting her hand, Rachel presses her bloody palm to the wall and marks a glyph in red chalk with the other. A thick line shimmers into view, encircling the walls at chest height.

"What are you doing?" I ask.

"Activating a ward anchored in the skeletons of three hundred people buried beneath the floor and walls."

"A passive soul source, then?"

"Yes, but that number of enchanted bones has created a very stable theorem that will last for decades and can be raised and lowered with little effort. No deceased soul can cross it. I'll shut it down after Mary is safely re-contained." Rachel wipes her hands on a tea towel. "Whatever happens, we can't let her escape."

I clench my fists. "We also can't keep her inside a bottle with Edie."

"I agree, though I promise she isn't harming Edie. Their necromic cycles will conflict rather than complement one another. If there was a way to link their loops, then the potential would be—" Rachel shakes her head. "Another time. Now, when Edie is released, her phantasmic essence will be enhanced and concentrated. Technically, for a few minutes at least, she will become a shade."

"You mean a monster?" I gasp. A shade is any soul that has been corrupted by magic. There are many accounts of spirits summoned by occultists, or contained in traps, who later break out and slaughter them in horrible ways.

"No, no, a bottle doesn't have that effect. It is more akin to becoming a temporary poltergeist, for lack of a better term. The shades you need to worry about are the result of failed magical experiments. They lose their humanity and hunger for more phantasmic essence until they become highly dangerous to the dead and the living alike."

Her hand touches my shoulder and I flinch, not realizing that I have backed away in horror. I can't imagine my Edie becoming anything like that.

"You don't have to worry. Edie won't be corrupted and she hasn't been bottled for long, so the effects will wear off after a few minutes. She will still be herself. She won't hurt us. Now, when I spin this" – Rachel gestures to the apparatus – "I need you to call to her. Talk to her about something she will recognize. Ask her to follow your voice. Can you do that?"

I nod, not trusting myself to speak. My fear for Edie is making me dizzy and panicked, but she needs me to focus. I don't know what I will do if something happens to her.

Rachel spins the zoetrope, activating the theorem and settling it in motion. The air around us changes, smelling of bone dust and the sea, a slick briny scent that coats the back of my throat. The hairs on my arms and the nape of my neck prickle and rise. I don't see the seal on the bottle crack but I know the moment Edie and Mary are released because the inside of the zoetrope and the cage on top of it become filled with fragments and dusty particles, all spinning in a blur of light.

"Talk to her," urges Rachel.

I start to speak, not knowing what I'm going to say until the words are falling from my lips. "Edie, do you remember when we took the bus out of the city for a picnic, just the two of us? You lay beside me on the grass and we turned clouds into stories. That's one of my favourite days ever because I got to spend it alone with you."

I look to Rachel and she nods her encouragement. Focusing on the spinning zoetrope I picture Edie as I last saw her, cheeks flushed in determination and her eyes wide with surprise. "I kept tickling your arm with a blade of grass and you threatened to push me down the hill." I laugh, despite my fear. "Remember that? I love curling up in front of the fire and reading together, or sitting in the sun spots in my front room. I want to make a thousand more witch bottles with you, and listen to your poetry. No one weaves words quite like you, you know? I always thought that was your own particular magic and I need you to bring that back to me."

There's a sound like rushing air that threatens to swallow my words. I keep talking, raising my voice above the maelstrom as the zoetrope spins faster and faster. The table vibrates. Dust rains down from the ceiling. Rachel is chanting but I don't concern myself with her and instead focus on Edie.

"I remember the first day I met you. You were sitting in a sunbeam in the attic and I didn't know then that you would become the greatest gift anyone could ever ask for—"

She is my greatest and closest friend. The best in the world but … I wish to be more. The realization of that slams into me, almost making me sob.

I *want* her. I *love* her.

I think I have since the first day that Merle invited her to join our attic coven. For weeks I wilfully chose to mistrust her instead of admitting my attraction. I was afraid because of all the things I adore about her: that smile of hers, the unfiltered gleam of emotion in her eyes, her profile against the lamplight. She is so beautiful and her mind is magnificent. She is my darling and I'm foolish not to have recognized my feelings when she was still alive.

I don't try to stop the tears that come as I speak to her of Merle and Bea and the coven and our sisterhood. We promised to always be there for each other and so she needs to come back to us, to me, because I can't do any of this without her. It is impossible for us to be together as a couple, for so many reasons, but I can't deny how I feel any more. I cannot admit the truth to her so I say the only thing I can. "I cannot go on without you, Edie."

Particles start to lift through the gap in the apparatus: flakes of flesh and bone, scraps of fabric, leather and metal. They coalesce in the air, stitching themselves back together. A nose appears first, cute as a button, cheeks and chin, lips and eyes and hair, and the serpent brooch I gifted Edie, cotton fabric and the glass in her monocle. A heartbeat. A breath and—

Edie falls into me. I press against her with a cry of relief, my nose to her neck, inhaling her perfume as I bask in the solid presence of her. My heart feels raw and beaten and ripe with relief because I have her back. My Edie.

I hold her for all of three seconds before she's ripped from my arms.

14

WHAT RACHEL KNOWS

Mary has materialized outside the apparatus. Something has gone terribly wrong. Wasn't she supposed to remain within the mechanism? She has Edie by the neck, an expression of vicious hatred searing her face.

"No!" I scream, my voice a broken cry.

Rachel moves to stop Mary. Unlit candles, glass beakers and chemical bottles fly from the shelves to smash into the walls. The large dresser pitches forward and crashes into the table. Rachel leaps back just in time to avoid being crushed.

Dragging Edie backwards, Mary opens her mouth, teeth glinting in the low light, ready to bite down…

Driven by panic, I grasp at Mary's gown and haul her off Edie, surprised by my own strength. Edie is on her feet in a second, arms extended and from her slams an invisible force that batters into Mary, sending her flying into the wall with a screech of anger. She hits the tiles and I'm momentarily stunned that a ghost made impact on something solid, before I remember the ghost line that protects this place and prevents Mary from leaving.

We are trapped here, with her.

Edie slumps, whatever enhanced phantasmic essence she was granted by the bottle trap already used up. I hope that means the same for Mary – except the room is shaking, furniture breaking and something like an ocean tide drags at me. My shoes lose grip on the floor and I'm sliding, wrenched painfully towards Mary's open arms.

With a deep-throated growl, Mary lunges and I know as soon as her grip tightens on my arms that we have made a mistake. She's not a normal ghost.

She changes as I watch, growing taller somehow, her back bowing unnaturally, limbs elongating behind the waxy distorted flesh. With every second that passes, she looks less and less human and more like an insectoid nightmare – the kind of ghosts I have read about in books on phantasmology.

The worst kind of shade.

I struggle against her grasp as she spins me like a giant spider wrapping a fly in silk and pulls me back against her abdomen. She smells of spoiled milk, decay and something unpleasant that I cannot place: a silky, cloying scent. The furniture is still shaking, glass shards swirling in the air. Edie shouts my name, horrified.

"Let Viola go." Rachel has a laceration to her forehead and cheek but her brow is set in a determined scowl.

"Lower your barrier ward." Mary's breath is hot and stinking on my face. "And I won't suck the life out of her."

"Even shades need a link to a living victim to drain their essence," says Rachel, calling her bluff.

A long arm snakes around my torso to hold deadly, sharp claws to my belly. "I'll gut her in that case."

"Don't you dare." The voice is Edie's. She's beautiful when she's angry – face like a storm and eyes flashing danger – and in this moment she is livid.

"Lower the ward, let me leave unhindered, and she'll live," Mary hisses. It is likely an empty promise, but there's a wild fear in Edie's expression and Rachel also looks pained, as if she knows that she has no choice.

Whatever happens, we can't let her escape.

But it seems that, for me, she will. Smearing the blood dripping from her hairline into her palm, Rachel moves cautiously to the wall, not breaking eye contact with Mary. The shade tenses against me, claws tightening, as if anticipating a trick.

Rachel swallows. "When I place my hand on the ward, you push her away. Fail to do so and I—"

"Do it, witch," says Mary.

Rachel slams her bloody hand to the tile. Magic flares and drops. I gasp as I'm shoved away from Mary with such force that I almost fall straight on my face but Edie is right there, catching me and pulling me close. I search for the harm done to her as she does the same to me. She looks exactly the same as she has since her death, not a hair out of place. The change is in her eyes: a deep, haunted look that wasn't there before. She softens and leans her forehead against mine as she breathes out a sigh of relief.

Even though we are still in danger I can't turn away from Edie. There's a strange feeling in my chest that has nothing to do with the weakness of my lungs. I am sure my face is a mess but I don't even notice the throbbing in my cheek bone because Edie has her hand on the back of my neck, the other on my waist.

I want to kiss her. I so badly want to kiss her.

And I have so many questions: what was it like inside the bottle? How does it feel to be able to affect the physical world again, however briefly? But now is not the time.

The air stills. Mary is gone. The laboratory is a mess of toppled cabinets and shattered apparatus and the zoetrope is buckled and broken, the cage above it crushed.

"Well, so much for that experiment," says Rachel, sponging the blood from her face with a tea towel she drags from the ruin of the kitchen.

"I'm sorry, *experiment*?" I ask, voice shrill, my apology about Mary's escape dying on my lips. "You mean to say that you've never attempted that before?"

"I've never had the need, but I know what went wrong with the extraction. And don't worry, it was not your part of the theorem that failed. I didn't realize that Mary had become a shade. Regular bottles are simply not designed to contain such potent phantasms, which was why it was cracking." Rachel starts to sort through the detritus spread around the room.

"But if I modify the third equation and place it diagonal to the crystalline structures of… No, it will compete and undermine the containment, unless…"

Finding a notebook and pen, she leans over the little table near the metal door, which is miraculously untouched, and begins noting down magical glyphs and equations. I watch her for a moment, so angry and scared that I don't know what to say.

Edie places a soothing hand on my back. "She had little choice but to bottle us both, Vi."

I know, but that only makes me angrier. I hate having no control. My bones have been stolen, someone killed Edie, I almost lost the girl I love, *again*, and I am entirely out of my depth.

"How did Mary become a shade?" I ask.

Rachel grimaces. "She's a spirit we've previously bottled, but that bottle was stolen from Rupert some weeks ago by someone who must have been experimenting with theorems far beyond their abilities. Shades are the result of mathemagical misfire. If an unbalanced or badly designed theorem backfires, then it perverts the soul syphoned to fuel it. The result is inhuman, angry and very hungry. Their phantasmic essence is limited and to maintain their influence on the material world they must feed on other ghosts, and the living, if they get the chance."

I remember, distantly, the overheard conversation between Rachel and Mr Spicer in his office. "Who do you think stole her bottle from the safe?"

"No idea; there was no sign of a break-in. Rupert is investigating but he is honestly far more concerned about the more organized, targeted thefts that are occurring now. Someone has it out for him and is determined to see him go bankrupt. Mary is my problem. I can't let her roam the streets attacking other souls."

"How are you going to stop her?" asks Edie.

"First I need a new form of containment. A ghost bottle simply won't hold a shade for long." Leaning back from her notes, she sighs. "Mary spoke intelligently. That's ... unusual."

"How so?" I ask.

"Normally shades of her type become mindless echoes of the people they were in life. All instinct and anger, no thought. But she is lucid and intelligent, calculating... I wonder..." Rachel looks at me, expectant and hopeful. "Viola, might I take some blood samples from you?"

"Whatever for?"

Adjusting her half-moon glasses, Rachel starts to set the room to rights. Leaving the dresser where it fell, she sets up two surviving chairs on the end of the long table that is still usable. Finding the copper kettle – now slightly dented – she lights the burner and sets water on to boil. "There is a belief among some of the more ancient ghosts that the blood or flesh of a death-touched can restore them to life."

Edie and I exchange a glance. We have certainly encountered at least one such spirit and if there is truth to it, then I could bring Edie back—

"It won't," Rachel goes on quickly and my hope sinks. "But

I have long wondered if there is a kernel of fact to it. If perhaps death-touched blood can somehow alter the corporeality of a spirit when expressed in certain parameters, even if only temporarily—"

"Giving ghosts a physical body, you mean?" asks Edie.

"Or to modify their phantasmic one to *behave* like a physical body at will." The kettle starts to whistle. Rachel fills the teapot and sets it on the stand to brew. "Death is irreversible; I can never restore true life, but I've been researching how to reestablish a ghost's ability to interact with the physical world without requiring them to become a mindless, hungry shade. Mary might be evil, but she's still self-aware, so it is perhaps possible."

Really? I cannot help feeling a fresh flare of optimism. We might not be able to bring Edie back from the dead, but if she could be more easily visible to the coven and other living people, then she could reclaim a little of the life she had. She and Bea could be together again.

I resent the wave of hurt that washes over me at that thought. I am a selfish creature. Yes, I want Edie for myself but I will not stand in the way of love. I care about her too much to ever do that. All I want is her happiness.

Rachel pours the tea, the steam wafting off the surface as she sets out milk and sugar. She has poured a cup for Edie and it means a lot to me that she has so effortlessly included her, even if Edie cannot drink what is offered.

"I've not had the opportunity to experiment with the properties of death-touched blood before but it might be the key to finding a way to contain Mary, as well as helping develop my work towards a restoration theorem. Your kind are so rare, Viola. Please let me take a few samples."

This means a lot to her, I realize. There is more than simple passion for science and magic driving her. Should I allow her this? The idea of letting her take a part of me to experiment on is unsettling, but the potential gains are immense. I glance at Edie, who meets my gaze, and in her expression I read both hope and concern. She steps closer to me, hovering protectively, but she doesn't speak for me. My blood, my decision.

"Fine," I say. "I'll do it on three conditions."

Rachel's eyes brighten. "Anything."

"Firstly, you tell me everything you know about being death-touched."

"Agreed."

"Secondly, if and when we need your help, you give it freely."

Rachel nods, stoic.

"And lastly, if you succeed in your experiments, then you will restore Edie's corporeality."

Edie's breath hitches. Reaching up, I take her hand and squeeze it reassuringly.

"I promise," says Rachel. "I will share what I learn with you." She digs out a tin of biscuits and places them in front of me. "Eat something first. The sugar will help prevent any dizziness when your blood is drawn."

I'm not hungry but I force a few ginger nut biscuits down and sip my tea as Rachel finds and prepares the equipment.

I take one of the chairs at the table. Rachel sits beside me and puts on some medical gloves. There is a metal tray and in it a large glass syringe with a horrible-looking needle and six vials.

"A sharp scratch," Rachel warns.

As the needle breaks my skin I blurt, "Have you ever seen a ghost with silver eyes?"

"Silver eyes?" Rachel repeats. "I can't say that I have. What does it mean?"

"I don't know." I'm unsure of how much to tell her. The pain in my arm flares and I swear I can feel the blood being pulled out of me by the syringe. I look away. "We read about it somewhere."

"I've never heard of it."

The rattling of vials being set into the tray makes my stomach clench. I am very ready for this to be over.

"What was the book called?" asks Rachel.

"I don't remember. Edie?"

Edie gives a little shake of her head. "It was a while ago," she lies smoothly.

I feel the needle being removed.

"Well, if you can remember, I'd be interested in reading it. Silver eyes. How extraordinary." Rachel presses some gauze to the puncture wound, folding my arm back on it. "Hold that there a moment."

She stores the six full vials beside her soul bottles in the metal vault in the wall. "Thank you. You have given me renewed hope in my work and a potential means to stop Mary before she becomes completely unmanageable."

I nod, pleased that I can be of some use to someone, but wishing I understood more. "Tell us about being death-touched."

"I know less than I would like," Rachel admits. "Writings on it are scarce and highly prized. As far as I understand, when a person crosses over into death and returns to life, they might gain the ability to see, speak to and touch the dead. You died recently in a fire?"

"Yes, with Edie."

I returned. She didn't. Yet another reason to feel guilty.

"I'm sorry." Rachel looks at Edie, her eyes rich with sympathy and kindness. I think something passes between them that I do not grasp because Edie suddenly drops my hand. I rise sharply as she turns on her heel and makes towards the stairs. I call after her, but she doesn't turn back.

What has upset her? Muttering an apology to Rachel, I hurry after my friend, but Rachel grabs my arm and presses a piece of paper into my palm. "We have a rotary phone; please call me."

Taking the paper, I nod and run. My chest heaves as I take the spiral stairs two at a time, and then I am emerging into the crypt and then the cemetery. Lightning forks over York. Warm storm water licks my cheeks as I hurry around the chapel, searching for Edie.

There she is, striding away along the gravel path. With the leaden sky swirling above her, she looks like a mirage, grey streaks of rain striking through her body.

"Wait!" I shout.

Only then does she look back over her shoulder with the

most delicate, mournful expression. Did I say or do something wrong? I'm terrified that being in the ghost bottle, or our conversation with Rachel, has irrevocably wounded her.

I catch her up at the cemetery gates, my hand finding her arm and hooking her back to me. "Will you slow down?"

"Please just let me go." She rips out of my grasp and the slight stings more than I care to admit.

"Go where?" I blink rain from my eyes. "What's wrong?"

Her laugh is hollow and broken.

"Talk to me." I'm soaked to the bone, hair limp, dress sodden. I don't care.

"There is no point. We are stuck as we are, or I am." There are tears in Edie's eyes, but they don't fall. The hurt on her face is mixed with confusion and something else that I'm frightened to acknowledge, because it might mean truly losing her forever.

She is not shackled to me. She isn't *mine* to long for.

"I know about Bea," I blurt.

"What?" Edie looks puzzled.

We stare at one another. She says nothing for a long time. There is only the beat of the rain on my shoulders and the rumble of traffic up Cemetery Road. Another jagged bolt of lightning splits the sky, lighting up the dull afternoon. Despite the chill, my skin feels hot.

"I saw you together on your birthday," I say. "You were kissing."

She dips her gaze, cheeks heating. "You weren't supposed to see that."

"I'm sorry it wasn't her." I struggle to speak what I mean. "If not for me, you could be together."

"Bea and I?" Edie whispers.

"It should have been Bea who became death-touched. Then you might be happy."

The haunted look has returned to Edie's eyes and for a moment I think she really might cry, but she doesn't. I'm not entirely sure that the dead can shed tears. "You think I should be with Bea?"

No, I want her to be with *me*. But how can I say that?

"I think you should be with whoever will make you happy."

Edie's face crumples. I've said the wrong thing, somehow.

"Do you know what I experienced inside that bottle?" she asks.

I shake my head, suddenly ashamed that I didn't immediately ask. Then, with dawning horror, I remember what Rachel said about soul bottles mimicking a necromic cycle. "Your death?"

"No. *Your* death." Edie grits her teeth. "I was back in the fire. I had to watch you die over and over in my arms as if my choice didn't change anything."

"What choice? What are you talking about?" I'm begging now, not even trying to hide it.

"I can't, Vi. I'm sorry. I can't talk about this."

Rain and wind whips wet strands of my hair into my face. I blink and her body dissolves into nothingness the way the Grey Lady's did at the theatre. Edie is gone. I am left standing in the rain, shivering. More than anything I want to feel Edie's arms wrapped around me, but I am alone.

I wait, but she doesn't return.

15

AN UNDESIRABLE ENGAGEMENT

When I arrive home, Pa is sitting at the kitchen table with a brew. He doesn't look at me. With shaking hands, I pour the dregs of the teapot into a cup for myself. There's no milk so I sip it black, bitter tannins flooding my tongue. There is bread on the counter but no butter. I am too exhausted and famished to care. Cutting two slices, I tear them apart and eat the morsels dry.

It is only then that I notice an open envelope on the table beside Pa.

"From Ma?" I ask, collapsing into one of the rickety kitchen chairs.

Pa grunts the affirmative.

Opening the letter – addressed to Pa and me, and written in Ma's neat handwriting on three sheets of paper – I scan through, quickly digesting the news and instructions for the cleaning and maintenance of the home, which of course now falls entirely to me. I miss my ma with a fierce ache. We do not see eye to eye on my future, nor do I enjoy the burden of womanhood she seems so determined to help me inherit, but I do not doubt her love for me.

Of Pa she asks only that he try to paint again. She has been to an exhibition of modern German art at the Burlington Galleries that had been labelled as "degenerate" by the Third Reich, and declares it a most delicious collection, utterly astounding and inspirational. She describes in detail several of her favourite pieces including a sublime painting by Max Slevogt of a panther taking down its prey. She has sent money, the advance for her modelling work, and asks that we use some to live on and the rest should go on new paints and materials for Pa.

"What will be your first subject?" I ask him tentatively.

He doesn't answer, doesn't even look at me. I can smell the alcohol on him: a creeping tang of aniseed and fennel blending with the musk of his unwashed skin.

"Might I have the share Ma sent for the household?" I venture. "I will pick up some fresh fish for tea."

Pa merely stands, drops his used mug in the sink and leaves the kitchen without a word. He doesn't even mention my cut lip and swelling eye. I know then that the money is already gone, drank away and pissed into the outhouse. Pa was on top of the world, on the cusp of incredible success and celebration and now he is a husk of a man who loathes the sight of his only daughter. There will be no new paintings.

This is my doing. Somehow, I have to make it right but with my only method of earning a living stolen, I am at a loss. We owe debts to almost every shop on Blossom Street and cannot rely on the charity of neighbours to keep us.

What am I going to do?

Although I can hear the traffic and the sound of our neighbours in their yard, I am alone. As the living can't touch the dead, without Edie I'm truly exposed to any other ghost that might wish to walk into our home and harm me. Rising, I hurry to check the wards I have in place. Powered by witch bottles set on shelves in the corners of the flat and anchored by glyphs, they protect against living intruders but little else. Certainly not ghosts or shades.

I need to fix that before a dangerous soul like Mary or the Grey Lady realizes that I am undefended. Retreating to my room, I write out a possible protective theorem, balancing the glyphs with those for "deceased soul" in two different alphabets. I itch to ask Edie to look over my workings, but there is still no sign of her.

Her absence is acute, a nasty weight in the centre of my stomach that I cannot shake. She was so hurt and I keep replaying it in my mind to look for clues as to why I might have upset her. Maybe I should have kept that I know about her and Bea to myself. I only meant to ease Edie's distress and let her know that I understand how difficult it must be to be separated from the girl she loves.

A girl she can no longer even touch.

I swallow, laying my pen down and putting my head in

my hands as tears burn at the back of my nose. I loathe this feeling: jealousy and guilt comingled with desire. It is terrible.

Heading back to the kitchen, I dig through the cupboard for the bag of salt I keep there. Salt has ancient protective properties and as I read somewhere that it can be used against dangerous spirits, I hope that it will add additional protective qualities to my magic. Finding a blade, I slice the soft base of my palm. The passive fuel found in witch bottles will not be enough to give the wards the strength they need to deflect the dead. I have to self-syphon.

Unless I use a soul bottle as power.

The shudder that runs through me at the thought dismisses that notion. I can't stand the idea of using a ghost that way, even if I could get hold of one. If both Mr Spicer and Rachel keep their soul bottles under lock and key, they are clearly precious and worth a lot of money – money I do not have. And as Mr Spicer is already short on his deliveries, I don't think he will give me a soul bottle to practise with, no matter how great my need. It is more likely that he will offer me a room at Spicer House and keep me safe behind their stronger wards.

Perhaps that is for the best. I would be safer there, but I cannot abandon my pa. Someone must make sure he eats and that the house is clean.

How can Mr Spicer bear to trade in souls at all? I simply cannot reconcile the kind and generous man, who has always been like an uncle to me, with the vision of a ruthless businessman who sells trapped ghosts to other occultists without a care for their fate.

Before I became death-touched, my understanding of ghosts was that they were shadows of the people they once were in life. Now that I see them, I know they are so much more. They are utterly *themselves*. Do some deserve to be bottled to make the streets safer? Certainly, yes. I have no sympathy for those like Mary. She hurt Edie and tried to hurt me. She can be bottled and syphoned to extinction for all I care.

But most of the dead are not like that. Just look at Edie. According to Rachel, and what I overheard myself, Mr Spicer doesn't care if a soul is innocent or not. Perhaps he doesn't realize how human the dead still are. I must talk to him about it, and soon.

For now, I will use my own soul as fuel and pay the price.

Many wards require a specialist paint to fix their power. I have a batch already prepared: a gloopy ochre mixture that I blend with drops of my fresh blood and paint on all the windowsills. Five glyphs in total, all linked by a relatively simple magical expression that should tie this new theorem into my pre-existing wards. On her return, Ma will think the pattern pretty and eccentric and Pa will barely care. I complete the protections with a thin line of salt across all the doors and windows. My efforts leave me weary and aching and deepen the throbbing in my face and body where Phillip struck me.

I can't block anyone from entering entirely, either dead or alive, but now any ghosts that mean me harm will be deterred and if they do persist and enter the flat they will trigger an alarm tied to my blood that will wake me if I am sleeping. Hopefully it will give me enough advance warning to defend myself, or flee. The new wards seem to take well but I won't know if they are successful until they are tested.

Exhausted and drained, I stagger back to my room as my lungs tighten. My atomizer helps a little but it takes hours for me to stop wheezing and my head throbs in pain. Night falls. Pa doesn't come home and neither does Edie.

I go to bed alone, tense and afraid. The silence in the flat feels too loud and the air too hot and I feel completely empty. Staring up at my bedroom ceiling, I imagine the curve of Edie's throat, her chin, the swell of her lips drawn into that coy smile she wears when I have said something to make her laugh. Salt hits the back of my tongue – I am crying. I want her in my arms, the distance between us so compressed that I can bridge it with a kiss and a confession.

With Edie on my mind I finally sleep and instead of dreaming of fire and death I imagine the peony, gardenia and amber scent of her perfume settling over me. Her lips at my ear, her fingers tracing down my arms, touching me in a way I know she never will but I still long for.

I dream of her and it makes the dark night bearable.

"Goodness, that's quite the shiner," Bea professes when I open the door to her the next day.

Looking at her in my doorway, brow quirked in surprise and concern, I understand completely why Edie is in love with her. She is always the brightest star in a hazy sky: dramatic and fun and not afraid to break the rules. As children I tailed her like a kitten after a ribbon. Now that we are almost adults, I still concede to her because a battle with Bea always leaves me feeling raw and uncertain.

She sweeps into the flat and up the stairs, depositing herself on the chaise-longue in the front room before taking the long-handled obsidian mirror from her purse and angling it to see the room. "Is Edie here?"

I take a seat opposite. "I haven't seen her since yesterday afternoon. I think she needs some space."

Bea's brow lifts. "From *you*?"

"We had a silly disagreement and she vanished."

"She'll come around." Bea takes my hands. "You know that Edie hates to be smothered."

My nod is reluctant, though Bea is right. I'm bitter towards myself for making so many mistakes, not only with Edie, but also losing the bones and failing even to read true for Mrs Aldridge and poor Christopher. Whoever means our coven harm could strike at any moment and we will have no way to see them coming, let alone deduce their identity.

Mary is loose on the streets of York and Rachel said there are other hungry ghosts like the Old Souls lurking around the Minster. Edie is savvy and smart, far smarter than me, but I worry. I can't help thinking of the way her mouth sounded out, "I can't talk about this," and the anguished gasp that escaped her before she vanished.

She is out there somewhere, hurting, and I cannot comfort her.

I could confide in Bea, I realize. But I don't want to tell her what I learned from Rachel just yet. Soul bottles would revolutionize the theorems we are capable of, but if I put the idea into Bea's head before I confront her father about his approach to the trade, then it will get even more complicated. I have so many questions of my own, and, as much as I hope that Rachel can find a way to make Edie corporeal, or at least visible to the living again, that discussion calls for a full coven meeting.

"Vi, darling!" Bea spools over the chaise. "I need guidance. Opening night is only hours away and I'm still playing the nurse and chorus roles with only a few meagre lines. Not enough to be noticed by the audience and certainly not to be mentioned in the press."

"Aren't you the lead female understudy?" I ask, my mind still on Edie.

"Well, yes, but Millicent is on top form, not a sniffle of a cold or hope of a sprained ankle." Bea teases a long strand of auburn hair over her shoulder and spins it idly around her finger. "And Andreas just told me—"

"Who?"

"Andreas Sweets. You saw him when you came to the theatre last, though how he got to be a leading man I don't know. He is so inconsistent. At times he is the finest actor I have ever seen and at others he is so distracted." I presume she means the deep-skinned, fine-featured actor whom the director scolded last time I was at the theatre, but Bea doesn't wait for confirmation that I know who she means before she continues. "He heard from Lil, who overheard Mr Mosley telling his assistant, that Mr and Mrs Fox-Morton will attend opening night."

She leans towards me, expectant. I return a blank expression. "Is that not good news?" I venture.

Bea explodes off the chaise and starts to pace. "No, it is a tragedy. The producers will never notice me unless I'm playing Juliet. I know all of Millie's dialogue and blocking by heart and I can certainly bring more passion and presence to the role than she does." Bea slumps beside me on the sofa. "Read the bones for me, Vi. Tell me how to secure a one-way ticket to America."

She looks so eager but all I can do is break her heart. "I can't. My knucklebone set is gone." I gesture to my split cheek and bruised eye. "Phillip."

Anger sparks in Bea's eyes. "That bully of a lad who used to pull your hair and steal your sweets?" Her fingers are cool on my hot face as she tilts my chin for a better look.

"This time he made off with the knucklebone set."

She stands. "He should not have hurt you. We need the coven together for this. Can you summon Edie?"

Summon her? She's not a jack-in-a-box. I can't wave my hand and draw her spirit to me, although I wish that I could. We are so rarely at odds. I desperately want to see her and know that she is well, though I'd never *force* her to be here.

"No, we..." I don't want to tell Bea the details of our quarrel because I don't want her to know I saw them kiss, and I wouldn't be able to bear it if she confesses her love for Edie.

That alone might break me. But York is a dangerous place for a spirit. What if the Grey Lady or some other horrible ghost catches up with Edie?

The sudden rap at the front door makes us both jump. I'm wary, fearing the worst. Is it Phillip? If it is, I will make him return my knucklebones and curse his manhood to wither for good measure. I'm halfway down the stairs, Bea hot on my heels, before I remember that it is midday on Friday.

Oh God, I completely forgot.

Mr Saunders. Lunch.

Pushing past me, Bea opens the door before I can stop her. Henry Saunders stands on the doorstep wearing a broad smile and another crisp linen suit. He tips his hat.

"Miss Spicer, what a pleasant surprise. I'm here to pick up—" His sentence cuts off as he catches sight of me standing behind Bea looking like a bruised, startled rabbit. "Miss Sampire, your face. What happened?"

I dip my gaze, heat rising in my cheeks, even though *I* have nothing to be ashamed of. "I had a run-in with a thief called Phillip Petty, a boy from around here."

"Did you report him?"

"No, I…" The thought didn't even occur to me. Perhaps I should have.

"Consider it taken care of." All charm and mirth drops from Mr Saunders' voice, his promise an implicit threat. I don't know what to say so I just stare at him, not liking this version of him any more than the soft, charming gentleman who has been trying to win me.

I have no doubt that he can find and punish Phillip and perhaps retrieve my knucklebones far more efficiently than the coven can; he is an accomplished occultist with far more experience. But if I allow it, then I will be indebted to him and I refuse to turn to him for help before my own coven. I desperately need those knucklebones though. Without them, I have no hope of a future at all.

"Considering the circumstances, I understand if you are not well enough to lunch—" he goes on.

"She's perfectly well." Bea drapes an arm over my shoulder. "Give us five minutes."

"What—" My coven sister manhandles me back up the stairs and sits me on the chaise by the front window, pulling make-up from her purse.

"I *cannot* go for lunch with Mr Saunders," I hiss. "Edie is gone, someone is trying to kill us, and I have to retrieve my knucklebone set."

"Henry will take care of Phillip." Bea begins gently brushing a little make-up around my bruised eye to hide the worst. "He is handsome, wealthy and entirely taken with you. Besides, he's a very skilled occultist. You could do worse. Also, this will be a good distraction from everything that is going on. You need to have some fun, Vi!"

I swallow, stunned and hurt. We have been friends for years, as close as sisters. Does she really understand me so little? "I'm *not* interested in him."

Or any man.

Bea's gaze catches on mine as she tilts my chin and holds it to the light so that she may apply lipstick to my mouth.

I want Edie. Her girl. Her love.

God, I am a terrible friend.

But is Bea much better? Has she always been this blind to my needs and feelings and I have never noticed before? Yes, she's always been like this, I realize. Our unspoken leader who always gets what she wants over anyone else and I have simply made excuses for her. I am not sure if I can any more.

Disappearing into my room, Bea returns a moment later with my newest afternoon dress and all but strips me in the front parlour to wrestle me into it. My hair is clean and brushed but Bea pins it back for me, smoothing flyaway curls. And I still say nothing. I don't refuse her. I don't tell her how I feel, afraid to provoke an outburst.

"You truly didn't find any trace of magic at Pa's studio?" I ask.

Bea stills, something dangerous flashing through her pretty features. I have surprised her. She's probably irritated that I'm questioning her. "No, nothing at all sadly," she says eventually. "I was hoping for a clue but there are no signs of theorems or any magic there." Bea's smile is soft. She takes my hands. "Don't worry. We're coven sisters, Vi, and we will get to the bottom of this, together. Try to have a good time with Mr Saunders and I will see you later."

"Later?" I ask, frowning.

"The play, silly. Opening night."

Tonight.

York Royal.

I cannot go back. My mind flashes to the claustrophobic backstage corridors and the haunting, towering nun waiting to tear the flesh from my bones. Returning would provoke the ghost's anger and be utterly foolish. "Bea, I can't…"

"Don't say you're missing my debut." Tears well in her eyes. "Vi, don't you know how much this means to me?"

"If I go, the main event of the evening is likely to be my slaughter by an angry nun." I'm shaking at the thought. "The Grey Lady is not the benevolent good luck spirit she's said to be."

Bea looks crestfallen but she nods. "I understand. I'm sorry to be so pushy."

"I'll make it up to you. I promise." My heart churns with guilt and yet there is a new sting of awareness that once again Bea is being very selfish.

Downstairs, Mr Saunders waits beside a sporty motor pulled up in front of the garage. He's surrounded by most of the mechanics working today, all admiring the handsome vehicle.

One of the mechanics whistles in appreciation. "A Frazer-Nash Shelsey, four cylinders. It has a tubular front axle with inverted semi-elliptic leaf springs."

Mr Saunders laughs at their delight. "Whatever you say, boys. I just liked the colour." He opens the passenger door for me. "You look wonderful, Miss Sampire. Thank you, Miss Spicer, for convincing her to take a chance on me."

Closing my door, Mr Saunders takes his place in the

driver's seat and produces a silk scarf from inside his jacket pocket. "It gets pretty windy. May I?"

Without waiting for an answer, he wraps the scarf over my hair, tucking the ends neatly around my neck. And then the engine roars beneath us and we're circling out of the garage and heading into the city.

16

SHE IS IN GREAt DANGER

We drive around the corner and, only a couple of minutes later, pull into the grand entrance of the Royal Station Hotel, an impressive building in the Italianate style beside the train station. A doorman greets us and takes Mr Saunders' keys as he opens my door and offers his hand. He locks gazes with me and I fight to suppress a flare of irritation. We could have simply walked here from my house.

In the hotel we are shown to a private dining room with a fine view over the city. The table is set for two and we are waited on by an older gentleman and two younger servers. I remain unimpressed. Silly shows of wealth like this are entirely vulgar, even if the wine is exquisite and being in such beautiful surroundings is rather thrilling. Still, as nice as my best dress is, I feel shabby in comparison to the other guests and horribly out of place here.

Without Edie, I cannot relax. How soon until I can make my excuses and leave to look for her?

The conversation between us is light and impersonal. Mr Saunders speaks enough for the both of us, telling me about his family business, his father, his home in London and the house he has rented in the New Forest. He talks as if I will see it one day.

I think of Edie and our last moment in the cemetery before she vanished. The more I go over it all, the more I feel like we were having two entirely different conversations. Bea has been so pushy and demanding of me lately. Am I guilty of being equally inconsiderate of Edie's feelings?

Edie was murdered, for goodness' sake. Someone killed her and here I am having lunch with a man I dislike. What am I doing? I shouldn't be here; I should be looking for her.

When the server clears the course and refreshes the wine, I stand, about to plead a headache and excuse myself, but Mr Saunders places a small, wrapped package on the table between us.

"A gift for you."

"Mr Saunders—"

"Call me Henry, please." He winks, and if I were even the slightest bit attracted to him, I am certain my heart would flutter. As it is, I only miss Edie more. I long for *her* smile, *her* touch, *her* attention. I have become a thing that wants only her. With her, I am home.

I need to find her.

I push the gift back across the table. "I really can't accept this. I have a headache. I must go—"

"Open it first." He sits back in his chair, waiting. "It will only take a minute."

Sighing, I pick up the package and know immediately that it is a book. Just a little token, then. That isn't so bad. When I unwrap it, the leather cover is worn and the pages thin. A book of classic poetry, perhaps? I turn it over and my heart skips as I read the gold stamped writing on the cover: *A Discoverie and Examination of Spirit Seers*.

I look up sharply, shocked. He knows? "How did you—?"

Mr Saunders smirks. "Rupert mentioned your new-found … situation."

I presumed, after everything, that Bea had told her father about my new abilities – Mr Spicer all but said so himself last time I saw him – but I didn't think that he would freely share that information with his clients, let alone Henry Saunders.

"Why would he tell you?" I fail to keep the suspicion from my tone.

Mr Saunders smiles wryly. "To justify his asking me to cease my attentions towards you. No doubt he is keen to keep you in York to work for him now that you can see, hear and touch the dead, and you cannot work for him if you are my wife."

Wife? I shudder, then seize on what he just said. "You wouldn't let me work?"

If I wish to, he could not stop me.

"Certainly not, and not in a job so grubby and dangerous as soul catching."

I hesitate, absorbing that information. He believes that Mr Spicer wishes me to become a soul catcher like Rachel? Why, because she won't indiscriminately trap souls to fulfil his quota? Mr Spicer wouldn't expect that of me, surely? *Wouldn't he?* a nasty, doubting voice inside me asks. He has a business to save and a reputation to uphold.

Mr Saunders tilts his head. "You do not approve of what Rupert does, do you?"

"No, I do not," I state simply. "I didn't know about the existence of soul bottles until recently. He's selling *people*."

"Ghosts are not people."

My hands are shaking as I think of Edie and how misunderstood she is. "Are *you* death-touched, Mr Saunders? Can *you* speak to the dead?"

"I cannot."

"Then you have no idea what they truly are."

He leans in. "Tell me. I am eager to hear your opinion on the matter."

I hate that I blush under his gaze. I hate that he gets under my skin in this way. Sitting, I flip through the little book without really reading it, using the moment to collect my thoughts and bank my anger. As much as I want to rage at him, this is hardly the place. Still, there's a bite of venom in my tone when I do speak. "Bottling and using ghosts as fuel for magic is as inherently wrong as slavery. It *is* a form of slavery and I will not abide innocent souls being taken and used in such a way."

"Then when Mr Spicer asks you to work for him as a soul catcher, you will refuse?" asks Mr Saunders, looking rather pleased.

I set the book down. "I will."

"Good. Because I have other plans for you."

This time I cannot meet his gaze. "That does not mean I will marry you instead."

"If your heart belongs to another man, then I will not stand in the way of your happiness—"

"There is no other *man*." I can be truthful about that at least.

"Then I will do whatever it takes to convince you that you belong with me." His smile is smooth and disarming and I think I actually loathe him. "The moment I laid eyes on your portrait in London I knew that you were part of my future."

I open my mouth to protest that my father's portraits of me are but a poor representation, but he holds up a hand, wishing to speak his piece. "Miss Sampire, you are not the only one who reads the future. I will be honest with you. We are on the brink of another war, one too late to prevent."

My skin flushes cold, and goosebumps chase up my arms despite the heat of the day. There is true sorrow and worry in Mr Saunders' eyes. Is he telling the truth? Is war coming? I have seen the headlines. I fear that he is right. We cannot face the horror of another great conflict. Oh God, Theo is of age. He will graduate university only to be called upon to fight.

Mr Saunders nods, as if he can read my mind. "I am developing a weapon that will give our soldiers the edge in the arms race to come. My father has granted me a loan. My friend

Mr Harrow, you remember him from when he came to work on the wards at Mr Spicer's house? Yes, well, we have founded a joint venture working to develop mathemagical theorems in new innovative directions. It is only very early days, but your insight and assistance as both a powerful diviner and now death-touched would be invaluable to our mission."

War. Theo torn apart on the battlefield. I can't let that happen. That will not be my brother's future. Tears spring to my eyes and I blink them away. First my coven is under threat, now my blood family. "You want me to trap ghosts for you instead?"

"I would never ask that of you. Never. But ... if it comes to that, we would use enemy souls, and it *may* not come to that," Mr Saunders quickly adds. "You have such potential, Viola. Think of the good that you could do and the lives you might save."

"You do not need to marry me for me to help you in your work."

"No, but I wish to." The look he gives me is direct and unflinching. He doesn't shield the desire he feels and I resist the urge to fidget in my seat.

I grit my teeth and jut my chin, refusing to let him get to me. "And if I can never love you?"

"Then I will settle for your companionship and, I hope, your friendship." He takes a sip of his wine. "Though, in time, you might learn to love me as I do you."

Doubtful.

If I had my knucklebones, I could divine his intentions

and ask if he would really be satisfied being married to me in name only. If I do not need to love him back, then perhaps this could work between us. Certainly, my family's financial troubles would be over, I would get to focus on growing my skills as a diviner, I'd be protected from whoever is trying to harm us and I can work to save my brother and millions of others from a terrible fate.

"I will … think about it," I say after a long moment, ignoring the horrible, empty feeling inside me at the prospect.

Mr Saunders' grin is wide, bright and boyish. "That is not a no."

"It is not a yes either," I chide, as I once again open the little book he has gifted me. It is an extraordinary thing, and very generous. Rachel said that there are very few written records about the death-touched and it means a great deal to have any information at all.

The book is older than I first supposed, the text printed close together in red and black ink in a similar format to early books of common prayer. I flip through carefully, noting the elegant, handwritten comments in the margins in a flourishing script.

"It has been mouldering in our family library for generations," says Mr Saunders. "I thought you might make better use of it, seeing as it is a personal account of your condition."

Condition, as if being death-touched is an affliction the same way my weak lungs bother me daily. Perhaps it is. I am finding my life more and more changed by it.

"Thank you, Henry." I say, meaning it, as I flip through more of the pages.

He hums in contentment at my using his given name. "There is a fascinating description of becoming death-touched in chapter four. It is so rare because someone has to die for you, forgoing their own life to save yours." His smile becomes sad. "I understand that your friend, Edith…"

It hits me then and I grip the table to stop myself from falling to the floor and crying. I did not become death-touched simply because I had a close encounter with death. I see the dead because I was brought back to life by Edie, at her own expense.

She died *for* me.

Because of me.

I feel utterly wretched without her. I want to demand answers and kiss her lips and thank her from the depths of my soul for saving my life. And then I would like to scream at her for letting herself die when it should have been me.

Edie, where are you? When I eventually get home, I crouch next to the bed and put my head in my hands. I am not sure how long I remain like that, motionless and numb. When I look up, there is a strange glint of light on my window. Frowning, I stand to inspect it. Streaks of ochre red bleed into view.

At first I think it is a theorem, but then they begin to form words not glyphs. Magic prickles the back of my nose. I smell bergamot and clove and then my mouth falls open in horror at what is written in the window for me to find.

Opening night will be her last.

PART 4
SOUL

The fourth, the soul bone, is about the essence of people, places and things.

Witch Bottle: sacrifice/power/control/ephemerality/transience/storage/a store of resources or power. Positive.
Glasses: sight/vision/clarity/revelations/new understandings. Positive.
Magpie in Flight: a messenger/message/communication/the soul/spirit/rebellion/challenging tradition/birth and rebirth. Neutral.
Gravestone: grief/loss/endings/letting go/transformation. Negative.

17

SHOOTING STAR

The entrance of York Theatre Royal looms ahead as I weave around people on the street, cross the crescent and hurry into the foyer. I didn't have the money to hire a taxi and so I came on foot and my lungs are ragged from my panicked rush across town, but I'm too late. The stage doors are closed. The performance is already underway.

My hands clench at my sides, palms sweating and head swimming as I fight for breath. I cannot pass out here, not when Bea is in danger.

Opening night will be her last.

The ominous message looms in my mind and can only mean one thing: Bea is the next target. Whoever jammed the door and trapped us in that fire also broke into my home and left me a warning. Why? To frighten me? To taunt us? Well, it worked. I am utterly terrified.

Perhaps it is a ruse, or a trick and they don't mean to hurt Bea this evening. But I cannot take the risk. If anything should happen to her, I— No, I cannot think it. I cannot lose more of my coven sisters.

An usher approaches me. "Good evening—"

"I need to get inside."

"I can let you in at the interval."

No. Bea might be dead by then. My eyes sting, tears threatening. I need to explain myself, but where to start and what to say without sounding like a madwoman? Seeing my distress, the usher softens. I realize that it's the same man from my last visit. "As you are a friend of Beatrice Delane, I'll sneak you in the side door."

"Thank you, thank you so much," I gasp and clutch my chest. My lungs are agony.

He leads me into the backstage area. I try to control my fear. I should *not* be anywhere near the Royal. The Grey Lady is likely lying in wait like a spider for a fly. I shudder at the memory of her nails biting into my skin, the smell of her, and the sickening gleam in her eyes. Just because the smock men came to my defence last time doesn't mean they will do the same tonight if she attacks me. And yet, I can't leave without protecting Bea first.

I will not abandon her. If I die, then so be it.

But how am I going to stop whatever is about to happen when I do not even know who is targeting us or how they mean to strike? Damn Phillip for stealing my knucklebones to protect his pathetic petty theft. I feel helpless without them.

The usher cracks the side door and we slip into the dark auditorium. Sound and light in a shadowy space followed by dusty air taut with the tension held by a rapt audience. Bea is on the stage as Juliet's nurse. A few audience members are disturbed by our arrival but quickly swivel their attention back to the stage.

I'm led along the back of the auditorium to an empty seat. Although there are no smock men present, nor any sign of the nun, the aisles teem with a motley collection of lords and ladies watching the performance in their finest. Ghosts. Why are they here? Do they know something I don't?

And then it strikes me that being dead and unable to affect the material world might be rather tedious. What do most spirits do all day? I am sure plenty of them haunt theatres, picture houses and dance halls simply for something to do. I relax a little, because they are likely not here for me, or my coven. They probably only want an evening's entertainment. I pray that none of these ghosts believe the ancient lie that my flesh and blood can return them to life. Contending with the Grey Lady, and Edie's killer, is threat enough.

How does our enemy intend to strike? Surely there is little that they can do while Bea is onstage and visible to hundreds of people. For the moment she is safe but that will not last for long.

Is Edie here? As upset as she is at me, surely she wouldn't miss Bea's big debut? Bea is the person most precious to her and she has attended many of her rehearsals. I can't see Edie anywhere, and that sends the worry in my stomach twisting painfully deeper.

I focus on the audience as I search for Merle. I'm faced by the backs of people's heads, for their attention is rightfully fixed on the stage, where Juliet runs rings around Bea's nurse. Even dressed as a matron, Bea is breathtaking. It doesn't matter that she is playing a smaller part, she is beyond radiant. If she goes to America, I will miss her terribly, but she deserves a shot at her dreams at the very least. And if I accept Mr Saunders, I will be saying goodbye to York to move south, in any case. Everything is changing.

I spot Merle. She's only a few rows from the front of the stage, elegant in a soft chiffon gown with her hair styled in a modern fashion for a change. She sits beside her father. Beside him is Henry Saunders.

"She is most certainly a seer," a voice behind me hisses, drawing my attention.

Tensing, I turn to see who is speaking and spot a finely dressed gentleman in a Georgian light blue silk ensemble. His companions, a pretty woman in a gown that looks like it came right out of a Reynolds painting, and another equally brightly attired man are looking my way.

I quickly turn my back, pretending I can't hear them.

"She might have no inclination to help us," the woman mutters.

"Then we will impress upon her the gravity of the situation," says the first voice. "I cannot abide the wallpaper. Chartreuse, for goodness' sake!"

Taking a risk, I slip out of my seat and continue along the back of the auditorium, moving away from the whispering ghosts. From here I have an excellent view of the galleries to the right of the stage, which are packed with onlookers. My focus catches on the two women in the front-most box. The first is middle-aged and of Indian descent, elegant and serene in expression as she watches the performance with clear enjoyment. Instead of a fashionable evening dress she wears a classic saree in pale silk that makes her glow in the light from the stage.

Beside her is a petite woman, younger by a couple of decades at least. She's leaning forward in the box, her arm on the railing. Her light olive complexion and fine features are exceedingly pretty and there is a gravitas to her that leaves me breathless. She too is dressed in silk, though not a saree. I cannot see the entirety of her gown but her neck, wrists and ears are heavy with jewels. She looks like a queen from another time.

My skin prickles, nerves tensing. I feel like I'm a gazelle catching sight of a lion on the hunt. And then the young woman's gaze leaves the stage and catches on mine, as if she has always known that I am lurking in the shadows watching her. I gasp.

Her eyes glint with a distinct silver gleam.

She doesn't look away and I cannot break her gaze, as if a theorem keeps me locked in place. My heart is in my throat. Her lips twitch into a mysterious, almost haughty smile. Is she mocking me or making a threat?

It occurs to me that whoever is after us, whoever killed Edie and broke into my home to leave such an ominous message about Bea, is certainly an occultist, because the message wasn't written in ink or paint or blood, but magic, and whoever left it was strong enough to breach my wards. That is how they will attack. Magic.

I don't see exactly what happens because I am staring at the woman with the silver eyes but a heavy clunking sound suddenly emanates through the theatre. Onstage there is a rush of motion followed by the crackle of snapping timber and a blood-chilling scream.

A heavy wooden sun, painted and emblazoned in the Capulets' house colours, hangs over the performers by only one rope, dangling directly above Bea and Millicent. Bea glances up, breaking character, as the last rope snaps and the sun plummets towards them.

There is a sudden blur of movement. A ripple of shocked gasps and fearful screams and a stagehand is— No, it is Tempest, the ghost who helped me when I was last here – moving across the stage faster than is possible. I lose sight of him, then realize that he has stepped *into* the handsome-costumed Romeo, sending Bea and Millicent toppling as the sun crashes with a deadly, sickening splinter, striking Andreas square on the back.

I cry out in shock.

"My God!" shouts a man in the audience as the theatre erupts into chaos. People are on their feet and many hurry towards the stage as staff appear from the wings shouting Andreas's name. Andreas himself is floored by the weight of the scenery, pinned beneath the wooden set piece. The falling sun struck his spine with two of the pointed spikes that make up its rays. Is his back broken? Has he been impaled? And where is Tempest? He was moving through Andreas one moment and then—

No, it is impossible. Impossible and yet…

"Help me get this off him," a gruff man in a flat cap bellows. His fellow moves to assist, all the while talking to Andreas, trying to reassure him. Andreas moves of his own accord, rolling over with apparent ease and showing strength I did not think possible. He simply pushes the giant stage piece off himself and as he does, he glances into the audience. That is when I see it: his eyes are silver.

Andreas stands. His form blurs and Tempest steps out of him. *Out*, as if they were sharing one skin. One moment Andreas is alone and the next Tempest is beside him again and Andreas's eyes have lost their metallic sheen. My mouth is agape, overwhelmed by a thousand questions as both man and ghost vanish behind a wall of people.

How did he lift that sun? It must weigh as much as two people, perhaps more. He is well built, not overly muscular, but with the natural strength of a young man who works his body as much as his mind. Still, it takes a hefty series of levers and ropes to move such a large scenery piece. He should he crushed beneath it, but he seems perfectly fine. And the way Andreas moved once Tempest stepped into him, too swift for the eye to follow.

Inhuman. Preternatural.

Silver eyes are the mark of a mirrored soul.

But what does that mean?

A groan of pain comes from the stage. Where is Bea? I can't see her among the crowd. Is she hurt? Someone lowers the heavy stage curtain, blocking the chaos from view. I'm hurrying towards the front of the auditorium before I realize I'm moving, driven by instinct and panic.

Too late. I was too late to do anything.

The soft touch of a hand finding mine and for a blessed moment I think it is Edie, but it's Merle, who has rushed down to me. "What are you *doing* here, Vi? The Grey Lady could—"

"Did you see his eyes?" I ask, pointing to the stage.

Merle looks baffled. "Whose eyes?"

I glance up at the box where the silver-eyed ghost and her companion are seated, but they're gone. Surely the fact that one of them has silver eyes like Tempest is not a coincidence.

There is a small set of steps at the furthest edge of the stage that leads into the wings. I take them, pulling Merle along with me. "Someone left me a message threatening Bea tonight."

A stagehand tries to stop us going backstage but I am not in the mood and shove him rudely away. Unprepared, he stumbles and blusters but we are already surrounded by a chaotic riot of voices and arguments, questions firing back and forth as blame is moved from one individual to another.

"Threatening Bea?" says Merle. "What are you talking about?"

I swivel and grip her shoulders. "Whoever is after us broke

through my wards and left a warning that they plan to kill Bea tonight, and she was almost just crushed by falling scenery. That was no accident."

Merle gasps, hand flying to her mouth, and then she's calling Bea's name, searching for her in the throng of theatre staff, stage crew and actors.

Our coven sister is sitting on the edge of a large storage crate, her head tipped forward, long hair pulled from its pins and trailing in a curtain so that I can't see her face. A woman with a make-up brush sticking out of her tight curls is carefully feeling Bea's skull, presumably for any injury. Seeing Bea unharmed relaxes something inside me a fraction, though if she hit her head she could suffer later.

"No swelling or abrasions," the make-up artist concludes.

Bea sweeps her hair from her face. "I didn't hit my head."

"You went down pretty hard. Are you sure you're not injured?"

In truth, she seems more irritated than shaken from the near-miss. Probably because she has no idea she was a target.

Looking up, Bea sees us approaching. "What are you two doing back here?"

"Are you joking?" Merle's voice is high-pitched and panicked. "You were almost *killed*!"

Concern and pity flashes in Bea's eyes, as if we're overreacting. "I'm all right, thanks to Andreas."

Her fellow actress has not been so lucky. The moaning is coming from Millicent. Grey-faced with pain, she holds her arm very gingerly as a man in a smart suit examines it.

"Broken wrist, I'm afraid," he says.

Millicent sniffs. "I can't possibly go back on."

"Certainly not. The bone will need to be set." The man helps her up and she thanks him.

"What happened?" a member of the cast demands to know.

"The ropes snapped," says one of the stagehands, holding up the frayed end of a thick rope. "It shouldn't have; they were brand new. I checked 'em myself not four hours ago."

Because this *wasn't* an accident. I have no doubt the ropes were sabotaged, probably with magic. Bea's watching me with concern. I know I shouldn't be here. I told her I wasn't coming.

"What about the show?" asks the pale-faced man playing Mercutio.

Bea slides off the crate, adjusting her costume. "I know all of Millie's lines and blocking perfectly."

"I think it would be best to cancel," I say loudly. "In case there are any more … accidents."

"This is a disaster," squeaks Mr Mosley the director, red-faced and frantic.

"We cannot disappoint our audience." Bea makes eye contact with me. I widen my expression and shake my head, trying to warn her, but she ignores me. "We have worked too long and too hard to cancel on opening night, especially with the press here."

"You and Andreas also had a fall, miss," the man seeing to Millicent reminds her, but Bea flaps her hand at him, dismissing his concerns.

"I feel quite well. What do you say, Andreas? Are you hurt?"

I hadn't realized that he'd come backstage but Andreas stands a little behind us, looking somewhat bewildered by the situation, though not shocked or upset. His pupils are once again a deep brown with no hint of silver.

Did I imagine it?

No, I did not. Nor did I imagine the silver-eyed woman in the audience. Does Andreas know what I am and what I saw? Good lord, is he death-touched like me?

No, Andreas *cannot* be death-touched because he would be corporeal and solid to ghosts but Tempest moved through his body and into him in a form of … possession. He turned Andreas's eyes silver and he made him faster and stronger.

"I'm not injured," says Andreas.

Bea smiles. "Then will you have me as your leading lady?"

"If Mr Mosley agrees, I would be honoured to go on with Bea as Juliet."

18

THE SHOW MUST GO ON

We watch Bea under the lights. I feel the shift in the crowd, still tense from the shock of the accident, now transported to Renaissance Italy. Bea's nerves have evaporated and she seems not to be Bea at all but the most essential form of Juliet Capulet. I know her to be a talented actress but, in this moment, she is extraordinary, especially with what just happened hanging over her. In her place I would be a mess. As it is I am so disheartened and disappointed that I could cry. I risked my life to come here and the least she could do is take my concern seriously. She is so utterly selfish it makes me want to scream…

"We should go," says Merle. "Before the Grey Lady learns that you're here."

She's right, but just because Bea is being a stubborn mule doesn't mean we should let whoever tried to kill her get away with it, or try again. Leaving the wings, I head behind the stage.

"Vi?" Merle whispers, stalking after me in a soft flutter of chiffon. "It's not safe. Viola!"

I round on her, teeth clenched, and hiss, "And it won't be safe until we catch whoever is doing this." She takes a sharp step back, hurt by my outburst, and I immediately mellow. Merle is not like her cousin, and if anything Bea bosses her around far more than myself or Edie. "I'm sorry," I say. "I'm stressed and scared—"

Merle takes my hand. "I know. What's your plan?"

"We need to discover how the stage piece was sabotaged and find the killer before the Grey Lady realizes I'm here."

The broken sun is leaning up against the rear wall backstage. It is huge. Two of the arms that make up the sun's stylized rays are splintered. On the back are several heavy metal rings through which the ropes once looped. Merle pulls on them, testing each one.

"They're intact," she confirms. "Maybe the rope was simply cut?"

I look up into the dark dusty gloom far above our heads where the ropes and pullies are hung. If we try to venture up there during the performance, someone is bound to stop us, but we can check the scenery itself for signs of magical tampering.

"Did you bring a witch bottle?" I ask Merle.

She fishes a small one from her purse and I take mine from the pocket of my dress. It is nothing special – a basic mix of bird bone, iron and quartz flakes squeezed into a narrow, flat flask.

"Revelation spell?" asks Merle. "But we don't have all the right herbs."

"I can bypass that with blood."

"Self-syphoning is for emergencies only," Merle scolds.

"Bea was almost crushed to death. This *is* an emergency."

Merle's chin dimples in displeasure but she doesn't object as I use a large splinter of wood peeled from the broken scenery to dig into the fleshy part of my palm until a trickle of blood slips down my wrist. Once both witch bottles are set up I use my blood to mark the auxiliary glyph for "revelation" on to the centre back of the sun, equidistant from the three hooks.

"Illuminate that which is hidden by design," I chant quietly. "Take what is mine and reveal secrets in kind."

The sharp dragging sensation begins through my chest, bleeding along my arms and slipping through my outstretched fingers. Pain melts through my lungs and my breaths grow shallower. I grimace, easing into the discomfort as a watery sheen ripples over the unpainted wood. Merle inhales sharply as glyphs slowly appear, like someone is burning a design into the surface. They keep appearing, a complex theorem constructed from potent master glyphs balanced by glyphs taken from a different alphabet. Both are systems we know well but I certainly don't have the knowledge to work them in this way. Merle examines the theorem carefully as I grit my teeth, struggling to hold my spell steady.

"Something is fighting me. This chain here." I point to a

sentence of auxiliary glyphs beneath the master theorem. "It's trying to hide all this. I don't think I'm strong enough to force it into visibility for much longer."

"Let it go, then," urges Merle. "You'll burn too much of yourself and get sick."

I hold on for a second longer, and then end my spell, slumping in relief as the magic releases. The exposed glyphs immediately fade. I lean into Merle for support, breathing slowly as my lungs rattle.

"I didn't recognize the signature," she says. "Did you?"

Closing my eyes, I picture the complex riddle of magical glyphs designed to sabotage the stability of the ropes and drop the deadly set piece on to the actors below. "No, they used Quentenian master glyphs blended with Cyrillic, both standard alphabets. The sequence layout, however, that was unique."

"Why didn't they simply tie the first two glyph expressions together?" wonders Merle. "Instead they balanced it with an additional equation. It's indulgent rather than efficient."

And that at least tells us something. No one, no matter how skilled, could power such a theorem with witch bottles alone, and self-syphoning a theorem of this size would be costly. Whoever did this has access to an alternative source: soul bottles.

"There was no remote activation that I could identify," adds Merle.

My blood chills because she is right. I sensed a secondary theorem to hide the visible magic from another practitioner, but there was nothing to suggest that the primary theorem could be activated at any great distance. Meaning whoever did this is certainly here tonight.

Are they still here?

Shadows move against the wall, accompanied by the sound of footsteps. Hurriedly, I use my handkerchief to wipe my blood from the wood. Merle supports me, as I am a little woozy on my feet after self-syphoning, and we have just enough time to slip behind some stacked boxes before whoever is coming turns the corner.

"What would you have had me do?" hisses a male voice that I recognize. That is the ghost, Tempest. "Nothing?"

"That is *precisely* what you should have done," snaps a woman in an accent that is possibly from somewhere in the Middle East. She carries immense authority in a delicious, ageless voice that cuts through the chaff around her. "You risked exposing us."

"Aside from Kavita, there was only one person in that audience who saw what really happened," Tempest replies, "and I have already introduced myself to her."

Is he talking about *me*? I hold my breath, listening closely. Merle looks confused and opens her mouth to ask a question. I silence her with a quick, sharp shake of my head. Of course, without the obsidian mirror in hand she can't hear the whole conversation.

Shifting forward, I risk peering around the boxes, hoping that the shadows hide us well enough. Three figures stand where Merle and I were only moments ago, examining the huge sun. I recognize the two women as the elegant Indian matron and her noble silver-eyed companion who were sitting in the front box during the performance.

"I am sorry, Meryem," says Tempest. "I did what I thought was right."

Meryem. The woman he's addressing, the younger of the two who looks like an Ancient Byzantine queen decked in jewels and precious metals, has layered skirts that sweep the ground. A loose veil trails over her shoulders and arms and, although it is badly lit backstage, the fabric still glistens like winter frost. It must be woven with precious metals and gemstones. She is petite and slight and yet, from their body language, it is clear that all defer to her.

"Do we intervene?" asks the Indian woman.

Meryem narrows her eyes. "Not yet."

Instinctually, I reach for Merle, hungry for support and reassurance. My friend curls her hand in mine, concerned but silent. Meryem moves ever so slightly and I catch the glint of her silver eyes. A mirrored ghost. She has to be mirrored with eyes like that.

"Can we trust her?" the Indian woman asks. "She's an occultist."

Meryem shakes her head. "An augurer at worst. We must approach carefully. There are not so many death-touched that we can afford to lose her."

With murmurs of agreement, they leave as a group and I slump back against the boxes, exhausted and confused and overwhelmed.

"Was that woman talking to ghosts?" whispers Merle.

I nod, my throat dry.
"Do they mean you harm?"
"I don't know," I whisper.
I don't know.
And that scares me.

19

MAGICAL RESERVES

"I see." Mr Spicer steeples his fingers and leans on his desk. A heavy wooden Victorian piece has stood in this office for as long as I can remember and is so large it takes up most of the space. The top is a dark green leather and he has arranged an interesting selection of occult items along the front of it. My favourite is a set of silver scales that seems to weigh value in spiritual terms rather than any financial worth.

Merle and I are sitting in the armchairs opposite Mr Spicer, the ones usually reserved for clients. Bea is a frenetic breeze to our left, still buzzing from the rush of being onstage and irritated about being dragged home rather than being able to celebrate with the cast. I'm just grateful that she's safe.

Mr Saunders leans against the window, hands in his pockets. Both men listened in silence as the three of us told them everything we know about the fire, the warning message in my room, and the threat against us. Other than the theorem on the sun at the theatre, we have no evidence except my reading of the bones, which I admit that I no longer have in my possession, thanks to Phillip.

"I will go by the Royal in the morning and take a look at the theorem on the back of the sun myself," says Mr Spicer. "As for your knucklebones, Viola… Henry, you may wish to pursue the thief, but I think it best to simply replace the set."

"Replace?" I ask, feeling both hopeful and disappointed. I cup my palm, smoothing a thumb along the ragged scab where I dug the splinter into my flesh to draw blood. The pain of the spent magic is a throb in my temples.

"Sets made of human bone are not common," Mr Spicer goes on. "But there are dealers on the continent who I can approach."

I would love to wield the power of the bones again, but I want *my* knucklebones. Will I even connect to a different set? The images may be different, the feel of them certainly will be. But it is still an incredibly generous offer. "Thank you, Rupert."

Outside, the heat of the day has once again broken for a night-time summer storm, the raindrops lashing the dark glass behind Mr Saunders like tears.

"It might take me some weeks, but I will find you a suitable set," Mr Spicer promises. "In the meantime, I would like you to stay with us, just until this is over. You will be safer here than at home."

"You believe us, then?" asks Merle.

"Oh, yes, and as angry as I am that you kept this information from me, I am afraid it might well be my fault."

His fault?

Mr Spicer exchanges a glance with Mr Saunders, who clears his throat and offers an explanation. "Someone has been targeting Rupert's occult trade for several weeks now. That is the true reason I am in York. Rupert is the primary dealer of souls in the country – if his network is disrupted it will have a serious impact on the supply of soul sources not only across Britain, but into the continent and beyond."

"Do you know who is behind it?" asks Bea.

"We suspect it's a rival dealer wishing to expand their business and poach trade."

I close my eyes, feeling a wash of dread as Mr Spicer stands and unlocks the safe behind his desk. Inside are three bottles. He removes one and places it on the desk. "Our greatest resource."

The glass is tinged green, contrasting with the stark red seal at the neck that keeps the ghost inside contained. Merle leans in for a closer look, as does Bea.

"What on earth…?" Bea mutters under her breath and I wonder what everyone else here can even see inside the bottle. For me, it is a whirlwind of dust and gore punctuated by a glimpse of a hand, eye or other fragment of the soul trapped inside. This one seems to be a woman with a snarl to rival Mary's.

Mr Spicer explains to us that soul bottles are a natural

extension of witch bottles and can be used as sources of power when working complex theorems that are simply too large for witch bottles to power. Instead of self-syphoning, risking soul drain and sickness, a bottled ghost is used like a battery. He speaks in a way that avoids humanizing the spirits themselves, talking about them like they are a valuable commodity, business and nothing more.

Merle chews on her lip as she listens, her whole body tense. Bea looks outraged and flustered. "Father, why didn't you tell us about this sooner?"

Mr Spicer hesitates, a question in his eyes. Bea answers with a tensing of her jaw and a slight widening of her eyes and then the moment shatters and father and daughter each look away.

"I didn't hide the information from you," says Mr Spicer. "It was there in the ledgers that Merle worked on, mentioned in the fine print and addendums of the books I gave you access to, but I didn't want to introduce the idea directly before you were ready. I wanted you to come to it on your own."

I want so badly to believe Rupert. He has always been so generous and he has taken care of us and allowed us the space to grow and nurture our magical practice.

"If you are one of the most prominent traders of soul bottles in the country, then it's likely that whoever attacked Bea tonight purchased the soul bottle they used to fuel the theorem from you," I say.

Mr Spicer's lips tighten and I realize that he has already considered this. "Henry and I will go through the ledgers.

We have everything in hand and will find those responsible. I want you three to remain in the house, safe and protected, until we have brought the perpetrators to justice." Mr Spicer puts the soul bottle back in the safe. "This is no matter for the police. This is a quarrel between occultists. Now, it is very late, we should—"

A commotion sounds from the front of the house. Hammering, as if someone is pounding on the front door, followed by the chime of the brass doorbell and a man shouting. Standing abruptly, Mr Spicer checks his watch – it has gone ten in the evening – and strides out of the office.

We follow his broad strides through the red rooms and into the front hall. The housekeeper, Irma, in a nightgown and robe, is squinting in confusion. "Are you expecting anyone at this hour, sir?"

"No, I am not." Mr Spicer holds his hands up, indicating that we girls should keep our distance. "Henry."

Mr Saunders produces a small pistol from his jacket pocket and trains it on the door as he double-checks the ward, then reaches into the pocket of his jacket and scrapes the seal on the little bottle inside. A twist of his fingers. The front door unlocks and unlatches on its own before slowly swinging open.

On the other side a man in a brown working man's suit and flat cap supports a second similarly dressed figure. It is a younger man, his head lolling, clothing dishevelled, his shirt ripped open. There, on his chest, a strange pale glyph burns with a chilling glow.

Henry lowers the gun. Mr Spicer lets out a grunt of dissatisfied surprise.

"We found him like this a couple of hours ago," says the gent in the flat cap as he hauls the other man inside. Both men are drenched from the downpour. "He's marked by the same theorem we found on the lads delivering the last stolen shipment, look."

"Another one?" gasps Irma with her customary disapproving tone. "I'll make him up a bed."

"Bingham?" Mr Spicer taps the bespelled man's cheek.

The man called Bingham raises his head in response, but his gaze is unfocused. He looks like my pa after a few too many at the pub: skin waxy and mouth slack. "Empty," he mutters. "There is nothing … nothing. I can't feel, taste. I think I am dead—"

"Who did this to you?" asks Mr Spicer. "Give us something, man."

Bingham's breathing is laboured. "Silver eyes."

"Get him upstairs," Mr Spicer orders.

Putting away his pistol and sliding Bingham's arm over his shoulders, Mr Saunders helps flat cap drag the half-sentient man up the stairs. Bea and Merle press themselves back against the wall to give the men the space to pass, their faces grim.

Silver eyes.

Those words lodge ice shards under my skin. I think of Andreas Sweets, Tempest and the beautiful Byzantine queen at the theatre. Are they involved? Is this their doing?

"Father, what's going on?" Bea stalks after her pa. "What happened to him?"

"Girls, not now." Mr Spicer pauses on the landing and looks down at us, then sighs. "Several of my soul catchers have either disappeared, or they show up incoherent and marked by an unknown glyphic theorem that seems to make it impossible for them to work any magic, let alone bottle another soul."

A chill winds through the stairwell. I'm shaking, half from exhaustion, but mostly from shock. "Have you warned Rachel?" I ask, worried for her safety.

"She knows," Mr Spicer confirms. "All my network are aware of the threat, but whoever is targeting me is still getting to them. So far our attempts to break the enchantments have failed. This is the most powerful theorem we've ever encountered, impossible to reverse-engineer. Which is why I need you to stay home. I couldn't live with myself if this happened to any of you. It's best that you retire for the night. Viola, if I might have a quick word. I know you are exhausted—"

"It's fine."

Bea looks concerned, and a little irritated that she is not to be included, but she quietly takes Merle's hand and they climb the stairs to bed without protest.

"Viola." Tears shine in Mr Spicer's eyes. I do not think I have ever seen him cry before. When he opens his arms, I step into them instinctually, breathing in his smell of tobacco and clean cloth. When was the last time my own father even spoke to me, let alone embraced me?

"Thank you for protecting my daughter," he says into my hair. "You are a wonderful friend to her and you know, don't you, how much you mean to this family? You are like a second daughter to me, Viola."

He breaks the embrace and, keeping his hands on my arms, sits back against his desk. "This threat to me is now a threat to you, and I am sorry for that." He pauses, as if choosing his words carefully. "In general, occultists, augurers and witches don't police each other's work. What another practitioner does is none of my business, unless they attack me or my associates. In that case, I must retaliate and defend myself." His hands slide down my arms to gently take my palms. His expression is sincere and filled with concern, but disquiet pricks along my neck and I cannot relax. "That is why I have always allowed you and the girls the space to grow into your own practice but now, dearest Viola, I must ask something of you. Edie's death was a great tragedy but she has gifted you with a rare and coveted ability. To see the dead is to hold great power."

"I don't feel powerful." The words are out before I can stop them, but it is the truth.

"But you are. In order to stop whoever is targeting us, likely the same person or persons responsible for Edie's death, I need to replace the soul bottles that these villains stole in their raids on my shipments."

And in that moment, I know what is coming.

"Viola, you have the capacity to become a talented soul catcher. I would train you myself, provide you with all that you need—"

"Can I have some time to think about it?" I ask, knowing that I'm stalling. I will never trap souls for him.

"Of course." He pats my hand fondly. "But don't take too long. We have enemies at our gates."

I finally head upstairs and find Bea and Merle discussing matters as they brush out their hair.

"At least now we know who is targeting us: those with the silver eyes," says Bea.

I'm not sure we can know this for sure. If Tempest, Meryem and the others did set the trap to kill Bea, then why on earth would Tempest and Andreas save her? No, Mr Spicer is wrong, but I'm too tired to explain everything I saw at the theatre, and recount my meeting with the ghost Tempest Lawson. If I am honest, my concern for Edie eclipses everything.

I see her face whenever I close my eyes. Her absence haunts me. While Bea and Merle ready themselves for bed, I sit with a view of the small but lush rampage of garden behind the house. Rain spatters the sill where a line of salt and magic protects us from the threats of the night.

It doesn't matter that I ache from the magic I used this evening. I cannot rest safely behind wards while other people solve my problems for me, and I cannot wait any longer to look for Edie.

No matter where she is, I will find her. As soon as Bea and Merle fall asleep, I slip out of the back door and into the night.

20

TORCH IN THE NIGHT

I have too much clouding my brain not to want to walk and walk and walk as my search for Edie takes me all over the city, through almost barren streets as the storm washes York clean. I forgot to bring an umbrella and I am soaked to the skin in moments, but I will not give up. At this hour, most of the people around are ghosts, or late-night drinkers spilling out of pubs as they close.

I cannot find her anywhere. The breeze has no answers.

About to brave the bridge and return home via Micklegate, I pause at the top of the steps down to King's Staithe where the Ouse Bridge Inn sits proudly on the banks. At that very moment the door of the establishment opens and Phillip Petty himself strides out. The pub closed a half-hour ago, but perhaps he is friendly with the landlord.

I am exposed at the top of the steps, frozen in surprise. All he need do is look up and he will see me. Instead, he pauses to light a cigarette, looking out over the Ouse. Light from the streetlights across the river dances through the grasping hands of the souls wrapped in its waters. I dare not get any closer. I have no proof that the river souls mean me any harm but there is something melancholic and strange about them that warns me to keep my distance.

Anger fizzes in my blood. I should confront him and demand he return my knucklebone set. But I have no theorems or charms prepared. I am alone, the streets are almost deserted thanks to the rain, and he has already proven himself far stronger than me.

Before I can formulate a plan to approach him, a figure walks along the staithe. A young woman. Phillip catches her waist and pulls her against him under the eaves where there is a little shelter from the downpour. Even from this distance I can see genuine affection shining in Phillip's eyes. It's unsettling to see him so tender and considerate. He kisses the woman and she wraps her arms around him and kisses him back.

He has a girlfriend. It is true that Phillip is not unfortunate-looking, for a man. I think very little of him because I have seen his cruelty and his callousness, but some girls like a man with a certain meanness, which Phillip has in generous supply. And his face is very fine when he smiles, as he does now.

The couple step to the side, turning to place the girl directly under the lantern protruding from the wall and I let out a gasp. Phillip's sweetheart is Mrs Aldridge's maid and nanny, the domestic who worked for Mr Spicer some months ago.

Lottie! That's it.

She's wearing a wool coat to keep off the rain. From deep pockets she takes out several items and hands them to Phillip. I see a flash of silver, a pair of earrings and something else gleaming that I can't make out. He slips them into his jacket.

What is going on? And then it clicks. I'd bet anything that the items Lottie just gave Phillip are stolen, quite possibly from her employers. He's probably convinced her to steal for him, and the Aldridges don't suspect her because they're so preoccupied with Christopher's illness.

My neck prickles, nerves alight with sudden alarm. Someone is watching me; I know it in my soul. I step back into a man huddled under an umbrella. We bluster an apology at the same time. He side-steps me. I spin on my feet and stop dead.

Dark robes, bloodshot eyes, and a wide grinning mouth.

The Grey Lady! I stumble back with a scream of pure fear, only half aware that my cry has Phillip and Lottie looking my way. This is a walking nightmare, a trick of the light. Paranoia and distress take me over—

"Miss?" The poor man I bumped into looks terrified and I realize I have just screamed in his face. I'm holding on to him as if he could save me but he cannot. There is nothing anyone living can do to protect me. Any second now the Grey Lady will sink teeth into my flesh, drawing blood and all they will be able to do is watch in horror as I die.

"Little seer." The nun's lips stretch into a wide, sickening grin and I know that she is real, only a few paces away and hungry for my blood. "I *need* you."

"Leave me alone!" I bolt, slamming into Phillip and Lottie as they reach the top of the steps, looking angered and puzzled. If they try to grab for me, they miss, and I rush across the ancient bridge and on to Micklegate.

My lungs swell against my ribs, painful and haggard, and I slow. The sound of my shoes hitting the cobbles rings in my ears. Even before the fire I was not keen on running and my muscles burn. I daren't turn to see if I am being chased as that will slow me down even more.

My best hope is to reach Spicer House before she can grab me and hope their wards keep her out. The road slopes gently up and I gasp in pain, a stitch blooming in my side. I don't have much more to give.

My body is failing, vision spotting dark at the edges. I've slowed. My sprint up the slope is more of a frenzied jog. I expect the Grey Lady to be at my heel but when I glance behind, the street is clear. Chest heaving, I cleave through the scream of my anxiety to scan the road, searching for her.

She's not here. She isn't following. Gasping with relief, I wheeze a few shallow breaths and stumble the final stretch. One moment I am five steps from the front door of Spicer House and then the Grey Lady, in her long nun's habit, materializes directly in my path. I cannot stop myself from running into her open arms.

Clawed nails dig into my back and scalp, gripping my

hair. My head is wrenched painfully back, my neck exposed, my frenzied pulse hammering. The nun's eyes are wide and gleeful with victory. I fight against her with a desperate cry but I am weak and exhausted.

"I shall live again." Her voice is horrifically soft in my ear. "And my child will live too."

Any moment now she will tear my throat out, lapping at my hot blood as it pumps from my neck, and I will die in a painful panicked gurgle. My death will be a mockery of Edie's sacrifice. I want to live, for Edie, as much as for myself.

Anger explodes through my veins, gifting me a last burst of strength. I narrow my eyes and grit my teeth, shaping my hands into claws of my own. I go for the Grey Lady's face and scratch. It feels horrible – her skin is sweaty beneath my fingers. I scratch at her eyes and she screeches. Her grip relaxes for a split-second. It's my one chance and I seize it, forcing her off me, but I cannot fight her off. I am not strong enough.

Green light flares in my face and I almost fall backwards but a hand reaches around my back, catching me and spinning me to my feet. The darkness is washed in chartreuse tones, a lamplight glow that catches on a familiar face.

Tempest Lawson. The green light emanates from the flaming torch he's holding. It's not an elegant lantern but a bundle of rushes tied together and soaked in oil, the kind depicted in old paintings and prints of Hogarth's London. He thrusts the flame into the Grey Lady's face and she recoils as if burned.

"Agnes, we've talked about this." Keeping her at arm's length with the torch, Tempest walks us carefully in a semicircle.

The Grey Lady rucks her lip. "She is not yours."

Although I am sweating and panting, I shiver at the haunted sing-song quality of her voice.

"No trying to eat *any* death-touched," says Tempest. "Not just Andreas and Kavita."

She growls then, a hissing sputter that guts the last of my courage. She means to attack anyway, and I do not know what a single flaming torch can do to save me.

"Wh-why does the torch deter her?" I ask him, uncertain how he can even have such a thing as a ghost.

"I was a link boy in life, guiding people home through perilous streets," Tempest replies. "Souls can manifest objects that were important to them in life, so I still carry my torch. Its light is protective, defending against necromic cycles, dangerous souls and shades."

"She's a shade?" I gasp, eyeing the Grey Lady warily.

Andreas steps from the shadows of the churchyard. "Nah, she's just mean."

"We'll take care of her," says Tempest. "Run."

I do, stealing a last burst of energy as he shoves me away from him and lunges towards the nun. Perhaps I should try to get around them and into Spicer House but Andreas and Tempest are fighting the nun on the doorstep. My own home and its wards are only minutes up the road and I am desperate to put distance between myself and Agnes.

Micklegate Bar looms ahead, a great gate with open arches for motor cars, buses and other traffic to pass beneath and a stone staircase on to the city walls that surround the oldest part of York. Since the fire, every time I walk in and out of the city, I'm cautious not to look at the ghostly severed heads strung from the parapets.

Is anyone following me? I risk a glance over my shoulder. My foot catches on a cobble. Tripping beneath the pedestrian arch of Micklegate Bar, I blink, shaken and confused. The sound of keys rattles in my ears. Looking up, I lock eyes with a girl, a year or two younger than me, her hair tidy under a white coif, her simple kirtle covered by an apron.

Her neck is horrifically broken. A jagged shard of bone protrudes from the side of her throat. I recoil in horror and disgust.

"The king is at the gate," she says and the world dissolves around me.

21

BENEATH THE BAR

I am no longer on the street but in a small stone room with rough-hewn furniture and pewter plates on a wooden table. A blazing fire dances in the hearth. Outside, cartwheels creak over cobbles and a flag cracks on the breeze. Hauling myself up, I look out of the window upon Micklegate Bar, but this is not the York I know. Smoke trails from a thousand chimneys. It is daylight and the streets are cramped and stinking, the buildings lacking any modern convenience. I feel as if I have tumbled into Kay Harker's box of delights to be transported back in time.

Have I completely lost my mind? Is this a hallucination?

"The keys." The girl's words make me spin with a gasp, my anxiety flaring. She's rooting through a wooden trunk in the corner, paying me no mind at all. "The king is at the gate and I have lost the keys."

Blood slips over her lips as she talks. Her neck is still at an awful angle, her spine protruding from the open skin. She hurries to the next chest and continues her search, pulling out reams of fine woollen cloth and wooden utensils. I sense her anguish and mortification as if they are my own. The terrible pang of my failure overwhelms me. The king is at the city gate and I do not have the keys to let him in. Father tasked me this and I have let him down.

I failed my father.

I shamed my entire family.

The fire. Edie's death. My parents' financial ruin. All my fault. This girl and I are not so different. Only, she has a broken neck. She is dead. Long dead. And I am not.

Beware the souls who show evidence of their deaths. Rachel warned me about ghosts like her. Just because she isn't attacking me like the Grey Lady doesn't mean that I am safe here. And surely these thoughts and feelings are *not* mine, but hers.

I am Viola Sampire. I am standing beneath Micklegate Bar in the year nineteen thirty-eight.

I try to see beyond whatever illusion has me trapped, blinking my eyes furiously and urging them to clear, but nothing changes. There is a strangled cry, not my own, but I'm the one making it. My heart rams against my ribs as a creeping sense of foreboding crashes inwards, smothering and cruel. I must escape, and quickly.

The Grey Lady wants my blood and Tempest and Andreas are fighting her and now I have fallen into another time and it is not safe because I am certain that this is a necromic cycle.

The clink of metal snaps my attention back to the girl. She has found the keys. The chamber around us melts into a winding stone stair. I'm running down the steps with her before I can stop myself. It's cramped and narrow and I trip, my ankle twisting under me and the steps leap up.

This is how the girl broke her neck and I shall break mine, stone slamming against my jaw as my body tumbles over itself.

Soft hands grab my torso – familiar hands wreathed in a peony and gardenia scent – hooking me back from the brink of death. Edie is here. She encloses me in her arms and we're stumbling away from the looming staircase and the echoing scream of the girl's horrible death. I try to speak but I am overcome with the pain of simply breathing enough air to remain conscious.

Is this still part of the illusion? Is Edie real? I desperately need her to be real.

Whatever magic had me trapped breaks open and the rain-slicked night bleeds into streaks of grey stone. Edie and I fall sideways. Soft hair on my forehead, the scent of her is all-enveloping. I am once again on the pavement beneath Micklegate Bar, soaked to the bone as I pant and shake against the girl I love.

There is no time to speak her name or even to take in the fact that she is *here* safe and well, before someone scoops their arms beneath mine and hauls me backwards, dragging me out from under the Bar to the corner. Raindrops kiss my skin.

"Hey!" Edie hurries after us.

I can't breathe. My lungs are tight and vicelike.

Whoever has me lets me go but keeps an arm firmly on my back to keep me steady. I look up into bright but dark eyes softened by crow's feet. It is the woman from the theatre, her silk saree somehow resisting the rain. *Magic*.

"You're all right, Miss Sampire, no harm done." Her voice is smooth and kind. Her hands trace a shape on my back and my breathing instantly eases.

"You're death-touched?" I stammer, barely aware that I'm talking.

A soft huff of amusement. "And you're good at getting into trouble."

I have no answer to that, and I turn away to face the girl leaning over me with panic in her eyes. *Edie*. She is so close that I can see the flecks of brown in wide eyes that search my face, a question in their depths. The relief that she is here, unharmed, is an overwhelming rush. I can't think; I don't care who is witness, or if it is a terrible idea and will spark the end of our friendship. All I know is that, if death cannot stand in our way, I must be bold for the both of us.

Sliding my arms around her, I pull her down to me and kiss her.

Finally, something within me exhales as our lips meet. She tastes sweet and familiar, like home, like safety, and I know that I've never felt anything like *this* before. Edie's shaking in my arms and her mouth is on mine, kissing me back with urgency, and for a brief moment nothing else exists in the world. When we finally break apart, she holds me just as tightly and I bury my face into her neck, drawing in the scent of her.

The shock of the Grey Lady's attack is like a hammer, striking through my numb terror. The relief that I am safe and reunited with the girl I love tips me over the edge. I cry in ragged, ugly pants. Edie's on her knees, arms like a vice shielding me from the world as I let the stress and pain of the past few days bleed out.

"I'm here. I'm here," she whispers and that only makes me cry harder.

Her soothing hand strokes my wet and tangled hair. When my breathing has calmed and my sobs are gentle hiccups, I pull back and look at her. "Where have you *been*?"

She traces the bruise on my cheek with her thumb. "I'm sorry, Vi. I'm so sorry."

"Sorry? I was so worried!" I push her off me and she has the good grace to look ashamed. "You could have been eaten by a shade like Mary, or dragged into the river, or caught in another ghost trap. You didn't even visit Bea!"

The name hangs between us, taut and sharp.

"I will never leave you again," says Edie, soft and sincere. I can still feel the tingling warmth of her mouth on mine and the anger bleeds out of me. I trace a finger down to her lips, over the upper, plucking at the lower, then flick my gaze up to meet hers. I want desperately to kiss her again.

But we are on the street, exposed and observed so I clamber to my feet, dusting road dirt off my wet dress. God, I ache all over and my head is agony.

The woman from the theatre has given us some space. I am certain that she is living, death-touched like Andreas and I, but the younger silver-eyed woman she is talking to now – the one who holds herself like a queen, head high and eyes glinting with pearlescent silver – is a ghost.

"My name is Meryem." The ghost walks over and offers her hand. Slowly, I take it. Her palm is butter soft and a jolt of something like electricity shoots through me as we touch. She doesn't let me go, instead tracing her nails over my skin like she's reading my future in the lines on my palm. Then, she gestures to the older woman. "This is my mirror, Kavita Jha."

Mirror. Silver eyes are the mark of a mirrored soul.

"Why doesn't she have eyes like yours?" I ask.

"Sometimes I do," Kavita replies. "But only when we share a body."

"Share?" I swallow nervously, remembering how Tempest stepped into Andreas's skin at the theatre. "As in possession?"

"More like symbiosis," says Meryem. "I do not deny Kavita her autonomy."

"How does that work?" I demand, hungry for answers.

"Curious little thing, isn't she?" Kavita smiles, but it is fond rather than cruel. "We are members of an organization called the Hand, who travel the world shutting down occultist networks who trade in trapped souls to fuel their magic. We work in pairs, one ghost, one death-touched, bound to each other by a unique magical seal in a process called mirroring. Only Meryem can possess my body, and only I can sustain her ability to work theorems without risking soul burn. It gives us extraordinary abilities and a way to fight dangerous ghosts and shades without needing to destroy other souls to fuel our magic."

Kavita smiles affectionately at Meryem, who smiles back.

"It is a partnership of equals," says Meryem. "Sacred and secure."

"Like marriage?" asks Edie, her voice catching.

Meryem's lips twist in amusement. "You could say that. For Tempest and Andreas, it certainly is, though most mirrored pairs are not sweethearts. Kavita and I are very close friends, as close perhaps as you are to your little coven."

The mention of my friends sours the atmosphere. Edie wasn't at Spicer House or the theatre. She doesn't yet know about the attack on Bea, that soul catchers have also been targeted, or that the culprits pursuing Mr Spicer's trade in bottled ghosts are standing in front of us.

"Someone has been intercepting Mr Spicer's shipments," I say. "You are responsible."

Meryem nods slowly. "We have freed every spirit that Rupert Spicer has attempted to sell in the past month. Catchers are a blight to the dead, but also to the living. It is our duty to put a stop to the trade."

"And to curse local soul catchers?"

Meryem's eyes darken, their silver sheen becoming sinister. Kavita's reaction is subtler, a slight tightening around her lips and eyes. Eventually, Meryem breaks the silence. "The theorem you speak of is not a curse. Curses are temporary. This cannot be broken. It is the first seal of three that I designed and it severs a practitioner from all phantasmic essence. They cannot syphon, not from the dead, the living, or even from themselves, meaning they can no longer hurt anyone."

Empty. That is what Bingham said. He was talking about himself.

"It severs their connection to their own soul," I say, trying to process what that might feel like.

Meryem simply nods. "It is the lesser evil. Occultists are dangerous. They experiment with theorems and when that backfires they create shades that go on to cause more damage and deaths. We stop shades when we find them, and free souls from necromic cycles where we can."

I glance up at the girl with the broken neck lurking by Micklegate Bar and realize that I somehow know her name – Sarah. Perhaps a side effect of falling into her necromic cycle. We are only a few steps away, close enough that I can hear her muttering to herself about the lost keys.

She seems so broken and lost and I know that it is not the same thing as the sealing theorem that Meryem and Kavita used on Mr Spicer's soul catchers, but it still shakes me to the core. I cannot let that happen to Bea and Merle.

"Do what you want to me," I say, "but please leave my friends alone."

"They're occultists."

"So am I!" I snap and Edie has to hold me back, cooing soft soothing sounds against my neck, her arms tight around me.

Kavita narrows her gaze. "You've syphoned from bottled souls?"

"Not... No." I think of Rachel's zoetrope apparatus. That was powered by trapped souls and I contributed to the theorem. Does that count? I don't think so. "I've only tapped into witch bottles and syphoned from myself, when I absolutely must."

A subtle shift in Meryem's expression: a soft fondness, as if I am a mere child that amuses her. I realize then that she must be centuries dead, her experience adding up to more lives than I can count. "Then you are what we call an augurer, which is still a dangerous practice. Do you know what will happen to you if you drain too much of your own soul to fuel magic?"

"We have always understood the risks," says Edie coldly.

"Then can Viola vouch for herself and her friends and promise us that they will never resort to bottled souls to fuel their magic?"

"Yes, of course!" I'm irritated that she would even suggest such a thing. And I have to believe this is true. Merle was horrified when she found out the truth about soul bottles, and Bea looked visibly shaken, almost sick. I trust them as well as I trust myself. They would never cross that line.

Kavita steps forward. "And when one or all of you are dying too young because you have been foolish and power hungry and consumed too much of your own soul for magic trifles. What then?"

"They wouldn't." I'm trembling. "*I* wouldn't."

Meryem twists her hand in the air and the next moment she is holding a stylus, like a long feather pen without the feathers. The shaft is narrow and tapers to a deadly knife point. "Come, Viola. Let me show you what is at stake. It will not hurt. I promise."

I don't trust them, not completely, but I am also too curious not to take the risk and I don't feel like I'm in control of anything any more. I'm so tired. Swallowing my fear, I let Meryem touch the tip of the stylus to the centre of my forehead.

"Imagine, if you can, an ancient city devoid of the dead, entirely stripped of its souls."

Magic roars, flaring bright in my vision as golden threads of shimmering light stream from the place where the stylus touches my skin. As if drawing in the air, the strands start to form an image. A vast walled city expands around us, the golden light settling to reveal sand-coloured walls and red-tiled roofs gleaming under blue skies. It looks to be a mixture of Roman architecture, Greek monuments, mosaics and gold and rich gardens. Life, bursting and ripe in its complexity.

And then the catchers come. I feel the change, the panic and pain and void left behind.

The city is dead. People still crowd the streets, motors, music on the wind and the elegant spires of ancient buildings still cast their shadows. Yet the city feels empty. My head spins and I would like to be sick.

When the image fades, Edie is holding me and I'm crying.

"Souls are not only the source of magic; they are keepers of memory." There is something in Meryem's tone that chases goosebumps over my wet skin. I realize now that York thrives because it is so rich with hauntings. Ghosts are more than just fuel for spells; their essence embodies their living experience and memory.

They are the heart blood of a place.

"You are aware, I presume, of the requirements to become death-touched?" says Kavita gently.

I don't look at Edie, but I feel her stiffen, tension in every line of her body. Does she know that I am aware of the sacrifice that she made for me?

"We know how it works," I reply.

"Then you can imagine how rarely the right ... conditions occur to give rise to a death-touched like you or I." Her smile is sad and serious. "We need death-touched, Viola. We are too few. There are only fifteen mirrored pairs in the Hand, which means we are forced to be transient and can help fewer ghosts than we would like."

The rain has slowed to a mere smatter of drops but the breeze has picked up. I shiver, and not because of the growing chill in the air. I am too overwhelmed to process this new information well. Sarah, the ghost under Micklegate Bar, spins on the spot, muttering, her neck at that horrible angle. Her existence is confined to this one place, condemned to experience her final moments on repeat until the end of time. That pulls at my heart. It is unfair.

"Is there no way to help her?" I ask, sniffing.

Meryem smiles softly, as if I have passed some kind of test I did not realize I was taking. "There is, though it is not known to many and can be performed by even fewer. Only a death-touched can free a looped soul and it is dangerous to attempt alone."

She exchanges a glance with Kavita, who shrugs. "She will need to learn it herself one day. Why hide it from her now?"

"Wait here," Meryem orders Edie and I, and the two women stride back towards the Bar. I know the moment they enter the loop because they sway a little, but otherwise they are unchanged. They don't disappear or alter in appearance and I realize that while I was caught in the loop I was simply wandering around under Micklegate Bar, completely unaware of my real surroundings and entirely vulnerable.

A few moments pass in which Meryem and Kavita seem to reorientate themselves and then they speak to Sarah. She ignored me, but when Kavita addresses her, she seems to listen.

"You're dead, sweetheart," Kavita tells the girl.

"No," Sarah protests. "I can't be. I have to find the keys, the king—"

"Has not been at the city gates for many centuries."

It takes a few minutes to convince Sarah, and I am relieved it is so late that there are few passers-by and none crossing on this side of the Bar. If anyone did walk by, they would see Kavita all alone talking to thin air. No doubt they would think her unwell or dangerous and call the police.

"You don't have to stay here." Kavita offers Sarah her hand. The girl takes it and, clutching the large iron key to her chest, allows herself to be led towards Edie and I.

I don't see the moment Sarah's loop breaks, but I sense it,

and then her neck is no longer broken. The look of stricken panic has vanished from her face to be replaced by something like awe as she takes in the street lighting and modern shopfronts. York must look incredibly different to her after hundreds of years in purgatory and she seems somewhat overwhelmed. "Where is my father?" she asks. "My family?"

"Dead, child," says Meryem gently. "Everyone you knew in life is long dead but some might have remained as ghosts like you and I. We can look for your father if you like, but if he moved on after death, then there are lots of free souls in this city for you to befriend. You won't be alone."

I watch Sarah process the end of everything she knew, her chin quivering and her fist gripping the key until her knuckles turn white.

"Are there many other souls trapped in necromic cycles?" I ask.

Kavita nods. "In a city as old as this, there are hundreds, but they're anchored at fixed points. It is possible for them to move if the area they haunt is disturbed so you do have to be cautious, but in general, if you learn where they are on your regular routes, you can easily avoid them."

Although I pass through here any time I walk into the city centre, I usually cross Micklegate Bar on the other side of the street. I've eluded this necromic cycle purely by chance. Maybe it was only a matter of time. I am truly blessed that Edie chose this moment to return to me, or I would have broken my neck.

"I was asking because I want to help them, not avoid

them," I say. "If they are suffering, surely we can't leave them as they are."

"We will do our best to free as many as we can, but it would take years to help every one of them. We don't have that kind of time. We are needed elsewhere. Occultists and the shades they create pose a greater threat."

"Come with us, Sarah." Meryem turns and walks away, taking the ghost girl with her.

Is that *it*? They mean to simply leave? My skull pounds, my thoughts spiralling. It is too much to process and I still have so many questions. "Wait—"

Kavita grasps my shoulder. "We'll speak again soon, Viola. I promise. You may warn Rupert Spicer that we are coming for him if you wish. It doesn't matter; it will end the same way. In the meantime, consider all we have said."

"Are you going to hurt our friends?" asks Edie.

Kavita laughs softly. "Hurt them? No, but it is clear that someone is trying to hurt you. We did not set the studio fire that killed you, nor did we spell a set piece to fall on Beatrice Spicer. We are investigating, if that is any reassurance, but be careful where you place your trust." She squeezes my shoulder gently. "Now, rush home, young seer. You never know when you might meet another hungry soul."

22

WHAt A SOUL NEEDS

I don't know if it's the aftershock of falling into a necromic cycle, our encounter with the Hand, or my first kiss with Edie, but I cannot get the key into my front door lock. A hand closes gently over mine, guiding my fingers to slide the key home. Edie steadies me, her breath against my neck, and the doorway yawns before us.

I don't cross the threshold, turning instead to face her. "Where did you go?"

Edie shrugs, lowering her head. "I needed to say goodbye."

"To *who*?" My heart pounds. Surely she cannot be thinking of leaving us?

"My family. My life." She sighs. "The places that I wanted to travel, the book I planned to write. I'm ... struggling, Vi. I don't know how to exist like *this*."

My heart burns for her. Her pain is my pain and I wish

I knew how to offer comfort. For so long my true feelings for Edie were impossible to pin down: flighty and fragile. If I looked at them too closely, they shifted away, avoiding my scrutiny. I know now that I've never felt anything like this for any boy, or any other girl, and it only took her death for me to realize how hopelessly in love with her I am.

"Hate me if you must," she says.

I snap my gaze to hers, confused. "I could never hate you, Edie. You saved my life. You *died* for me." There are fresh tears in my eyes. "You sacrificed your life for mine. I am alive because of you, and I can't ever pay you back."

Edie looks at me from under dark lashes, her lips parting slightly as her breath catches. She steps away. "I don't need payment; you're my best friend."

I go inside, wet and shivering, pulling Edie with me. As soon as the front door closes, she hangs her head when all I want is for her to look at me.

"Do you regret it?" My voice shakes. I have to know or I won't survive the guilt.

An expression of such hurt bewilderment crosses her face that I lose the strength in my legs and sink down on to the stairs. She follows, kneeling in front of me. "Do you really think that I could stand to live in this world without you?"

Edie's brow softens, head tilting as if waiting for me to understand. And in that moment, I do because there is something at war in her eyes: words left unspoken for too long, a glimmer of a terrifying but delightful truth, and regret as deep as an ocean. I think about her pressed close to me at night, the evenings spent cajoling me to eat as I healed, reading to each other in the chaise, and midnight stories to soothe me to sleep.

"What about Bea?" I whisper. "I thought that you and she—"

"There's nothing between us," Edie is quick to reassure.

"But ... you kissed her."

"She kissed me and I let her because I believed that the girl I really wanted would never like me back, not in that way. I was lonely and stupid."

I smile at her with a new knowing. Her eyes flare wide and startled as a rabbit's – as if she's been caught doing something she shouldn't.

"But ... we, we can't, Vi." She shakes her head, leaning away. "It's too late. I should have said something when I was alive and now ... I'm just an echo. You deserve more."

"You're *not* an echo." I take her hand, desperate. I refuse to come so close to what I want only for her to slip away. What is death in the face of love?

"I don't feel the cold any more. Did I tell you that?" Edie rubs a thumb over my knuckles. "I don't feel the rain. I can't eat. The world is right there but I can barely sense it."

I pinch the back of her hand hard until she yelps.

"Oi! That hurt!" she accuses, glowering at me.

"Exactly." Taking a deep breath, I lean in to her and curl my arms around her back. "And you feel this?"

Her, "Yes," is barely a whisper against my neck but it sends pleasant tingles chasing over my rain-damp skin. There's a catch in her voice that I don't think has anything to do with sorrow. Leaning back, I lift my hand to her cheek. She inhales – the softest of gasps as I brush her skin.

"Viola." Her whisper is a warning and an invitation in one.

"Tell me if you feel this." I lean in and hesitate, giving her a moment to turn away if this isn't what she truly wants. Instead, she pulls me in.

Kissing Edie for the second time is like the first breath of air I took after the fire: full of desperate, hungry relief. I want to embrace her sweetly, but the feel of her lips on mine has me crushing her close and kissing her with need; nothing else in life, or the afterlife, matters in comparison. There's a warmth in my chest that I can't contain, coupled by a sense of completeness I've been chasing my whole life. This is what I need.

Her.

She tastes of sweet mint and strawberries, and her mouth is warm. In proximity to her, every part of my body feels more alive. I kiss her and I know myself better. I need to brush my fingertips over the soft skin of her neck. I do, and she makes a moaning noise that I swallow down. I kiss her until we're both breathless. When we finally break our embrace, she lets out a delicate exhale that makes me want to pull her mouth to mine all over again, but I sense that she wishes to say something and so I wait.

When she speaks, it's just my name, and no one has ever said my name like that before. The sound takes the thrumming light inside me and sets it blazing.

"I would have died for you in return," I say, cupping her cheek.

She leans into my palm, eyes fluttering closed, an expression of pained serenity on her face. "I know."

Edie doesn't need to sleep but she wants to lie with me. We recline on my bed wrapped up in each other, the sheet kicked back and the window wide to entice the rain-cooled breeze to freshen the room. Dry and warm, I kiss her hair and she snuggles close as I tell her about everything that transpired since she left me at York Cemetery.

"You won't work for Mr Spicer, will you?" she asks when I have finished.

"Not as a soul catcher."

"And Mr Saunders?"

"He will have to find another death-touched witch to be his bride. I belong with you."

Edie makes a small whimpering noise as I run my fingers over her collarbone. I follow my touch with a trail of kisses and she melts against me, winding her fingers through my hair. I want to lie here forever, unchanging and immortal, and show her how much I need her, but our meeting with Meryem and Kavita plays through my mind.

"What should we do about the Hand?" I ask.

Edie sighs. "We wait, for now. They're serious about stopping Mr Spicer's trade in souls."

"You think we should let them?"

"As long as they don't actually hurt *him*."

"The sealing magic they mentioned, it's brutal, Edie—"

"We won't let that happen. Not to Rupert and certainly not to Merle and Bea, but let them shut down the soul trade in York. It's for the best." Edie kisses me, soft and deep. I nip at her lips as she pulls back. "We need to focus on who targeted Bea at the theatre, and find who killed me. I don't believe it's the Hand, which means we're right back where we started."

"We'll get them," I vow, then hesitate, not sure how to say what I mean. "When I find out who is responsible, I will end them. I will kill them, for you." Leaning in, I kiss her forehead gently. Then her nose. Then her mouth. I don't want to scare her but I need her to understand the kind of person I am. "I will do whatever it takes to keep you safe. No matter what that means and no matter what that makes me."

PART 5
WORLD

The fifth bone is the world bone, representative of the wider environment.

Mountain: mountainous terrain/high ground/a defensive position/the wilderness/an impasse or blockade/perilous terrain/responsibilities/burdens/a difficult journey/perspective/increasing wealth/greed. Negative.

Walled Garden: a garden/a settlement/civilization/abundance/community/safety/a short journey/history/humanity/predictability. Positive.

Canyon: a canyon, crevasse or cave/hidden resources/unexpected pathways/instability/debt/failure/separation/obstacles. Negative.

Storm: a body of water/transport/emotion/unexpected or sudden change/the unknown/progress. Positive.

23

GIRLS AT THE GRAVESIDE

The churchyard around St George's Catholic Church is empty save for Edie, myself and Mr Petty the old landlord, who chose to accompany us to pay his respects. I also suspect he's feeling guilty over his nephew's poor behaviour and wants to keep an eye on me, but he doesn't mention Phillip and so neither do I.

They don't often bury people in this churchyard any more, for lack of space, but Edie's family are respected members of the congregation and once donated money to have the stained glass repaired, and so this is where Edie was laid to rest. Everything looks very pleasant and calm, the way churchyards often do with neat, clipped grass and flowers planted at the verges. The gentle breeze stirs the ivy creeping along the older gravestones. I find it strange and horrible to think of Edie rotting below ground when her soul walks beside me, looking like she's still breathing and alive.

I don't know if it's considered healthy to visit one's own grave but she wants to be here and there is nothing I can do except support her.

Mr Petty goes ahead, pausing to smell the honeysuckle that has escaped a nearby yard to trail along the churchyard wall. With his round cheeks, moustache and laughing blue eyes, he's a hard man not to like. The good-humoured landlord was only too pleased to join us this morning and, in the absence of Bea and Merle, his presence does make our visit here feel jollier, like we're simply going for a nice morning walk. Although they never knew each other well in life, his and Edie's deaths were only six months apart. If anyone can understand her struggle, it's him.

Leaning in, I quickly kiss her cheek. She flushes pink and it's the prettiest thing I've ever seen. She looks at me, a fragile smile on her lips, and it feels less like being observed and more like being touched. I become so incredibly aware of every part of my body that I want nothing more than to reach for her hand. I restrain myself, unsure of what Mr Petty will make of our relationship.

She was laid to rest in a lovely position to the west. The freshly turned earth has settled and grass is already growing. Her family have placed flowers in two stone jars either side of her headstone: a riot of larkspur and delphiniums likely grown in Mrs Turner's garden.

Her parents loved her dearly but they didn't understand her. If they had, they wouldn't have chosen such an ornate and fussy headstone. It is bone white, not yet beset by lichens and weathering. The mason has done a fine job with the columns and pediment, carved as if draped in floral garlands, meeting at an ornate cross. Below is the inscription: BELOVED DAUGHTER.

"It's *very* Catholic," I say. "But I do like the angels."

Edie shakes her head. "It must have cost Father a fortune."

It occurs to me that funerary rights are not so much for the deceased but for those left behind. Edie does not want this fuss. She has always been rather frugal with her earnings, goodness knows why. I spend money as soon as I get it.

How would I wish to be remembered? I've been imagined by others so often – Pa's portraits of me, Ma's hopes for my future, Mr Saunders and his idea of me as the perfect witch of a wife. Only my coven knows me as I truly am. It is to them that I would entrust my remains. When I die, they can strip the flesh from me by boiling, disarticulate my skeleton and etch glyphs into my bones to create powerful impresa to anchor their spells and theorems. That is how I would like to be remembered.

"Vi! Edie! I'm sorry to interrupt, but do you know that child?" calls Mr Petty. He's walked back around the side of the church and is squinting towards the end of the yard where a little blonde head ducks behind a nearby gravestone. Edie and I exchange a glance. It's certainly the same child from Betty's and Mrs Aldridge's house.

Whatever is she doing here? Is she haunting *us* now?

"Let me," says Edie. With a gentle squeeze of my hand,

she approaches the child with caution so as not to spook her. Beckoning, the child skips off with Edie.

Mr Petty and I follow. The churchyard isn't large but around the back of the main building there are a few more recent burials. The little girl stops at a small headstone, as white and clean as Edie's but far simpler, with a cross and epitaph. Someone has left a teddy, damp from yesterday's rain. It is propped up, alone and sad.

"Norma Anne Warren," I read aloud. "You're Norma?"

The girl nods sombrely. She was someone's daughter now laid to rest beneath dirt and turf as her ghost walks the world alone. Her short life is etched on this headstone. She died this year. She was nine. It seems terribly unfair.

"I'm sorry," I say with a sad smile.

Norma Warren.

Warren.

Why do I know that name? Sometimes I think that I have met this child before, but then most children look so similar to me. Norma bites her lip and sways softly, as if she's about to be scolded. She's nervous.

"I'm not angry about the tea," I say quickly. "I know you didn't mean to do it."

The child frowns and shakes her head, her cheeks flushing. Clearly, I've said something wrong, though I can't think what. Why doesn't this girl talk? The other souls I've encountered do, but not her. She's distressed, gone from smiling to stormy as she gestures quickly with her hands.

"She's speaking in sign," says Mr Petty.

"She's deaf?" I ask. "But she understands what we're saying."

Norma gestures to her mouth. She must be reading our lips.

"Let me try," says Mr Petty, crouching to Norma's level and giving her a reassuring smile. "My sister is deaf. She moved away when she got married, lives in Norwich and it's been a good decade since I've signed much, but I can try. What do you want me to ask her?"

"Ask her why she's been haunting Mrs Aldridge," I say, but before I even finish speaking Norma is jumping up and down and signs so quickly that Mr Petty has to ask her to repeat herself.

Warren. I *do* know that name.

"I read the bones for a Mrs Warren earlier this year," I say, the memory returning. "She lost a valuable silver frame that contained a photograph of her daughter." A daughter that had died only two weeks before. "Was that you?"

Norma nods again.

"I remember that," says Edie. "Didn't one of the household staff steal the photo to sell off the frame?"

"The junior maid," I reply. "I retrieved it from her room that afternoon. Mrs Warren cared little for the frame's value only for the photograph of her daughter."

The back of my neck prickles with unease. Two sick children. One dead, one in decline. And now Norma is haunting the mother of the still-living child. That cannot be a coincidence.

"Do you know why Christopher is sick?" I ask her.

Norma signs, looking hopefully at Mr Petty whose bushy brows snap into a frown.

"I think she said something about his food, that someone is mixing a substance into it that is making him ill."

Nourishment. Exactly as the knucklebones divined, but I never anticipated poison.

"You *meant* to spill my tea," I whisper as the pieces come together. "Norma, was there something in my cup that would have hurt me?"

The little girl nods quickly and signs something and I know she means "yes" by the relief on her face. Which means that someone put poison in it to kill me, or at least make me terribly sick. Who? It had to have either been Mrs Aldridge herself, or the maid, Lottie. As far as I know there was no one else in the house and it was Lottie's job to prepare and serve the tea.

But why would she try to poison me?

To protect herself. I am relatively confident that whatever items she handed to Phillip outside the pub the other night were stolen. Lottie worked for Mr Spicer, but when she left, did she go directly into employment with the Aldridge family, or is it possible that she worked for the Warrens in the interim? Mrs Warren did tell me her maid's name at the time, but I took little notice and, as it was the girl's day off, I didn't meet her in person.

"Is Christopher's nanny and maid the same girl who looked after you when you were sick?" I ask Norma.

The child is trembling, poor thing. Then she signs

something to me and it's far more complex than a simple "yes".

"What do you mean by the long-necked woman?" Mr Petty asks the child with a growing look of horror and confusion. "Lottie prepares the meal and then, after the boy eats, the monster with the long neck comes to hurt him and I… That's what I can understand."

Monster? Long neck? Murder.

There seems to be an awful lot of *that* going around.

"My God," I whisper. "It makes sense. Lottie and Phillip are in a relationship. He's convincing her to steal for him from the houses where she's employed. She's poisoning the kids to keep her position for longer so she can pilfer things more easily, or maybe to distract from the thefts. What are a few missing trinkets when your child is dying?"

"That's evil," says Edie.

"I agree, and I suspect we will need to find out more about who Lottie really is to understand her motives." Motives the knucklebones would have easily spelled out for me now that I know what questions to ask. Phillip warned me that he protects his assets: he is a thief and his girlfriend is a child killer, and I rather think keeping that secret is worth killing for.

I kneel in front of Norma. "When you spilled that tea, you saved my life. Thank you."

A sob escapes the little girl. She throws her arms around my neck. I can feel her shaking as I hold her close.

24

UNDER THE BED

Mrs Joan Warren is a smaller creature than I remember, grief having weathered at her edges the way time wears on stone. If she is surprised to see me on her doorstep after so many months, she doesn't show it, only invites me inside. The ghosts follow. Norma has held tight to Mr Petty's hand since our meeting at the church, as if he is her only lifeline. He's such a big man that he has to stoop slightly to walk alongside her, but he does so without complaint.

I am served lemonade with ice, the heat making the glasses sweat. We sit on the veranda at the back of the house looking down over the long garden where two older children play around a pagoda. The minster bells chime in the distance, cheeping birds dance over the rooftops, and the borders are resplendent with hollyhocks and lupins refreshed by yesterday's rain. The blaze of colour sways in the soft breeze as bumblebees drone between the blooms. The lemonade is crisp but sweet and very refreshing and everything feels at odds with the shadowed, melancholy nature of our hostess.

Mrs Warren doesn't ask why I am here, only states that it is good to see me as she rarely has many visitors. She feels more like a ghost than ghosts do, perpetually distracted and not entirely present. I want to ask for chairs for Edie and Mr Petty. It's strange to be seated when they have to stand, but I don't. How would I even begin to explain myself?

Mrs Warren trusts in my abilities. I have no doubt that she will believe me if I tell her that there are ghosts present, but I'm not entirely certain how to approach the subject. I've never had to tell anyone that I can see the spirit of their recently deceased child before and I do not know how she will take the news. I'll admit to feeling nervous but not put off. We have no choice but to pursue the truth. This might very well be linked to Edie's death after all; we just have to find the connections.

I decide on a gentle but direct approach.

"Joan, I have something to tell you."

A beat later Mrs Warren swivels her head to look at me with watery blue eyes.

Norma, hand still in Mr Petty's, looks at her mother with the oddest expression: fondness, yes, and sadness, but there is a touch of anger there too.

"I came to ask you about your daughter." I sit forward in the cane chair. "I hate to ask, but can you tell me how she died?"

A crinkle forms on Mrs Warren's forehead and she draws away from me. "Norma caught a winter chill and never recovered. She could hardly eat; she struggled to breathe. We tried doctors, we prayed, but nothing helped. Then, two weeks before Christmas she had a seizure—" Mrs Warren absently smooths the fabric of her skirt over one knee so that the hem sits correctly. "Why do you want to know?"

"In the time that Norma was sick, did anything go missing around the house?" I ask. "I know it's a strange question—"

"You mean, did that wretched maid pilfer anything else from me while my daughter was dying?" Mrs Warren sniffs into a hastily drawn handkerchief. "Aye, she took a pair of ruby earrings, my late father's watch and a ring. At least, I cannot find it in the house and it has been weeks now."

It's been *months* since her daughter's death. I wonder if time has ceased to matter to her. Unlike Mr and Mrs Aldridge, she has other children: two laughing girls playing hide-and-seek among the ferns and flowers. Does she look at their faces and see her lost youngest?

"Did you report her to the authorities?" I ask.

"No. We should have – the jewels were worth rather a lot, as was the watch. I know we should pursue an enquiry and try to track the girl down, but it all seems so meaningless after losing Norma."

I understand her completely. There isn't a treasure in the world that I wouldn't trade to bring Edie back and give her the life that was stolen.

"What was your former maid's name?"

Mrs Warren leans on one elbow, pressing a hand to her brow as if to calm a raging headache as she scrunches her eyes. "Charlotte something-or-other. I forget."

"Lottie?" I say, my throat dry.

Mrs Warren nods and the blood rushes in my ears. I believed Norma, but here is yet another confirmation: the same name, at least.

Edie lets out a little breath, her face serious and shadowed. "Was there an inquest or an autopsy?"

I ask Edie's question. Mrs Warren shakes her head with a sigh. "We never had any real answers. It wasn't a steady decline. She would recover for a short while but before she could build up her strength she would sicken again."

Edie and I exchange a look. Norma's pattern of symptoms sounds identical to Christopher's.

Norma has been listening to her mother speak with her strange stoic silence, but she moves now to sign to Mr Petty who interprets for me. "She wants you to look in her room. Under her bed."

I frown. "Upstairs?" I have no notion of how we're to manage that without raising suspicion and I make the decision to be honest.

"What's upstairs?" Mrs Warren asks, looking at me rather expectantly but she's clearly puzzled.

Breathing out slowly, I gently place a hand over hers. "I don't only read the bones. I also see spirits and … she's here, Joan. Your Norma is here with us now."

I look over at the child and give her an encouraging smile.

Mrs Warren sits upright, as if she might see her daughter with her own eyes. "Truly?"

"Yes, it is a new skill and so forgive me if I am handling it badly. I do not mean to upset you. But your daughter has a request, an important one, and I would not refuse her."

Mrs Warren is shaking her head. "No, no, we cannot deny her. What does she want?"

I hesitate and glance at Norma again, who signs at me, urging me to hurry. "She wants us to look under her bed."

"She told you that?" Mrs Warren frowns and for the first time I sense mistrust. "She *spoke* to you?"

"In a way. She is signing. There is another ghost here, a Mr Ambrose Petty, who is kind enough to interpret for me."

Mrs Warren visibly relaxes, her confidence in me restored. She never told me that her youngest daughter was deaf. The only way I could know is if I am being truthful about seeing her ghost.

"Could you sign that again, please?" I ask Norma. "But slower."

With a little huff and a roll of her eyes to indicate that I am being *very* tedious, Norma makes motions with her hands that I attempt to copy. Her mother watches hungrily, her eyes watery with tears that start to fall as she hurries to sign back, far more fluently than I. Whatever her reply, Norma signs something else and I copy it.

"I will show her, dearest," Mrs Warren whispers, then stands. "Come along."

Silently, we all follow. Edie stays close to me and I long to trail my hand over hers. I want only to be with her, retreating into a cocoon of sheets and whispers, but we have a job to do here: lives to save and revenge to take.

Upstairs the house is airy with large sash windows and gauzy curtains that dance and stir light into motion across wallpaper with green and pink roses on a cream background. The last time I was here it felt homey and loved, the grandeur of the furniture softened by children's toys on the landing. This time the house feels more open, the cosiness of winter and roaring fireplaces has given way to the decadence of summer flowers. This is – was – a happy home, full of contentment. The building has joy built into its bones and I hope that offers a tonic against the choking misery of this family's bereavement.

That sensation changes as we approach the back of the building where Norma's bedroom is situated with a view over the garden. There is a worn teddy and a dog toy with a pink velvet tongue on the dresser. Clothes in the wardrobe. Colour on the walls. And a wooden bed with fresh, clean linen, even though Norma will never need it again.

Although the space looks cheerful enough, there is a deep sense of unease that blankets the room. I can barely stand to be in here. *A terrible thing happened here*, I think. Of course a little girl died. But there is more to the story, I know it. *She was murdered.*

I kneel and lift the bed pelmet. There is a little dust and several boxes but nothing else.

"Might I move these?" I ask Mrs Warren.

The lady of the house consents and helps me shift them out of the way. Once the under-bed is clear and I have an unobstructed view it is impossible to miss the markings on the wall behind the headboard. "There's something here."

We pull the bed further back to better reveal it. I stare, head spinning and mind thundering with fear and concern. A red handprint stains the wall, slightly smeared. Above each fingertip and on the open palm are glyphs painted in bone white. Interconnected lines link them, and below the palm glyph is a short equation, the anchor that ties it together.

A hand. *The Hand*. Are they behind this or is it a coincidence?

Mrs Warren gasps in horror. "Please tell me that isn't blood."

It probably contains some blood, but not much. It's been here for months and if it were, this room would be filled with flies attracted by the smell of decay.

"It's paint," I say with confidence. I've made a similar pigment to this many times before. A potent mixture of ochre and herbs that channels magical theorems well and fixes their action long after the paint itself has faded or been cleaned away.

"What do the symbols mean?" asks Mrs Warren.

I wish I knew. I don't recognize some of the elements, but upright hands usually feature in protective magic, quite possibly why the Hand have named themselves as such. What if this is them? No, I find that hard to believe. They have such grandiose ideas about protecting death-touched and ghosts from shades and occultists that I cannot see them deliberately hurting a child. Why would they?

This working isn't protective. I can feel its insidious intent lingering in the air. Hovering my own palm over it, fingers outstretched, I note that the print was likely made by someone of my size and stature – quite probably a woman.

"Might I borrow a pen and paper?" I ask Mrs Warren. When she leaves the room to oblige, I take the opportunity to speak openly with Edie. "What do you think?"

"The glyphs over each finger bear some resemblance to the Enochian alphabet developed by John Dee in the late sixteenth century," she says with confidence. Languages have always been one of her key interests and she has studied glyphic alphabets in some depth. "But this is far more elaborate, as if someone has developed it beyond mere glossolalia and into a true magical language."

Edie crouches to examine the theorem and my skin itches. I do not like her so near to such nasty magic, but she can handle herself. This theorem is not designed to hurt *us* – that much is clear. "Enochian was said to have been communicated to Dee and the scryer Edward Kelley by angelic beings and was primarily intended for control."

"Control?" I repeat. "As in, control of the child?"

"Perhaps, but that wouldn't make them sick." Edie stands and frowns. "The anchor at the base is in Quentenian. It means– "

"Half a soul," I finish for her.

"I think this is a syphon directive."

"A what, lass?" asks Mr Petty.

"Syphon," Edie repeats. "A magical term relating to the drawing of power to fuel theorems."

Mr Perry nods slowly, hands on his hips. "Seeing as I only understand one in two words you're saying, I'm going to go stand over here with Norma and let you get on with it."

"Edie, how can this theorem be a syphon?" I ask. "Surely it would need a soul bottle to fuel it, or several witch bottles, unless it's activated by self-syphoning but why—" Words die on my tongue as my gaze trails from Norma, pale and slight as she clings to Mr Petty, to the soft, sad expression on Edie's face. I understand.

The bones told me that Christopher's issues lie with ingestion and food. And I remember what his mother said: "*Lottie has him on a special diet and we've seen some improvement, until we don't.*"

Edie looks grimly at the faded theorem. "Usually magic designed to act on another person is anchored in an impresa that they wear, bone being one of the most potent materials, but the right ingredients could easily have been ground down and added to the paint this was marked with."

The grit in the ochre. It's not herbs but bone. Maybe animal, possibly human. Ground to a fine powder and mixed in.

"She would still need to tap directly into their soul," I say.

"That could be done by taking their blood. Or feeding them some of the paint. The connection would be temporary, but if Lottie keeps dosing her victim, then she would have access to their phantasmic essence with ease."

God, that explains why the children waste away. If Edie is right, this changes everything. Lottie didn't poison Norma just to steal from her distracted and grief-stricken parents; she tapped directly into the child's living soul and syphoned from her as if she were a ghost trapped in a bottle.

I'd thought Christopher's sickness couldn't possibly be connected to the studio fire, because who would stop me divining the cause of a child's illness? That isn't true any more. Lottie has everything to lose. She knew that Mrs Aldridge had hired me to read the bones to find out why Christopher is sickening. She must have realized that I would eventually catch her, and then possibly connect her to Norma's death too. After all, it was me who divined her thievery when she worked for Mrs Warren. So, she tried to stop me by starting a fire and locking me and my coven in the studio before I met with her employer. Perhaps she meant to kill us all just to be safe.

No wonder Lottie was so shaken when I showed up on the Aldridges' doorstep. She probably thought she'd got rid of me. When poisoning my tea failed, she asked her accomplice Phillip to beat me and steal the knucklebones so that I wouldn't be able to expose her. The bones divined that the perpetrator was close to us. Well, she used to work for the Spicers.

I feel sick and I'm shaking all over. Lottie is responsible for Edie's death. I have a name and a face. I take a step back, lean on the bed frame, and try to settle my breathing.

Mrs Warren returns with a pen and paper. "I shall call the

police. They will need to see that mark, though I don't know what they'll make of it. I'm not sure I know myself."

I copy the hand and glyph theorem with as much detail and accuracy as I can, taking care to note the colours and textures in the margins. We cannot rely on the police. They do not believe in magic and witchcraft and can do nothing to save Christopher. It is on us to put a stop to this.

Mrs Warren's eyes are red-rimmed and suddenly she wears the true weight of her grief on her face, as if she is Atlas shouldering the burden of the world. "Is that...?" She closes her eyes and a single tear falls on to her powdery cheek. "Is that why my daughter died? Is Lottie to blame?"

"We don't know," I lie, folding the paper and handing her back the pen. The last thing I need is a heartbroken and vengeful mother taking things into her own hands. "But leave it to us. I vow that whoever is responsible won't get away with it." There's a cold hard edge to my voice as my anger bleeds through.

Outside, the sun is hot. I tilt my face up to its warmth and bite back tears.

"Vi?" Edie touches my arm and I lean into her. She catches my head, pulling my temple against the side of her face. Every conclusion that I've arrived at about Lottie and the children and the fire, she has too, and we stand in that knowledge for a long moment, mourning all that it means.

"We have to stop Lottie. Today," I say.

"Vi—"

"It's about more than revenge," I blurt, needing her to understand. "It's too late for Norma but we can still save Christopher."

And I want revenge for Edie.

One thing is for certain, we cannot do it alone.

"We need to call on Merle and Bea," I say. "But I don't know if we are strong enough, even with the three of us working together."

"Then we recruit help. But first let's fill the coven in."

25

CONFRONTATION AND CALAMITY

It's early evening but York is still wrapped in muggy heat. With shades drawn against the sun, the Aldridge house looks drowsy. We're about to shake that calm. Rachel Tussle meets us in the street outside wearing a leather bandolier set with five bottles held in loops across her plain blouse. I told her everything we know over the phone when I called to ask for a favour in exchange for the blood she took from me.

"The boy is very weak," warns Edie. "If Lottie uses any magic and is syphoning from him, then it could kill him on the spot."

"She won't get the chance," says Rachel. The Aldridges have a wrought-iron front gate. Using chalk, Rachel marks a theorem around each post. She works quickly, syphoning directly from the lowest bottle on her bandolier.

"That's a rather nasty charm," says Merle, who is following the chalk glyphs closely.

Rachel smirks. "If anyone with bad intentions towards the residents of this property crosses this gateway, they will instantly regret it."

"A failsafe in case she tries to run," says Edie, sounding impressed.

Bea's grin is dark and gleeful. "Oh, that *is* clever."

We each pass through the gate with no ill effect. Striding up the garden path, I take a deep breath, look over my shoulder at the incredible witches who have my back, and hammer on the front door. Seconds later it opens and I am face to face with the person responsible for Edie's death.

I have thought of this moment over and over and the thousand horrific deaths I will enact on them when I find them. Lottie must see the storm in my eyes because she takes a cautious, instinctual step away, like a squirrel sensing a hawk. But she's the predator here and I know, in this instant, that I don't care if Rachel has to syphon from the dead to stop her. If that makes me a monster, so be it. I want Lottie to suffer.

"I'm sorry, Mr and Mrs Aldridge are not at home." She's still attempting to maintain the steady, politely neutral expression expected of a domestic maid, but her mask almost breaks as she tries to shut the door in our faces.

I put my foot in the way and slam my palm against the wood, forcing my way in. "We've come for *you*, Lottie."

She backs up into the hall. "M-me?" Catching sight of

Rachel, the bandolier of glass bottles across her chest, she turns sickly pale. "I'm not…"

"Occultists don't have many rules, Charlotte Fleet." Rachel steps forward and the air prickles with dangerous tension. "But syphoning from living *children*?"

"Who is it?" a man's voice calls from one of the adjacent rooms. A chair scrapes on wood.

I raise my brow. "Ah, the lord of the manor *is* home after all."

"Please don't." Lottie turns on her heel, maybe to try to escape, maybe to fetch her employers for help, and almost runs into the florid-faced Mr Aldridge, his wife just behind him.

"You again?" he sneers, catching sight of me. "I already told you: we're not paying you. Get out."

"Your maid is poisoning your son," Merle states simply. "Just like she poisoned Norma Warren, the daughter of a former employer."

Mrs Aldridge's eyes flare wide and a strangled cry escapes her. Lottie stills and whatever blood is left in her face drains. Oh, she recognizes her victim's name all right. The panicked, trapped look in her eyes shows her guilt.

"Preposterous!" Mr Aldridge snaps, but there's doubt there too.

"I'm guessing that Christopher's sickness came on after you hired her?" I say. "We spoke to Mrs Warren. Before Lottie worked for you, she had secured a position in the Warren family, poisoned her youngest daughter and then made herself invaluable as the child's nurse so that she could steal trinkets and valuables from the home."

"Lottie?" Mrs Aldridge sobs. "Is this true?"

Technically, there is more evil to Lottie's actions than our quick explanation, but poison isn't far off the truth and it is enough to force the Aldridges to act.

"Look in the kitchen, or in her room, and I bet you'll find an ochre paste that she mixes with his food. It will contain ground-up bone and dried yew berries, among other things. What do you tell them, Lottie, that it's home-made peanut butter?"

The young woman is shaking her head but the truth of it is plain on her face – agony, terror, guilt. She's been caught and she knows it.

"You don't understand," she stammers. "I don't want to hurt anyone."

Mr Aldridge is suddenly dangerously still. "Winifred, telephone the police."

A sudden burst of movement. Lottie bolts for the door. My hip slams painfully into the sideboard as she shoves me and staggers down the front steps. My lungs constrict, my pulse leaping. She can't get away!

"Stop her!" Mr Aldridge roars.

Bea tries to make a grab for Lottie, but misses, her fingers clutching on air. Rachel just lets her go, lips twisting into a satisfied smile as Lottie reaches the front gate, tears it open and then she's on the other side and—

Unsteady on her feet, Lottie staggers and clutches her head

as she stops and gasps. Rachel's ward is working. A second later Lottie is doubled over with a groan and vomits on to the road.

A nasty charm indeed.

"You had better come back," Rachel calls. "The further away you get from the house, the worse it will hurt."

Lottie takes another few steps, then drops to the pavement and grasps at her stomach. Looking back at us with stark, tempered panic, a bead of fresh blood rolls from her nose over her lips. She's going to run anyway. I can see it in the set of her body as she struggles to her feet.

A figure lunges from between the clipped hedges and grabs her, hauling her backwards towards the garden. Lottie's wail of pain becomes a scream of raw anger. The young man is rather strapping, his chin smeared with dirt. A gardener, perhaps.

"Good man, Carter!" bellows Mr Aldridge, hurrying down the front path. "Don't let her get away."

Lottie fights against Carter, legs flailing as she screeches out curses. Her eyes are wild. "You don't understand!" she shouts. "She'll kill me. Mary has to feed. She'll drain me if I don't give her the boy!"

A horrible feeling comes over me, the anticipation of something terrible. Mary? Does she mean the shade that Rachel tried and failed to bottle?

Suddenly, the gardener gasps and reels back, releasing Lottie. I'm not entirely sure what she has done, but she moves in a quick jerking motion and now he's clawing at his skin and wailing. Magic. Lottie used a theorem of some kind, and the effect was both instant and brutal.

I think that I cry out, shocked and horrified, but I'm not quick enough to stop her from trying to run again.

Rachel is. Confident and unshakable, she shapes a symbol in the air and whispers a word that I am too far away to hear. Lottie trips, falling face-first on to the path. There is a horrible crunch as her forehead hits the paving slab and she lies still. When Rachel rolls her over, Lottie's face is a bloody mess.

She's sobbing. "Please, she'll kill me. I only did what I had to do to stay alive."

Mr Aldridge is trying to help Mr Carter. His face is now covered with painful red lesions that have swollen so much that he cannot open his eyes. That was a nasty curse Lottie used against him.

Alarm rings through my mind. If Lottie used magic on Carter and she's syphoning from Christopher, then every theorem she works drains a little more life from the boy. He could be dying alone upstairs right now.

Turning, I shout for Edie's help, push past Mrs Aldridge and sprint into the house. The stairs pound under my shoes. I stop on the landing – not sure which way Christopher's room is – and lean on the banister, forehead on the back of my hands as I suck in fresh air. The adrenaline will keep me going.

Edie appears, leading me to the middle bedroom with jovial wallpaper and the heavy scent of sickness. There is a little boy in the bed, no more than six or seven years old, looking startled and afraid by my sudden intrusion. He's a slight thing, sallow-skinned and sunken-eyed. His face is far too thin, missing the round soft cheeks of a healthy child. He backs further into the pillows.

"Who are you?" he demands, his voice weak as he tries to sit up. "Where is Lottie? Why is Daddy shouting?"

"All is well. I'm a friend." There is no time for niceties as I check him over. He isn't suffering a seizure or any obvious immediate effects from Lottie's recent use of magic. "Christopher, I need to look at the wall behind your bed. Would that be all right?"

He frowns, screwing up his little face. "Why?"

"I'm checking for monsters."

He nods then, lifting himself from the pillow and I can see how much effort that requires. Pulling back the covers, I smother a gasp. Beneath his pyjamas his limbs are skin and bone, as if he's starving. Which he is, because Lottie is syphoning his vital life essence.

"He's dying," Edie whispers.

Not today. I pull the boy into my arms. He smells like sour milk, a strangely familiar scent, and his skin is clammy and hot to the touch. I carefully move him to the armchair beside his chest of drawers, well out of the way of the bed.

"Christopher!" Mrs Aldridge is in the doorway, Merle and Bea right behind her, and then she's inside the room, taking her son into her arms.

I grip the wrought-iron bed end and pull. It scrapes on the rug. Without a word, Bea and Merle help me. My breath hitches, chest aching, but we keep pulling until the wall is exposed. Edie whispers a curse. Bea gasps.

"What is *that*?" Mrs Aldridge's voice is shrill with panic.

The rust-red handprint sits low behind Christopher's bed, identical to the one Edie and I uncovered at Norma's house. The paint here seems even darker, the colour of dried blood, and it is thick with what I presume is ground bone. It thrums with fresh, active power that makes me feel sick.

"Oh God," says Merle. "We have to break it."

Taking out the witch bottle I brought, I crack the seal and press my thumb to the top, drawing from the essence within as I shape the raw glyphs for "end" and "shatter" in the air. The pull of the syphoning theorem wavers but holds. It is too deeply rooted, and fuelled by too strong a soul source, to be easily ended by a mere witch bottle. I will need to offer part of myself to stop this magic.

"Together," says Bea, pulling the bed frame even further back to make room for her and Merle to crouch beside me. "She cannot be stronger than all of us."

"Take from me," says Merle, offering her hand, a cut on her palm already welling blood. Bea uses the small blade to open a wound on her hand, and I do the same. Blood pooling, I open the witch bottle entirely and cup it in my bloody palm. Bea and Merle drip their life essence down on to the bottle. It hisses as it makes contact, as if the glass is sizzling hot, and I feel the surge of power grip me, hauling something vital from my heart.

My coven sisters' strength flows into my spell. I cannot

see magic, but I can feel it. Threads of power wind from our co-mingled blood, connecting our coven on a soul-deep level. I glance at Edie who is standing close, disconnected by death but always here for us. Her eyes shine with pride and determination and concern. I fold myself into Merle and Bea's friendship, blanketing myself in their love and trust. Although I am at the helm of our counter theorem, I am not steering alone. Merle and Bea are with me and, as I shape my glyphs again, I know, even before Lottie's dark theorem breaks, that it stands no chance against the wave of our combined intention.

Christopher cries out, back arching, chest raised as the syphon directive shatters so forcefully that the wall behind it bears the brunt. Spiderweb fractures crack through the plaster. The paint that makes up the handprint bubbles, the glyphs streaking as if they're being scattered by a powerful wind, but the air is still. When it's over, the theorem is still visible, but very faded.

Christopher slumps into his mother's arms, his breathing more even.

Merle rests her head on my shoulder. I pull Bea in for a hug. There are tears on her cheeks. We rest for a moment, breathing deeply in relief. I feel like I have run five times around the city. The strength of the theorem we just cast, and the essence we needed to feed into it, are momentarily overwhelming.

"Is it over?" Mrs Aldridge asks quietly.

Bea wobbles as our coven of three breaks apart. She puts out a hand to steady me. I am dizzy myself, my bones watery and lungs struggling.

"It's over," I tell mother and son, breathing deeply.

It's over.

And then the sense of relief prickles to fear. Something isn't right. In fact, it is most certainly *wrong*. Bea curses, the word harsh and strange in her mouth and then I'm swivelling on my heel to face the door and the monster stepping through it.

26

MARY, MARY, QUITE CONTRARY

What little humanity Mary retained in the crypt is long gone. Magic riddles her elongated form, cracking under her sagging, waxy skin. Her neck is horrendously stretched, long and pale, as it swivels unnaturally atop a body still draped in her printed gown. Hooked arms with spindly claws stroke the air. The eyes are yellow and gleaming, and she is much larger, body bowed and crooked in a way that reminds me of a huge praying mantis.

Mrs Aldridge is the first to move, throwing herself in front of her son to shield him.

"What is *that*?" Bea gasps, her voice choked with horror, grabbing my arm.

"You can both see her?" I ask, shocked. I've automatically stepped forward, shielding Merle and Bea as Edie rushes to us.

"We see something," Bea confirms. "It's… God, it's…"

The shade looks more horrific than any ghost I've encountered before, even than those caught in a necromic cycle who bear the wounds of their deaths. Mary's beady eyes roam over us as she brings her full misshapen bulk into the bedroom, scuttling, slick and quick, a deep clicking resonating in her throat as she grabs for the child.

Mrs Aldridge screams, fighting for her son as he's torn from her grip. I don't know what everyone else can see but Edie and I witness the true horror as Mary's face opens, jaws unhinging unnaturally wide as she latches on to the boy's chest like a leech. He beats at the shade with his fists, his feeble blows passing right through Mary's strange flesh, and yet she is grasping him firmly, seemingly unbothered by the presence of anyone else. Her throat works, as if swallowing blood, although she hasn't broken the skin.

Life. She's drinking his life.

But we ended the theorem on the wall…

We were wrong. Lottie hasn't been syphoning from Christopher herself. I remember what she said downstairs when confronted: *Mary has to feed; she'll take me if I don't give her the boy.*

Hunger. I recall the sensation of painful emptiness and the cramps in my stomach when I sat in the hothouse downstairs and rolled the bones to divine what was making Christopher so ill. But it was *her* hunger that I felt then – Mary's.

The shade is syphoning from Christopher, and Lottie is responsible. I remember something Rachel said, that shades cannot feed on the living without a link, which means that the handprint theorem behind the bed *is* a protective ward, of a kind, but it was not put in place to protect the child. It is there to protect Lottie and redirect this shade's attentions, offering Mary a connection to Christopher so that she can make a meal of him.

The boy begins to convulse, a seizure wracking him. The room is filled by a mother's terrified screams, Bea's confused shouts and Merle's panic. I barely hear them. Edie and I move in tandem. I aim for the shade's neck, not knowing if I can still touch this ghost but hoping that I can because if we can't stop her, Mary is going to drain Christopher beyond the point of death.

My fist smacks the back of the shade's neck and it's like punching a sack of flour, the flesh pillowy but tough. It does nothing to dislodge Mary from the child and I fall away. Edie has placed herself in the boy's way, her body melting through his in a way that makes me feel nauseous. She's fighting where he can't, reaching through his flesh to dig her hands into the shade's jaw, trying to push her off the child.

With a furious clicking, Mary strikes, catching Edie and throwing her across the room. I scream Edie's name as she hits the wall and flies through it, disappearing from view.

And then Edie's struggling back through the wall. "Stop her, Vi!"

"Get Rachel," I scream at Bea and Merle.

Merle scrabbles to obey and Bea steps up to my side, entwining her still bloody hand with mine. There's a determined focus on her face. She's with me in this, prepared to lend me whatever power I need. But I have no idea which theorem to use against this creature. I am not equipped to fight shades, and I have no means to trap her. I will have to improvise and on-the-fly magic will cost us both.

First, I need it distracted.

"Mary!" I shout, desperate. The shade pulls back from the boy, head swivelling to search me out. "Don't do this."

"Bone in his belly." Her voice has changed too and puts me in mind of rotting flesh splitting from an overripe plum. "Bone, ground and spelled. Bone in his belly makes him *mine*."

Bone in his belly.

"If you're hungry, snack on me," I call. "I'm death-touched, very tasty. Just leave the boy alone."

The entity rucks her lip into a sneer, mouth rippling and neck pulsating.

"Christopher!" Mrs Aldridge cries as the now silent child drops into her arms. Is he dead? No, he can't be. Surely I would see the moment he dies as his soul would leave his body. Unless there is nothing left because this creature has consumed it all?

I cannot think like that. Christopher will live.

Raising my cut palm, I slick my thumb against the wound, teasing fresh blood to the surface. There is no time to spin an elegant theorem. I will have to work with raw glyphs.

The monstrous shade swings back to the boy but before she can latch on to him again, I smear my own blood on my bottom lip and shape the Quentenian glyph for "defend" into the air. When I speak the command word, power tears through me like lightning. I think I scream. Bea certainly does, our connection allowing me to rip energy from her soul as well as mine.

A pressure crushes us and I realize that it is the ghost hammering on the tentative and invisible shield the burst of magic created. It won't last long. I am not strong enough to hold it, even with Bea's help.

Just in time, Rachel appears at the top of the stairs with Merle and Mr Aldridge in tow.

"What on earth is going on—" he blusters, and then he staggers to a stop at the sight before him. "Christopher!"

He dives for his wife and child, shielding them as best he can as Mrs Aldridge wails her distress.

"Mary Bateman," Rachel shouts, drawing the shade's attention. She has an empty bottle in her hand, magic already spilling from her. The air changes, the atmosphere charged and then Mary's flesh starts to flake and blister, skin lifting from her arms and claws disintegrating; the fabric of her gown and her waxy flesh shreds and swirls into the air as she comes apart.

Thank God! Rachel has managed to modify a bottle to contain a shade. *Please work*, I beg silently. *Please*. I slump against Bea, gasping with relief. Edie's arms fall around my shoulders, as we watch the monstrous ghost twist into the bottle.

Rachel is sweating. Moisture stains her collar. She grits

her teeth in determination, then her eyes widen a second before a cracking sound breaks through the room. The glass bottle shatters in her hands, slicing deeply into her palm. In an instant, Mary's hideous form resolidifies within the room and she is enraged.

"You cannot trap me, witch," she hisses.

Rachel jumps backwards but she is not quick enough. Mary's sharp claws slice into her side, cutting beneath the bandolier and through the fabric of her blouse. Blood blooms from the site and Rachel collapses.

"Rachel!" I shout but Bea acts. A protective ward flares from a hastily conjured theorem painted on to Bea's arm using the blood from the cut she made earlier. The glyph flares against her skin as she throws herself over Rachel.

Mary rears back and turns her attention to the still unconscious Christopher again. She's going to kill him and we cannot stop her.

The wail of more than one siren cuts through the air. Rachel is scrambling in her pocket for something: a pouch. Reaching inside she throws white crystals at the shade. Mary howls, her sickeningly pale face peppered by glowing burns. Salt!

Christopher chokes, frail body spasming, and then he throws up all over himself. The sour taint of vomit hits my nose, making me gag. The mess is creamy brown like some kind of oatmeal or porridge and reeks of acid and bile.

Mary pauses, head lifting. Then with a horrendous, creepy clicking, she scuttles towards the far wall and disappears through it, cracking the plaster wall and shattering the window.

A brief silence rings through my skull, a quick respite from the hideous sounds the monster made, and then the sobs and wails hit me. Mrs Aldridge cries her son's name as she cradles him against her. Rachel is cursing through the pain of throwing salt with a palm cut to ribbons by shattered glass.

Edie … is she hurt? No, she can't be, she's a soul, but, yes, there is a mark on her arm where Mary grabbed her. Is that normal?

"Edie, are you—?"

"I'm perfectly well," she reassures me.

Why did Mary leave? If ground bone was mixed into Christopher's meal and he expelled it, then that might have broken the hold Mary had on him. It is my best guess. All that matters is that the shade is gone and the boy is alive.

There's a shout from the hallway downstairs. "Police!"

I sigh, leaning into the supportive embrace of my coven. It's going to be a long afternoon.

PART 6
ROOT

As the sixth bone, the root indicates the foundations behind a question or answer.

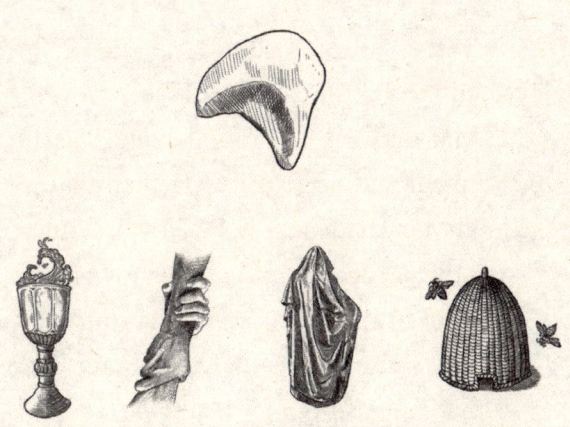

Chalice: domesticity/the home/family/shelter by friends or family/to offer hospitality/drink or consume/contained emotions. Positive.
Clasping Hands: love/romantic union/partnership/shared values/kindred/close friendships. Positive.
Velled Figure: enemy/adversary/betrayal/pride/pessimism/negative thinking/disharmony/trust issues/dominance/striking out alone/loneliness. Negative.
Beehive: a group/an institution/obedience/submission/shelter/industry/teamwork/reward/success. Neutral.

27

AFTERMATH

"We really ought to take you to a hospital," groans Bea, adjusting her grip on Rachel, who is slumped against her, bleeding on her dress.

"No hospitals." Rachel winces. She declined the opportunity to go to York General with Christopher, who was transferred for observation, and Lottie, who was placed under arrest but was also in dire need of medical attention. We should argue, I know we should, but Rachel is our senior, older and more experienced, and I am so shaken from what happened at the Aldridges' that I don't say anything.

"Keep pressure to slow the bleeding," Edie encourages Rachel, who glances at her through her half-moon glasses.

Merle checks the wards as we enter Spicer House. They're untouched. The building is secure. I cannot see the magic protecting us but the tension coiling through me relaxes a little as we step over the threshold. We turn on lights to illuminate frenetic painted surfaces and bold colour.

Rachel can't easily manage the stairs, so we haul her into the red rooms beyond the curtain to the elegant sofa outside Mr Spicer's office. She slumps into it, sucking in her breath as she pulls up the remnants of her blouse to reveal two nasty gashes across the bottom of her ribs where Mary's claws caught her. Her palms are also badly cut from where the glass bottle sliced into them. I peel blood-slick cotton from around the gashes on her side as Edie watches. Bea fetches what we need to clean and disinfect Rachel's wounds and plenty of fresh towels.

"Father is out on business; we're on our own for a while. Irma is heating water for us. Here." She hands Rachel a palmful of pills and a glass of water. "For the pain."

Rachel swallows the medicine down without protest. The hot water arrives moments later and Bea carefully cleans the blood from Rachel's stomach with a flannel, turning the bowl water murky copper. Rachel starts to shiver so I drape several of the fluffy towels over her shoulders. The deep orange tincture smells of cinnamon and turmeric and goes on to Rachel's cuts as an oily paste that Bea then bandages.

The exhaustion of self-syphoning is beginning to hit us. Merle looks dead on her feet and Bea has heavy bags under her eyes. My own body feels treacherously heavy.

"You next," Bea says to me, sitting on the floor and pulling my cut hand into her lap. She smooths the tincture on to my palm with gentle fingers. It stings for a moment and then the pain softens to a dull throbbing. Her touch is considerate and caring. When the bandage is in place, she moves on to Merle, who leans against her, sleepy-eyed.

The memory of what it felt like to be linked to them by magic, our souls pooling together to fuel the theorem that broke the syphon, washes over me. Tears build behind my nose, blurring my vision as I take Bea's hand in mine and treat her cut with the tincture. I was so angry at her for her attitude at the theatre, and for putting pressure on me to go out with Mr Saunders, but that bloody line on her palm represents so much – love, care, sacrifice. Without hesitation, she gave her own phantasmic essence, spending time and health, to help me throw out a raw glyph to protect a child. She smiles softly at me, our bond unspoken but fully acknowledged. She has not always been a good friend, but she was there when I needed her.

I am nothing without Edie, Bea and Merle.

"My sisters," I whisper as I tie Bea's bandage. "I am so grateful for you."

"Love you too," Merle whispers sleepily, and I smile through a blur of unshed tears. My heart is a well, overspilling in a flood of emotion. Bea spins the obsidian mirror to reflect Edie. Merle grabs hold of the handle as well and they smile at her. Edie kisses my neck, my cheek. I pull her closer still and for a long moment the four of us are entwined together. Three living, one dead, but always one coven. One sisterhood.

Bea's expression slips quickly from surprise to a knowing smile as I sweetly kiss Edie's lips and Edie kisses me back.

I blush a deep crimson, fearing Bea's anger. "Bea, we—"

"Took you long enough," she interrupts, and her smile is genuine enough. I curl Edie's hand into mine, thankful that Bea isn't angry Edie and I are together. Merle looks like she has a question, but when she speaks, it's not the one I expect.

"The thing that attacked Christopher, was that a shade?"

Rachel nods. "Unfortunately."

"Is that why Bea and I can see it without the obsidian mirror?" says Merle.

"Their nature makes them unique among spirits in that they can interact with the living, sometimes becoming visible as they attack," Rachel says, from her slumped position on the sofa. She leans back a little, her breathing shallow. "Mary is stronger than any I've encountered before, not that I've been acquainted with many. I'm sorry, Viola. I thought I'd created a bottle that could contain a shade but it was another failure. Merle, I'd like to look at your uncle's soul-bottle records. Can you access them?"

"Do you mean the ledgers?" asks Merle. "They're in the office."

With an exhausted groan, Rachel hauls herself to her feet and opens Mr Spicer's office. The door is unlocked, which surprises me. We follow her in. The room is full of shadows and the soft scent of magic. Although I have been in here many times, this moment feels somehow different, like we are breaking the rules. The desk is clear, any important papers locked away.

"Where are they kept?" Rachel slumps into Mr Spicer's desk chair.

Retrieving a set of small keys from behind the painting of a fairy ball, Merle unlocks the dark wooden cabinets on the far side of the room and starts to pull out ledgers. "It's one of these. I remember documenting the loss on the original acquisition record when the bottle was stolen."

Merle passes a heavy ledger to me, and I hand it to Rachel at the desk, leaning over her shoulder as she flips through it. The handwriting is small and spidery but perfectly even. Each sale is recorded in black ink with details of the item, the amount paid, and who purchased it. Mr Spicer's acquisitions for the collection are in red.

"There." Edie taps my arm, sending a jolt of adrenaline through me. "Bottom right."

"Mary Bateman, the Yorkshire Witch," I read out loud.

At the bottom of the record, inscribed in Merle's neat handwriting is *LOSS, THEFT* and a date. The financial loss is tallied beneath and the number makes my eyes widen. Soul bottles are worth an awful lot, but this one seems even more dear than others recorded here.

"Lottie used to clean this office," says Bea. "I expect she saw the opportunity to pilfer a soul bottle and took it."

"I wonder what she planned to use it for?" says Merle.

"Well, whatever it was, she messed up the theorem, which is how Mary became a shade in the first place," says Rachel, scanning the record. "Executed by hanging on the twentieth of March, 1809. Trapped by Simon Tussle at the Female Prison, York. Simon is my father; I remember him talking about this one. He gave Mary ample opportunity to change her ways, but even before she became a shade she kept attacking the other ghosts lingering in the new museum. In life, Mary Bateman was a famous fraudster, thief and murderer. She started out stealing from the wealthy houses she worked in—"

"Sounds a lot like Lottie," mutters Edie.

"Kindred spirits," I agree.

"—and had a reputation for divination," Rachel goes on. "Mary followed the prophetess Joanna Southcote for a time and defrauded her followers, eventually poisoning a woman to cure her of an apparent spell, for which she was executed."

"Uncle traded two books from the Mexborough House collection bound in her skin after her dissection in Leeds." Merle searches the shelves for an older ledger and flicks through it, stabbing the page triumphantly. "Here. An edition of John Cheeke's *Hurt of Sedition* bound in the skin of Mary Bateman the Yorkshire Witch six years ago to a collector in Chicago."

I shudder. "Books bound in skin? That is disgusting."

"Agreed, but esoteric objects like that are in high demand, especially when the skin belonged to such a notorious witch."

"I think we've found who set the studio fire," says Bea, pacing the office. "Think about it. Lottie probably stole Mary's bottle with the intention of selling it on herself. When she realized that would be almost impossible without Father tracing her, she opted to use the bottle as a soul source instead. It all went horribly wrong and Mary started killing children and so Lottie tried to stop Vi from divining the truth by setting a trap for us at the studio."

"And then at the theatre," Merle adds.

Of course Lottie would do anything to keep her secret. She killed Edie. I don't care that she is likely out of her depth, or that she justifies feeding Christopher and Norma to Mary to save her own life. She is a killer and a coward. I want five minutes alone with her in her damned cell to carve an apology out of her bones and then I will kill her anyway because "sorry" will not undo the damage she has wrought.

I don't realize that I'm shaking until Edie's cooling fingers find my neck, her touch tempering my fury.

"I feel so stupid." Merle's voice is small. "I have helped keep some of these records. How did I not realize soul bottles are different from basic witch bottles? I … I thought the name Mary referred to the creator of the bottle—"

Bea gives her a comforting, empathetic grimace. "None of us worked it out, Merle; don't be so hard on yourself."

"It is not your fault Rupert has been keeping secrets from you," says Rachel. "Perhaps now he will see your true value."

I help Rachel up and, as I shift to the side, I hear a short, soft clicking sound. The topmost drawer on the right-hand side of Mr Spicer's desk has released and is a little open. I shouldn't look inside. It is private and full of personal effects, but something makes me pull the drawer out. There, in plain view, is a familiar silk pouch.

My flesh feels split, skin charred and throat distended with the croak of a cry I can't quite force out. Disbelief mingles with dread, a thought I cannot fully grasp. I snatch up the pouch.

Can it be?

"Is that … your knucklebone set?" Merle looks as surprised as I feel, and Bea looks positively horrified.

Opening the pouch with shaking fingers, I tip eight bones into my palm, feeling the familiar, friendly weight of them. I turn the root bone to see the clasped hand motif and the veiled figure with the small chip of missing paint at its feet. Even if I couldn't feel them resonating for me, eager to be put to work, I would know them as mine.

Phillip stole them, so how did they get here, of all places?

"Oh, my dear." Mr Spicer is in the doorway looking at me with too soft eyes. "I so wish that you hadn't found those."

28

IN PERFECT TRUST

My heart stutters and for a moment Mr Spicer looks like a stranger. Surely he can't mean what I think he does? And then his serious, almost dark expression lifts into a jovial smile.

"I wanted to surprise you with them tomorrow." He tosses his jacket on to the empty chair and opens his arms to me. "Henry suspected the scoundrel might try to sell them on and he was right."

"You bought the set back from Phillip?" I stammer, automatically falling into his embrace.

"Not quite. I told him I must think about it and then reported him to the chief constable. Phillip Petty made a run for it when the police raided the house he's staying in, not surprising, seeing as they recovered a significant amount of stolen property from his digs, including your knucklebone set." Mr Spicer releases me from his hold. "He got away but they're looking for him and, in the interim, the chief happily released these to me yesterday. I was planning on returning them with much pomp and ceremony."

I clutch the bones in my palm, closing my eyes in relief at their familiar coolness. It's less like being reunited with an old friend and more like being handed a weapon designed just for me. And yet I don't feel the same agonizing attachment to them that I once did. When they were taken from me, I felt powerless. I've since realized that I am anything but, with or without the bones.

Rachel is right: this isn't over.

"It is a good surprise." I smile weakly. "Thank you."

"So, to what do I owe the pleasure of a sundown meeting in my office?" He turns to Rachel, who is still sitting in his chair. "My goodness, what happened to you?"

"Shade attack." Rachel winces. "Made from the soul of Mary Bateman, the ghost stolen from your safe all those months ago. The thief was your old maid."

"The maid? I should have suspected. Look, let me take you to hospital, Rachel. You are bleeding on my upholstery."

Rachel shakes her head. "I need to get back to the lab and work on another solution for a reinforced bottle. This shade won't be easy to contain—"

"You're in no fit state to work tonight. Please accept my hospitality." Mr Spicer pats her shoulder gently. "Irma will make up a room for you."

Rachel gives in and Mr Spicer rings the pull cord on the

wall, part of the old-fashioned system for when a house this size would have had many servants rather than one.

"Bea, what's this?" Mr Spicer takes his daughter's palm, noting the identical bandages on all our hands. "You know better."

Bea snatches her hand away. "We did what we had to, to save a child's life."

"I don't want you in harm's way. Especially if there is a rogue shade in the city." He rubs his face, showing his weariness. "This is the last thing we need, what with my soul catchers dropping like flies."

Salt. Bone. Magic. Secrets. Answers in the palm of my hand but I am too scared to divine our fate. Horror lurks at the gates of the city and within the walls, creeping into our nightmares, skulking in shadows and waiting until we expose our soft bellies to their claws. I am dazed and mixed up, exhausted and overwhelmed.

I am just a girl. Can I change anything for the better?

I am certainly no match for a shade, but I know people who are. This moment is an impasse. I am at a crossroads and I must choose which path to take. On one side of the coin is the option to stay silent and leave the matter to Mr Spicer and Mr Saunders, but that is a coward's escape.

Am I truly protecting Merle and Bea by keeping my knowledge of the Hand a secret?

I look to Edie because she is always my north star. There's worry in her eyes and her lips pinch as she reads the question in my expression. Then she nods, a gentle, almost imperceptible gesture but it makes me feel braver.

"I'll take care of the shade," I say, then swallow hard as every pair of eyes in the room turns to look at me.

Mr Spicer's expression softens. "Viola, seeing the dead isn't enough to prepare you to face such a monstrous ghost. I'm afraid that your knucklebones will help you very little beyond divining its location."

He's treating me like a child again. In one breath he tells me that I am strong and talented and asks me to risk myself to trap souls for him. And in another he's babying me. Women bleed, bear children, tolerate violence and insult. We fight every day of our lives, and yet we are called weak. I am so tired of it. Either I am capable, or I am not.

I slip all eight of the bones back inside their silk pouch and put them carefully in my pocket. Mr Spicer's mouth tightens, deepening the lines there.

"Whatever question you're about to ask, I don't have the answer," I say quickly.

From his expression, I know Mr Spicer suspects the truth: that I have encountered the adversary meddling in his business. He can't know that, not yet, or he could retaliate and the last thing I want is all-out war. Merle, Bea and Rachel are certain to get mixed up in it. I need to play this carefully.

I have something the Hand want – me. It is clear that death-touched are rare enough to mean something important to them, and therefore I may be able to negotiate for both sides to walk away unscathed. If Mr Spicer agrees to stop his trade in souls, then Meryem will have no reason to continue to target him and they will have no need at all to go anywhere near Bea or Merle.

"Will you trust me with this?" I ask Mr Spicer.

The silence stretches as he considers.

"Uncle." Merle comes to my side and cradles my bandaged hand in her own. Her tone is serious and firm, a reminder perhaps that we are not children any more. That we faced a shade and lived, that we broke an expertly crafted syphon theorem, that we – that I – am capable.

"Very well," says Mr Spicer. "But don't put yourself at risk and I would ask that you at least get a good night's sleep first."

Biting the inside of my cheek, I nod. Now I just need to work out how to contact Meryem and the Hand. The simplest approach would be to return to the York Royal and speak to Andreas, but there is no way I can go anywhere near the theatre until I know that Tempest has convinced the Grey Lady not to attack me. I could ask Bea to speak to him on my behalf, or set up a meeting, but then I would have to explain more than I want to. I love her but I don't trust her not to tell her father what she learns. I'll have to work something else out.

My head fogs and I stagger a little as a wave of exhaustion hits me. My lungs tighten instantly and I begin to wheeze.

"To bed with you, girls," says Mr Spicer. "Before you succumb to soul burn."

"We didn't push ourselves that far," protests Bea.

She didn't, but I might have.

I shake my head. "Pa will be expecting me home."

That isn't true. I have not seen him in days and I suspect he is avoiding me, preferring to spend his time in the pub.

"It isn't safe," says Mr Spicer. "You shouldn't have left the last time I asked you to stay."

"I have decent wards set up at home."

He regards me with a serious expression but I don't waver. Then he sighs and opens one of the glass cabinets along the walls, taking out an item on display there. A bracelet made from tiny golden beads interspersed by carved bone impresa, each one etched with minute magical glyphs. It is a beautiful piece and exquisitely made.

"For protection." Mr Spicer threads it around my wrist.

"This is worth a fortune—" I protest, and my lungs catch painfully.

"As are you, my dear girl. If you are leaving our wards, then wear it for the sake of the people who love you and don't want to see you harmed."

Before I can argue he latches the catch, and the metal and bone settle against my skin. The soft hum of magic flows through me along with a palpable sense of relief. With my bone set once again in my possession, I can finally reclaim control of my life.

One vital question remains. How am I to contact the Hand?

"They're most likely watching the house, so I doubt it will take long." Edie settles me gently on my bed. Nothing has ever felt so good: soft pillow, cotton coverlet and Edie close by.

In the end, we resorted to setting up a beacon, a simple

spell easily worked using a witch bottle, no soul syphoning required. The beacon is set up on my windowsill, its magic released as a gentle wash of power across the street. It is a message addressed to the Hand: *I want to talk.*

"I'll check the wards and make sure the salt lines are still in place." Edie kisses my forehead and is gone.

Doubt prickles at me. The bones were shoved into the desk drawer, like an afterthought, as if Mr Spicer wanted to forget about them.

I so wish that you hadn't found those.

He only said that because he wanted to be the one to give them back to me. For all his faults, and our differing opinions on bottling souls, he has been good to me. Exhaustion hits like a brick wall, shaking my ability to think clearly. Right now, I can barely string together a sentence, let alone divine the truth of anything. Our questions will have to wait for tomorrow.

When Edie returns, I grab her wrist, pulling her on to the bed, her knee at my hip, arm beside my head to hold herself up. Hair tickles my temple as she tilts my chin up, drawing my lips to hers. I stretch, moving into her embrace and pulling her down as I kiss her back.

The touch of her lips is soft, sleepy and sweet. The weight of her is the greatest comfort. As much as my exhausted body wants to sink into unconsciousness, every touch of her skin on mine lifts me up, keeping me present. My fingers find her waist and pull her shirt up, teasing underneath to the soft skin of her back. I inhale her little gasp and kiss her again and again.

I would like to take Edie dancing. When this is over, we shall go to a dance hall, or one of the smaller clubs where we can have privacy. I want to kiss her in the shadows as music moves through and around us. I want to do so many things with her.

It strikes me quite suddenly that she can still travel, and why wouldn't she? She is a free soul, not bound to York like some other ghosts seem to be. I will go with her so that she will have someone to talk to about the marvels of Egypt and Syria, and far away India, Indonesia and Australia. I will turn the pages of books for her, write her letters for her, tune the wireless; we will sit quietly and watch storms together. I will do everything I can to help her feel connected and part of the world again.

Just because she is dead doesn't mean that she cannot *live*.

Tracing the side of Edie's face with my finger, I marvel that I can touch her at all. It feels like the greatest, best gift. Smiling sadly, she takes my hand and presses her face into my palm, kissing the skin beside my bandage. We exist like that for a while. When did it become her comforting me again? I am afraid that, even in death, she does more for me than I do for her. I do not want this love of ours to be unbalanced.

I think then of Rachel Tussle and her experiments. It is ambitious, for sure. Ridiculous in its impossibility. Except… Except…

"Edie, if there was a way to interact with the world again, permanently, would you take it?"

She tilts her head in thought. "It depends on the price I would have to pay."

I am taken aback. "Why would it cost anything?"

"Because all magic has a price; you know this. If I am not the one to pay what is owed, then the debt falls on someone else." She kisses my forehead and then my cheek. "Sleep, Vi. Rest. I'll keep watch."

She kisses my lips and I drift into dreams with her arms around me.

29

THE WITCHING HOUR

Shortly after three in the morning my eyes fly wide open, my heart pounding. I expect the flames and heat and smoke of my nightmares to chase me into wakefulness. The wards are alerting, a soft, grating alarm trailing after the scent of magic in the air. As soon as I register that I'm not in mortal peril, the agony of my exhaustion slams into me. I need to sleep some more but Edie's worried frown has me sitting up on my elbows.

"Someone is breaking in," she whispers.

I hear it now, like fingernails on glass. Someone is attempting to pry open the hallway window. Perhaps Pa has lost his key and climbed up the guttering to the flat roof over the garage. Good lord, if he falls, he might kill himself.

I haul myself to standing. My entire body protests, vision spinning. Edie has me. After a second, I can stand on my own and pull on the dressing gown draped over the chair in the corner.

Edie stops me leaving the room. "Let me go ahead."

I refuse. "We stick together."

She grumbles, but I will not let her risk herself for my sake. If it is a common thief, then the charms etched into the windowsills should deter them. They will not get inside. But if it is an occultist or witch able to bypass my theorems, then they might very well be powerful enough to see and trap Edie. I won't let her walk out there alone.

We creep out of my bedroom, glancing warily down the corridor. The sound comes again, this time with the muffled crack of breaking glass. I resist the urge to call out for Pa, because it is very possible, even likely, that he found a bed elsewhere for the night. He has never been good at being faithful to my ma. If it is not him, then it is better to stay quiet.

I need a weapon. Creeping into Theo's room I root around under the bed, coming up with his old cricket bat. I don't know if I am strong enough to swing it, but it is better than nothing. My head pounds and the world flutters dark at the edges of my vision. I might not even have the strength to get back on my feet.

Stand up. Everything is moving. I think I'm going to be sick. The exhaustion is too much.

"Edie," I gasp, and she is there, pulling my arm over her shoulder and getting me back on my feet. Together, we slip into the corridor as silently as possible.

I'm trembling, fear threatening my lungs with an attack.

There is a bright moon tonight, enhancing the glare from the streetlamps. Up ahead, his back to me, is a large, distinctly masculine figure drenched in moonlight. Phillip stands in the shadows of my home, unwashed and sour.

There's broken glass on the floor from the window he shattered to gain access. It glints like snow in summer, strangely beautiful. How did he get through my wards? They would have been uncomfortable to cross, inflicting a deep sense of dread and making him feel like he wants to be anywhere else but here. If he pushed through, then something strong is fuelling him.

We did send his girlfriend to prison. Whatever horrors he plans to enact in revenge, I will not go silently, or without a fight.

"I've got you," Edie whispers in my ear, bolstering my confidence. She's here; I am not alone. I can do this.

Sensing my movement, Phillip turns. "Viola, wait—"

I don't hesitate. Mustering every drop of my strength, I swing the bat, cracking him in the face. The crunch of bone is deliciously satisfying. His head snaps back and, falling sideways, Phillip hits the wall and collapses, clutching his broken face. The momentum threatens to send me pitching after him but Edie keeps me upright. Blood trickles over Phillip's lips. His nose is a mashed mess.

"What do you want?" I demand, swinging the bat high over my shoulder, ready to strike again.

Phillip raises his arm to protect his head. "I need your help."

Did I hear him correctly? "You want me to *help you*? After you and your evil girlfriend murdered children, set the fire that killed my friend, and then you beat me and stole my knucklebones to prevent me exposing you—"

"Fire? We didn't set any fire." He's pale and quivering. "I swear on my life, we had nothing to do with that. I... The children. Lottie said it was the only way to keep Mary from killing us. We're guilty of that, but the fire wasn't us and I don't give a shit about your weird bones. I only took them because someone paid me to."

A chill washes over me. What did he just say? Someone *paid* him... That doesn't make any sense. I have the knucklebones back in my possession. I could roll for the truth, catch him in his lies, but I'm so used to being without them that I left them in my bedroom. Now I'm stuck here with a vicious, wounded bully who is surely looking for any opportunity to gain the upper hand. I can't risk turning my back.

"Tell me who hired you or I will curse you to die, slowly. And I will make it hurt."

I can do no such thing, but he doesn't know that. Though, who is to say I couldn't if I really tried? I'm so angry my skin feels hot, like I could ignite.

"I never saw who it was." Phillip spits something that looks suspiciously like a tooth on to the floor in a clod of blood and saliva. "I got a note with instructions and part-payment. I was to get the bones from you and leave them in a postbox on Micklegate. The rest of the payment came the next day in an envelope through my front door."

"Do you think it could have been Mr Spicer?" Edie whispers, echoing my own treacherous thoughts.

Surely not. I don't want to think him capable of that.

"What motive would he have to take them?" I ask her.

My divination skills would have been of use to him of late. I might have identified Lottie as the thief, and warned him of the Hand's intentions.

But he had my knucklebone set in his desk drawer and we only have his word that he meant to return them to me at all. I don't like that I feel more inclined to trust in relative strangers than in someone I have known most of my life, but at least Meryem and the Hand have been honest with me.

"I don't know, but something isn't right," says Edie. "If Phillip is telling the truth, Rupert didn't get the knucklebones back from a police raid. Phillip delivered them to whoever hired him."

Oh God, I feel sick. Could Mr Spicer have really hired Phillip to steal the knucklebone set from me? "I don't want to believe it," I whisper.

Edie looks close to tears. "The evidence isn't in his favour."

"I know."

"Who … who are you talking to?" asks Phillip.

"The girl you had a part in murdering," I snap. "Tell me about the fire and how Lottie set it."

"It wasn't us!"

"Lottie knew Mrs Aldridge was coming to see me that evening about Christopher's sickness—"

"The first we heard of the studio fire was street gossip."

Maybe Phillip senses the air move as I raise the bat, or he hears my hiss of irritation, but he recoils, protecting his head and face with his arms. "It's the truth! Please, that monster is going to kill me. You're the only other witch I know. I didn't know where else to turn—"

There isn't a lot of light to see by. I risk getting closer and that is when I notice that his injuries were not caused by my well-placed strike alone. His hand is bloody, presumably from when he broke the window, but there are dark bruises all over his neck and chest, visible through his torn shirt.

"Was Mary's the only bottle that Lottie stole from the Spicers?" I ask, needing to know.

"Bottle, yes, but Lottie took a dark mirror too. The kind that allows communication with spirits. She didn't mean harm; she only took the bottle because she thought it might be worth something. But it was empty, or so we thought until…" He swallows and closes his eyes. Tears leak down his cheeks, mingling with the blood.

"At first Mary was interesting, even kind. She knew things about magic and the spiritual world. She was convincing, manipulative, and promised us wealth and power if we followed her instructions. She taught Lottie magic, *real* magic, but then Mary changed. She grew hungry and she threatened to feast on us if we didn't provide … alternatives."

"And you chose children?" I say coldly.

Phillip hangs his head. Does he think that if he acts remorseful then he'll get away with it like so many men seem to? It's easy to blame Lottie, but he was profiting the same as she was. He is far from innocent.

They didn't set the fire.

Or so he claims. It could be more lies.

Roll the bones and divine the truth.

Before I can work out how to get to my knucklebone set without giving Phillip an opening to attack me, he shrieks, a sudden, terrible cry of fear that has me staggering back into Edie. She swears and curses, pulling me against the wall as a horror hooks its claws around the broken window frame. There's a pale face with that too wide, rictus grin, fleshy pulsating neck and insectoid body clicking beneath a filthy gown.

Mary. Distended and inhuman, she hunches over, her overlong neck craning up to a bulbous head with ill-defined features. She's missing her ears and nose. Her mouth is a gash on her face below beady, hungry eyes. She still wears a white apron and a cap over her stringy hair, a mockery of what she must have looked like before magic corrupted her soul.

Phillip is screaming, clawing at the wall as he begs for mercy. Blood flows down his chin, his voice garbled by his broken nose.

I have wards. Mary can't get in. There is a salt line—

The shade inches through the open window. Her head first, then her torso. With horror I realize that when Phillip smashed the window he also disturbed the trail of salt I'd carefully placed on the doors and windows in the apartment.

"Kitchen!" Edie shouts. "Now, Vi."

Because that's where the remainder of the salt is. Which means pushing past the shade to reach it. Don't overthink. I must move.

For what feels like a century, I can't do anything. Time is syrup-thick and cloying, my body frozen by a whitewash of panic. And then Edie's hand is in mine and she's pulling me along as Mary's bulbous head swivels to grin nastily at Phillip. Three steps, four, and then we're ducking beneath the shade as it swipes for us, its claws narrowly missing my scalp.

The kitchen door crashes open and the small space is washed in cool light from the moon. There is no time to light the lamps but I know my way around. The salt bag is on the pine dresser. I find it in seconds, heart sinking at how little is left, and almost trip over one of the spindly dining chairs. Kicking them out of my way, I start to lie the line at the kitchen door.

Phillip shoves me roughly to the floor as he climbs over me, babbling and useless, to hide beneath the kitchen table, knocking a pot of cutlery to the floor in his hurry. A wail in the corridor sends goosebumps chasing over my skin. The sound reminds me of the Grey Lady, though what we're facing is so much worse.

Cursing Phillip, I scrabble for the bag of salt and hurry to complete the line, using more than is necessary in my haste. A pale face emerges from the dark of the corridor. Mary pauses in the doorway, her lips rucking up in a sneer of disdain. Her elongated, clawed fingers scuttle and click against the door frame as she leers at Phillip and I on the floor, panting and panicked.

"Get out of here!" Edie shouts. She is nothing against a shade and yet the defensive anger in her tone bolsters me, as does the fierceness in her eyes. Edie would do anything for me and I for her and the strength of that connection gives me courage.

"Give him to me." Mary's voice clicks and clatters against her teeth.

"No, no, no," Phillip whimpers and scuttles further under the table, putting more space between himself and the abomination at the door. "Please, Viola, I swear we didn't set that fire and I'm sorry for everything I did to you. I'm so sorry. Don't let her kill me."

Blubbering, pathetic fool. I really don't care what happens to him.

"L-Lottie is dead," he chokes, his terror breaking into tears. "Mary killed her in her cell, drained her and now she—" He hiccups through his sobs. "Lottie is gone. She's dead."

Lottie is dead.

A flare of angry satisfaction wells inside me. I don't care if Phillip claims they had nothing to do with the fire. Lottie had motive and means. The woman responsible for Edie's murder is gone, or at least she is no longer among the living. Perhaps her soul remained earthbound. If it did, I will break my vow to never bottle a ghost and trap her myself. Maybe I'll lock her into a spirit sink for the rest of her afterlife.

"She failed me," says Mary, her razor claws leaving deep

grooves in the wooden door frame. "I taught her the secrets of the craft and in return she promised to make me anew and nourish me, offer up souls for me to feast on and make me strong. She failed. What good are you to me now, Phillip, except as nourishment?"

"P-please," Phillip stammers.

"Give him to me." Her gritty tone becomes a whine.

She stretches her arm – I lose sight of the limb behind the door jamb and then her claws extend through the kitchen wall. What? NO! She can't cross the salt line…

Except that she is not crossing it at all, she's going around it. I thought the salt only needed to cover openings. What a fool I am. At the Aldridges' I saw her melt through the wall to escape, so why did I think that only salting the doors and windows would be enough to keep her out?

Tipping more salt into my palm, I hiss as the mineral stings my cuts, and desperately throw it at her, spitting out a word of power to give it additional emphasis. Magic bursts from my bones, a flare that ties into the raw glyph I cast. My head throbs, lungs catching, and the salt disperses and strikes. Bright light sparks where it hits her, like fragments of a shooting star falling to earth.

Mary shrieks in pain and unbridled fury. Phillip is sobbing. Ignoring him, I get on all fours and pour the remaining salt into a thin circle, working quickly in the dark. I can barely see what I am doing and Phillip is in the way. I include him in the circle because if I leave him out he might well break the line trying to get inside my protections.

Grains slip between cracks in the floorboards and I curse. Can I even make an unbroken circle? I'm running low on salt. I'm not going to have enough. Phillip shrieks as Mary swoops down on us. Her flesh is so pale it is almost luminescent in the moonlight, like the pallid, wet flesh of a corpse.

"Take her instead of me!" Phillip wails and he shoves me forward towards the advancing shade. Edie screams my name in panic. My foot flails out, slicing through the half-complete salt circle. Phillip's grip is strong enough to bruise as he uses me as a shield.

Slimy coward. Light glints on metal: a dinner knife that's been knocked from the table. Grabbing it, I hold it backwards and slam the blade blindly over my shoulder.

There is resistance as it hits with a horrific meaty thwack followed by a surprised agonized cry. Phillip's grip on me slackens and I roll away from him. I got him in the neck. He gurgles around the dinner knife, blood pumping from the wound. And then his cry fails, and his breath releases, red foam blooming on his lips. I make no move to help him. He collapses, a blood pool slicking the kitchen floor.

Within seconds, Phillip Petty bleeds out.

I really couldn't care less. He deserved what he got and then some.

A soft pale wash shimmers from his body as a fine mist that coalesces beside his corpse. His ghost looks haggard – chin stubbled, his coat torn – but his fear is gone and all that is left is meanness. There is blood under his fingernails and his teeth are sharp, as if they've been filed.

"Bitch," he hisses. "I will make you pay."

But he died too quickly. Mary did not glut on his phantasmic essence and now she is turning her attention back to me in search of a meal. I have no way to defend myself. But I have not ingested the bone mixture, nor been marked by her as a target. Can she even drain me? I can't risk finding out.

Pure panic strikes me, coupled with the white heat of my anger. I hate that I am so helpless. Edie grips my arms, pulling me away. We both gasp as bright chartreuse light fills the kitchen, illuminating Mary's horrible face.

Phillip's grimace shifts from angry revenge to pathetic fear and he skips backwards through the solid table. With one last look at his cooling corpse on the floor, he turns tail and disappears through the wall.

Tempest hovers in our kitchen between the stove and the pantry shelves like a beacon, ghostly torch held high above his head. "By the pricking of my thumbs." A satisfied smile stretches his mouth and, for a moment, he looks a touch inhuman himself. "Something wicked this way comes."

30

NOT A GIFT

The justice Tempest measures out is swift and sure. The brilliance from his torch sears Mary as if it were acid not light. With an angry, pained hiss, the shade retreats, scuttling until she is pressed up against the salt line in the kitchen doorway.

"Mary Bateman," says a clear voice behind her.

The shade swivels her overlong neck to look into the hall. A handsome, dark-skinned face emerges from the shadows. Andreas Sweets holds something in his hands, bracing the object against his chest. It looks like a small book, but I don't think it can be. There are hinges one side and, as Andreas flicks it open in a smooth, clean action the two polished surfaces inside gleam. It looks like an oversized, rectangular compact mirror. Far too big to be practical or to fit into a purse, and not made of regular silvered glass but of obsidian, like the ghost glass that allows non-death-touched to see the dead.

Exactly like that, I realize.

"Edie, cover your eyes," warns Tempest. "Or you'll be drawn in too."

Edie obeys, though she is shaking.

Mary's head lowers on her insectile neck. Her mouth opens, teeth glinting in the lamplight. Andreas raises the double mirror as if he's holding up an open book for Mary to read.

"That's it. Look at how pretty you are," he says. "I bet it has been a long time since you saw yourself."

The shade hesitates. The strange, hungry clicking in her throat catches and fades. Something changes, I am not certain what, but Mary's movements slacken. Her arms drop at her sides, head tilting slightly. Stillness settles over her. She is like a statue, frozen, staring into the open obsidian mirrors before her.

"What's happening?" Edie holds on to me, alert and wary. "Is it over?"

"You may open your eyes," says Tempest.

Andreas speaks in a language that makes me think of French, but most certainly isn't. There is a harshness to it not found in romance languages, yet it is just as smooth as French and has a nasal sing-song quality. Before I can try to recognize any of the words, Mary disappears.

It happens in the time it takes for me to take a breath. Inhale, Mary pitches forward ever so slightly. Exhale, she is gone.

"Where did she—?" Edie whispers, and then we both see her at the same time. Mary's likeness stares out at us from within the double mirror in Andreas's hands.

"Wh-what is *that*?" I ask. "You condemn occultists for trapping souls but that's—"

"This is called a rhu tasi. It is entirely different from a soul bottle," says Tempest. "Shades and ghosts contained within it are not in pain. Time does not pass for them. It is a kind of sleep."

"And that is better?"

"Yes," whispers Edie gently. "It is better."

I squeeze her hand, knowing that she has been inside a bottle and experienced the agony of being trapped in an artificial loop.

Andreas brushes a thumb along the top corner of the rhu tasi and there is a soft, almost inaudible, click. He seems satisfied. "The shade is contained."

I swallow, nervous, as I remember the bottle shattering in Rachel's fingers. "What if she escapes?"

Tempest snorts, amused, then sees that I am deadly serious. "Our magic is stronger than that. She is like an insect trapped in amber. Her prison will be sent back to Constantinople where we have an aperture, safe from the outside world. She will not escape."

An aperture?

"Oh, goodness," says a bright voice in the doorway. "A corpse."

I lift my head to see Kavita and Meryem looking down at

the cooling body of Phillip Petty on our kitchen floor.

Meryem raises her brow. "Well, this *is* a mess."

Before I can defend myself, or argue, soul burn gutters through me, hollowing me out completely, and I collapse into Edie's arms.

I wake to sunlight on my face and a ghost beside my bed. It is not Edie. Meryem sits like a guard watching a prisoner. When I move, a cobweb-thin membrane of healing charms slips from my forehead, dusting ashes on to my pillow. As I brush them off, the bone and gold impresa bracelet at my wrist slips down my arm. Having it makes me feel a little safer, as if my coven is always with me.

I notice that *A Discoverie and Examination of Spirit Seers* sits on my bedside table rather than in the drawer where I'd placed it. Has Meryem been reading it? Does she disapprove?

"It is not the gift you think it is." Her voice is pebble round and soft. It echoes somewhere deep inside me.

I prop myself up on my elbows, wincing. My body aches everywhere, my joints stiff and swollen and my head feels muffled. "I never thought it was a gift."

Does she think me so naïve as to believe Mr Saunders gave me that book purely out of concern for me? He wants something from me, as does everyone, it seems.

Meryem sits back in the chair, somewhat slouched, her body angled towards where I'm lying. For a moment I don't see her as the ancient soul of some great noble lady. She is just a woman only a decade older than myself. I picture her in a modern sundress, a cocktail in hand as she sits on a balcony in the sunshine and becomes someone I could be friends with. And yet she is a powerful ancient spirit who commands magic I can only dream of.

"Where's Edie?" I ask, sitting up properly.

"Close by, don't fear." Meryem's pretty features tense into a smile that doesn't feel altogether natural or sincere. "I wanted to speak with you alone."

"You mean to scold me."

"Why would you think that?"

"You're giving me the same look my ma does right before she tells me I ought to marry Henry Saunders because he has decided he wants me."

"That occultist?" Meryem wrinkles her nose in disgust.

I can't help huffing an amused laugh because there, finally, is a true and honest reaction. "You don't approve?"

"Not in the slightest. Do you want him?"

"Not in the slightest."

"Good, because we plan to deal with Henry Saunders and his father the same way we will deal with Rupert Spicer. Occultists like them do too much harm to be left unchecked." She motions to me, as if I am a piece of evidence in a trial to convict them.

I frown, confused.

"Viola, Mr Spicer didn't even teach you containments or boundaries to reduce the risk of soul drain when self-syphoning, a lesson that would have saved you." Meryem clicks her tongue in disapproval. "This is why occult practice must be preserved for only death-touched mirrored in a symbiotic syphon that preserves the phantasmic essence of both members. In syphoning from yourself with no symbiotic soul to support you, you have pushed your body too far, draining more than you can spare. If you experience soul burn again, it will kill you."

I have promised never to syphon from the dead and I would certainly not do anything of the sort to anyone living, even though I now know such a thing is possible. So, if I cannot self-syphon, what does that leave me with?

Stop using magic. That is what she is saying to me. I must abandon magical practice and live an ordinary life.

Sadness wells within me, a deep loss pitted with regret. I don't want an ordinary life. I was made to take control over my future. For a long time the coven offered me that chance – magic is the power to shape the world around me, influence others and make a living for myself – but I have been foolish and squandered what was offered.

No, I cannot think that way. Even without theorems I have a rare ability. After all, what is so ordinary about seeing the dead? Or being able to read the knucklebones? I might not rely on them so much now that I am death-touched, but there lies my future. Seeing the dead is my miracle.

Edie is my miracle.

If I cannot use magical theorems again, then so be it. I will find a way to leave my mark on the world and make a difference to those I love.

"You want me to join the Hand," I say. It is not a question and I do not pose it as one.

The silence stretches between us and then Meryem stands and offers me her hand. "Come with me."

I struggle into my silk bed robe, stretching muscles that feel as if they have been too long asleep. I don't want to rely on Meryem's help, but I need it as we walk down the corridor to the front room. Soul burn has dealt me a heavy blow.

The front room looks as it always has: sofa and chaise, walls packed with paintings, a gap where the upright piano used to sit, and my parents' old desk. Except that, other than Edie, who stands at the window looking out at the traffic clogging Blossom Street, it is filled with strangers.

Tempest and Andreas sit together on the sofa, Tempest leaning into Andreas, who has his arm over his chest, his nose against his neck. Kavita sits alone on the chaise.

I look beyond them all to Edie, who has turned from the window to face me. The sun is radiant behind her, softening her form. A heartbeat later she's in my arms. "You're alive. I was afraid…"

"I'm alive." I breathe her in, tears pricking at the corners of my eyes. She kisses me and I tense, nervous because we are being observed. Then I decide that I do not care what Meryem, or any of them might think. I love Edie. I will kiss her and I don't care that she is a girl, and a ghost. She is the love of my life.

When we break apart, I don't see judgement in anyone's expression, only understanding, and my cheeks flare with embarrassment over my misunderstanding. Of course, Tempest and Andreas are a couple. With everything going on

I had forgotten. There will be no judgement here.

"Are you…?" Edie swallows, strokes the hair from my forehead, her concerned expression searching.

"What?"

"You killed Phillip, I just… Are you OK in yourself? Taking a life is a great burden."

I blink. Surprised. I'd not forgotten about Phillip but I'm more concerned about how to dispose of his remains without ending up on the end of a hangman's noose than any sense of guilt or regret. Perhaps that will come later, but I doubt it. Phillip was my enemy. He did terrible things and tried to kill me. I killed him instead.

"Will you think I am a bad person if I admit it doesn't weigh on me in the slightest?"

Edie says nothing, only kisses me again. Her lips soft but solid, a tether keeping me grounded in the chaos of what I've learned and everything we have yet to deal with. Like the fact that Mr Spicer might not be the kindly uncle I have always thought him to me.

"Viola, you don't need to concern yourself with Phillip Petty's remains. It's taken care of." Kavita stands to test my temperature with the back of her hand as Meryem did. "Your fever has broken – that's good, but you're weaker than I'd like."

She looks to Meryem and something passes between the two women that I don't understand, but the atmosphere in the room shifts, tension brewing like a storm.

"We need to talk about what happens next," says Meryem

calmly, gesturing for us to sit on the chaise. We do, side by side, Edie's hand curled into my palm. "We seal every practitioner of the occult we encounter because they are a danger to themselves and to others. They could accidentally or purposefully make a shade, or harm themselves through soul burn and resort to draining the phantasmic essence of ghosts or of other living beings to sustain themselves. They become little more than parasites and we cannot allow that. No one else takes care of death-touched and vulnerable ghosts and without us, shades would kill far more people than they currently do."

I swallow, my throat thick and sore. "You're going to seal our friends, aren't you?"

Meryem sighs. "There can be no exceptions."

I stand abruptly, forcing Kavita away from me. "Then seal *me*. Here and now, do it."

"Viola—" gasps Edie.

"No, they said there can be no exceptions. I'm an augurer. I've self-syphoned more than Merle or Bea combined. I already have soul burn." I open my arms, presenting a clear target.

Tempest and Meryem exchange a glance, but no one moves.

I drop my arms. "Oh, so there *are* exceptions. Because I am death-touched and so I have value to you. You want me to join you. You won't seal me."

"Is that such a terrible fate?" asks Andreas. "There are great benefits to mirroring with a ghost. The damage that you have already done to your phantasmic essence will be reversed. You will be able to practise complex mathemagics without worry and walk the streets without fear and when actively possessed by your mirror you will have phenomenal strength and stamina and, in time, you might also come to manifest phantasmic essence at will, a skill unique to mirrored death-touched."

I frown at that, not understanding what he means. "Manifest?"

Out of nowhere, Kavita draws a pair of double knives. They materialize from nothingness in the time it takes for her to circle her wrists in the air. Andreas smiles and opens his palms, holding them up as silver trails of light traverse his skin. A moment later he's wearing a pair of gauntlets embossed with elegant circular markings.

"They do more than look pretty," he says. "Which you'll find out if we are ever in combat together."

A single flex of Andreas's hands and the gauntlets dissipate. Kavita disappears her knives with the same effortless gesture. "There are also many benefits for the ghost you mirror with," she says. "They can manipulate their own density, become visible to the living or touch material objects for brief periods."

"We can eat and drink too, and it actually tastes like something," adds Tempest, as if that is the most important boon. He winks at Edie but she doesn't smile, and I realize that the Hand have achieved through mirroring with a death-touched what Rachel hopes to do with her restoration theorem – give ghosts a genuine connection to the living world.

"Viola, your choice is simple," says Meryem. "Help us stop Rupert Spicer's trade in souls, become part of a mirrored pair and fight occultists around the world. Or we can seal you today and you can live out the rest of your days without magic or spirits."

"Without spirits?" I whisper.

But I already understand. Edie is pure phantasmic essence, pure soul. If I am sealed, I'll no longer be death-touched and will lose my ability to effortlessly see, hear and touch her. That would be the worst possible fate. No matter what happens, I cannot lose her.

"That's not much of a choice," snaps Edie.

"Perhaps not, but it is still a choice." Tempest drapes an arm over Andreas's shoulder. Andreas tilts his chin and meets Tempest's lips. The kiss is sweet and tender, not the first and not the last but one in a lifetime and afterlife of kisses. They break apart, smile at one another and I see only trust and care between them. They are each other's mirrors, companions for life, and perhaps into the afterlife.

I could have that with Edie.

"Yes, we fight angry shades and nasty occultists," says Tempest, turning back to us. "And occasionally we have to track down and convince stubborn newly created death-touched adolescents that we are not evil. It is not an easy life, but overall the perks certainly outweigh the dangers."

"We support and care for our own," says Meryem. "We are a family."

A warm spark kindles in my chest, easing some of the trepidation I feel. But what about the girls? "We have a family. Merle and Bea. My coven. I won't abandon them." This is it, the moment to make my bargain. I know what Meryem and her people want from me now. It is all I have to barter with. "I will join you and mirror, but only on the condition that you spare Merle and Bea. They didn't know about soul bottles; they've never used them and don't deserve to be condemned."

"Do they not?" asks Kavita. "They certainly do not deserve your loyalty."

"Stop trying to turn me against them!" I snap, annoyed.

Andreas looks pained. "Haven't you worked it out yet? You must know that Phillip and Lottie didn't bind the door to trap you in the fire that killed Edie and made you death-touched."

"Nor did we," adds Tempest.

They believe Phillip? He's a liar, a thief and a killer. He and Lottie had the perfect motive to want to silence us. Doubt prickles up my neck. But someone paid him to steal my knucklebones, bones I found at Spicer House.

I remember the spread I rolled the night that Edie and I learned that the studio fire was no accident.

The curtain – for a secret not yet revealed.

The hive – for a group or community or family.

Broken earth – for shattering, division and strife.

Whoever did this is close to us.

As close as friends.

As close as sisters.

Some revelations strike like lightning, shocking and

painful. Others creep in slowly, leeching in like floodwater until they rise so high they drown you. This is both at once, a bolt followed by seeping dread.

"No—" My voice catches. I won't believe it. I can't. It's impossible, because the coven always comes first. We would never hurt each other. Never.

Seeing the painted horror on my face, Edie is frantic. "Who? Who was it?"

She loves too deeply, trusts too much. I am just enough of a cynic that I worked it out eventually. I don't want her to know. I can't stand to see the heartbreak on her face when she learns the truth, but I can't keep it from her. That would be equally unfair.

"Edie," I whisper, taking her hands in mine.

"Just say it," she begs.

I can't. The words choke in my throat.

"Shouldn't it be obvious by now?" says Meryem calmly, as the silence stretches. "The studio fire was set by Beatrice Spicer."

PART 7
TIME

The seventh bone stands for time, be it the present moment, fleeting, eternal, ancient history, or the far future.

Curtain: revelation/secrets/the recent past/display/
a performance/a question/surprise/the unexpected. Negative.
Snail: the ancient past/slowness/longevity/slow change/
steadfastness/prevention. Positive.
Obsidian Mirror: that which is hidden/ghosts/the future/
newness/hostility/fragility/truth. Negative.
Fire: malleability/intuition/hope/determination/passion/
speed/the fleeting/the present moment. Positive.

31

PROBLEMS AND PLEDGES

Meryem's words ring in the air like a death knell. I see Edie process them, her features dancing through confusion to shock and doubt.

"Bea Spicer. *Our* Bea?" Edie's hands tremble in mine. "She almost died herself that night and someone just tried to assassinate her onstage—"

"I'm sorry." Kavita's voice is gentle. She seems genuinely saddened for us. "Every practitioner, no matter if they are an augurer or occultist, leaves a unique essence that we can trace. The spell work on the sun set piece at the York Royal matches the signature of the theorem on the door at the studio. The same practitioner is responsible for both."

"There are no theorems there," I protest automatically.

Kavita's expression fills with pity. "And who told you that?"

Bea.

Bea went to the studio to look for magical residua and said she found nothing. Or course we believed her. What reason would we have to doubt her?

"Are you saying that she lied?" I ask.

Meryem tilts her head thoughtfully. "Why don't you use your knucklebones to confirm the truth?"

She is right. It seems I have become so used to being without them that I forgot I have the answers at my fingertips. It takes me only a moment to retrieve the set from my bedroom. Sitting on the front-room chaise, I hold them out, ready to throw. There is a knot in my throat and an ache in my stomach.

Why would Bea cast a theorem that threatened her own life, not once, but twice? Especially at the theatre. Why stage a second attack on herself? What was the benefit?

I don't need the bones to tell me that. All I need ask myself is what matters to Bea the most. Once I would have said our coven, but in recent weeks that hasn't been the case. All Bea talks about of late is the play, her dreams for her career, and her desire to be onstage and onscreen. She dreams of moving to America and making it as a movie star.

Of course. Bea *wasn't* the target of the sabotaged set piece – Millicent was. Her injury secured Bea the lead role after weeks of coveting the limelight. Bea was desperate to stand out and be noticed by the Fox-Mortons and now she is their star.

She must have left the magical message on my window. The last I saw of her that day was her waving me off with

Mr Saunders. It would have been easy for her to sneak back upstairs and leave the false threat against her life for me to find, thus throwing off any potential suspicion that she might be responsible.

Mr Spicer had to know there was no real threat. He knew. God, he *knew*.

"Did Merle know?" Edie asks me, her eyes pleading. "Ask if Merle knew."

My guts clench. I can't stand the idea that Merle was in on it too. Perhaps she knew about the theatre trick, perhaps not, but I'm confident she had nothing to do with the fire.

"We already asked the bones that, remember?" I comfort Edie. "She had nothing to do with the studio fire, at least."

The knucklebones. When I read them to try to pinpoint the culprit, they answered that the person responsible was close to us – a friend – I just never imagined that it would be someone so dear to my heart. But why set the studio fire? Why was she trying to kill us?

I cannot ask that, not yet. First, we must simply know if what the Hand, and my instincts, claim is true.

A deep breath to still the thrashing of my heart and I sink into the resonance of the bones. Wetting my lips, I ease the knucklebones around my palm, embracing the space inside myself where magic talks. A cool sensation bleeds into my hand. The bones are always cold to the touch, no matter what, and the fact that has not changed brings me renewed confidence.

"Did Bea Spicer set the fire and use a theorem on the studio door to lock us in the night that Edie died?" I grip them lightly for a second longer, letting my question ring through them, then throw them high.

I sense the arc they make in the air, a rising and falling, like breath drawn into lungs. I don't open my eyes until they have struck the rug at my feet with a soft patter. Ripples of phantasmic essence move through me and, when I look down it is to the sensation of roaring flame and smoke in the air.

My eyes water as I blink the vision away, smelling Bea's perfume so strongly it becomes a cloying, sickening scent I could choke on. It is a yes or no answer and a quick glance makes me clasp my hand over my mouth, sucking in breath as I shatter.

At the centre of the spread the root bone shows the veiled figure, our adversary. Around it, settled like the face of a clock, the other bones signify the snail, the walled garden, a witch bottle, the quill, the scales, lungs, an eye – and I feel the truth, no matter how heartbreaking it is.

I might be sick. Bea has betrayed our trust and destroyed our coven.

"I'm sorry, Edie. I'm sorry."

She reaches for me, a sob rushing out of her as a single tear falls on to her cheek. For the first time since she died, the girl I love is crying.

Edie bites her lip. "I need to hear it from her, Vi."

Gently, I swipe the tear from her cheek, watching as it melts into my skin. "I do too."

Meryem ghosts forward to embrace me and then Edie in

turn. We let her hold us. She is a stranger still, but perhaps in time she will become an ally and even one day, a friend. She smells wonderful, of the spices and florals of a lost past. Of promises, and hope and a future.

"You both have much to think about." Kavita takes a clay disc the size of a large coin from her pocket and holds it out to me. The front is stamped with an illustrative emblem – a hand holding a torch that looks very like Tempest's. "Rest and recuperate and when you are ready to give us an answer, break this token. We'll come to you."

"Despite what you now know, do not go seeking vengeance," Meryem warns. "Your former friends are well armed with potent spells and have proven they know how to use them. As tempting as it is to confront them, please wait for us. We will systematically take apart their network, but we need a little more time to prepare."

"We'll wait," I say, although I don't know if it is a promise I can keep.

Kavita hugs us too, her arms reassuringly solid. Then she and Meryem merge their flesh and ghost through the wall of our flat.

Tempest takes Andreas's hand. "You belong with us, Viola. I hope you realize that."

And then, as swiftly and silently as they arrived, the Hand are gone and all I hear is the echoing silence of our exhaustion.

A sunbeam breaks through the curtains. The light plays over Edie's face. I know that she can't feel its warmth. She casts no shadow. The motes of dust in the air move through her rather than around her. She is real, and yet not present. Part of this world and the next.

Beautiful.

My stomach flutters. Despite the betrayal and pain we have suffered, just being with her is like the most blissful luxury. I need nothing else in this world but her. I know, without doubt, that I want to spend the rest of my life by her side.

"Edie, I want to take up Meryem's invitation to join the Hand."

She swallows, her lip trembling, and I think she's going to cry for the second time since she died.

"You don't agree?" I ask, heart stuttering in disappointment and worry.

"I think it will be safest if you do join them." Her eyes are glistening. No more tears fall but she looks as if she's fighting a war within herself. "I like Tempest and Andreas especially and they will protect you in a way that I simply cannot—"

And I know in that moment why she's struggling to hold herself together in the face of what is, admittedly a life and afterlife changing decision, but frankly one that makes utter sense. She has it in her mind that I would desert her.

"Me? I meant *us*. I won't mirror with any other soul but yours. If you agree."

There's a flare of hope and relief on her face and then something melancholic settles into her eyes. "Oh, Vi, this has gone too far."

"Too far? I don't understand—"

"My death was not your fault, you must believe that by now. You're ruled by guilt!"

I put my hands on my hips. "Guilt? Edie, I am ruled by *vengeance*. I want Bea to pay for what she did to you, and Mr Spicer for protecting her, and I want to be with you—"

"I'm dead! I can't *have* you!"

I laugh, and perhaps it is curt and tinged with a touch of frustration, because she has me so utterly in her grasp I don't know what she means. Surely she knows how much I love her as both a friend and as my sweetheart.

She pulls away. "I'm unchanging. Stuck as I am."

"That hasn't stopped us from being with each other."

"But you *will* change. You'll age…"

"Edie, you can change too, not your physical appearance so much, but your thoughts and ideas aren't static. You can think for yourself as any living person does. Look at Tempest and Andreas. They make it work. Death is merely another form of life and if we mirror, you will have some way to make your mark on the physical world again."

"At what cost to you?" sniffs Edie. "Working for the Hand will be dangerous."

"And if I don't, they will seal me and I will lose you forever." A panicked, broken-winged fluttering bursts through me. I dispel it, knowing that this moment, more than any other, is a time to be brave and state plainly what I want.

What I want is Edie – whatever that takes, whatever the cost.

I take her hands again. "I will say this as many times as I must. Every day, if I have to." Gently, I stroke the pad of my thumbs over her knuckles, as if I can read my future there. "You have me. You have my friendship, my companionship and love. You have my heart – every beat of it calls to you and you alone. You have my body."

I throw in a rather wicked smile and she has the good grace to blush. It looks beautiful on her. "And now I wish to tether my soul to yours for the rest of my days," I tell her, meaning every word and needing her to believe me. "Not from a sense of obligation or guilt, but because you are the person I love most in this world and I don't want to spend a single day without you. I don't know, my dearest Edie, how to speak plainer."

"Vi, I—"

"But if this is all too sudden for you, if you don't want to be my mirror, I understand," I quickly add, not wanting to risk losing her over this. "It is a commitment akin to marriage, and I know you and I both pledged never to wed—"

"A man. Never to wed *a man*," Edie corrects.

"Well, yes, but—"

"It's not the bond itself that worries me." Edie looks at me through lowered lashes. "Viola Sampire, you are the love of my life, and afterlife. I have been yours since that first day in the attic when I sat beside you and you were mean to me."

I stick out my bottom lip. "I was *not* mean."

"You were, and I knew then that I was doomed." Edie smiles a cat's grin, wily and needy. The moment is soft and quivering, alive. Our hungry lips find each other. I kiss her mouth, her jaw, the bare skin of her collarbone and she makes a noise like she's sinking. There is a desperation in my throat that I've never felt before and then I'm under, and drowning has never felt more like flying.

"I wanted you for so long I never thought you would ever." Edie's throat bobs as she swallows. "That we would ever … and then my life ended and what you and I might have become felt lost because how can we make this work?"

The question isn't the end of something but a plea to allow for a beginning, as if Edie is asking for permission to do the impossible.

"It is a little unorthodox," I admit, knowing I'm beaming from ear to ear because she loves me – like a sweetheart, like a lover. Like a wife. "We can learn, together." I wind my fingers around the lapels of her waistcoat, feeling the metal serpent brooch. I wonder, when we are mirrored, what phantasmic objects we might both manifest. "Are you afraid?"

"I'm afraid *for* you. It will mean a lifetime of risk."

"Well, if I die fighting a shade or occultist, then I'll stay earthbound for you as you did for me," I vow. "What sort of afterlife could I have without you? I don't think you realize, there is nothing I won't do for you, Edie."

She looks at me for a long moment. "That's what I'm afraid of."

I realize then that it is being in love, the simple act of existing for another so utterly, that is the greatest and most perfect gift. Edie loves me. She loves me and I love her. In the face of all we have lost, that knowledge is what gives me the courage to meet our fate.

Because a lifelong friend, a sister, someone I trusted with our lives, killed her. For what? I need to know. I cannot breathe. My anger flares like embers smouldering in a woodland, the fire stoked to fresh flames. I swore that when I found out who was responsible for Edie's death that I would make them pay.

The Hand said to wait, but I have never been patient.

32

COVEN

Merle pokes her head out from the contemporary gallery, a book on glyphs in hand, as I storm into Spicer House. She's dressed in a full-length wrapper dress, her hair piled high on her head. The sight of her makes my heart ache.

"Oh, thank goodness you're here. Uncle was going to send a runner—"

"Where's Bea?" I demand.

"Uncle's office." She spins as I push past her. The contemporary gallery has been rehung with a series of larger paintings that are vibrant in their violence. Abstracted bodies slashed and twisted in red and yellows. The faces are blocks of blue and grey. I don't know the artist but it's as if they have dragged my soul from me and plastered it across the walls, putting me on display.

"Why are you crying? Vi—" Merle frowns, confused. "What's going on?"

Pushing past the curtain and into the red rooms, I stop in my tracks as the office door opens and Bea strides out. She's elegant in a new summer dress but her expression is more guarded than usual. The burning anger I feel at the sight of her keeps me locked where I stand. I can barely breathe. My lungs tighten.

Not now, please not now. Except this feels different to the attacks I normally suffer. My heart rate thrums in my ears and everything is too clear and sharp. The walls are closing in. I am so anxious. Edie is here too, racing after me through the streets, her own anger simmering beneath her skin. She doesn't crowd me but I wish she would. I want her weight against me, crushing until all I can smell is her hair and skin. I want to hide behind her.

But I am here to defend *her*, avenge *her*.

I glower at Bea. "You set the spell that locked us in Pa's studio."

She doesn't look surprised or outraged. The only reaction is a slight parting of her lips, the quiet exhale of relief. I can see the truth in her face. She has been waiting for this ever since the bones were returned to me. She knew that her luck would run dry, her tactics would fail and the truth would out.

My eyes fill with tears. This is the last, worst part. What was I expecting? That Bea would deny it and I would have to present our evidence and force her confession? Yes! I want her to feed us sweet lies that I'll desperately want to believe.

I want her to manipulate me as she always does, allow me to make excuse after excuse for her terrible friendship, because it is safer and easier to let her get away with everything than to confront her. Even though I know better, that this time there is no excuse, I still want her to lie.

"I knew if you had your knucklebone set that you would ask the right questions eventually," Bea says too calmly. "Which is why I hired Phillip to take them."

"Please tell me you didn't." Merle's hand flies to her mouth.

Bea's jaw firms. "He wasn't supposed to hurt her; he did that on his own."

"Why?" Merle chokes. It strikes me that she really did not know what her cousin was doing. That at least is some relief.

"Because Father forced me to." Bea swallows and raises her head, refusing to look away. "He wants a death-touched to better serve his business. Rachel and her father have a code they refuse to break and there are not enough working soul catchers to meet demand. He thought if I were death-touched I would have special insight into the spirit world, and death-touched flesh and blood has other magical uses he wishes to explore."

The curtain, quill and scroll. The search for hidden magical knowledge: that of the death-touched. With the resources at Mr Spicer's disposal, it is no surprise that he found out how my kind are created. Henry Saunders could have told him as much.

Magpie in flight paired with the seedling. New beginnings. Rebirth.

I recall Bea's admission when she first saw Edie's ghost reflected in the obsidian mirror: *"It should have been me."* In that moment I'd thought that she was saying that she should have died in Edie's place. She was being a friend and grieving and feeling the same guilt that I was. We survived and Edie died and we would do anything to change that.

How wrong I was.

That day in the attic Bea meant that Edie should have died *for her*. Not for me.

"Father has always had a plan for us," Bea goes on. "Do you think he gave us access to occult resources out of the goodness of his heart? He was training us, subtly shaping us in the ways he wanted."

"Keep going," I tell Bea. "We want to hear everything."

Licking her lips, she sighs. "I was to become his death-touched soul catcher. He wanted to marry you off to Henry, or another suitably powerful client, to improve his connections. Edie—" For the first time since we confronted her, Bea's resolve seems to break. She dips her gaze, her lips trembling. "Is she here?"

Neither Bea nor Merle has an obsidian mirror to hand.

"Yes," I tell them, turning to Edie, whose face is a mess of emotion. "And she wants the truth as much as I do."

The last time I saw Bea, she was like a sister to me. The new summer dress of hers makes her look older, as does the way she's curled her hair with a deep side part.

"Edie was supposed to die for me," admits Bea. "Father asked me to find a fourth, a coven member whom I could seduce and who would love me enough to give up her life for mine."

Her romance with Edie was nothing but manipulation. She was trying to cultivate devotion, trying to make Edie fall in love with her so that when she put our lives in danger, Edie would sacrifice herself for Bea and bring her back as a death-touched.

"Edie, I never deserved your love, and I know now that I never had it," Bea addresses Edie though she cannot see her. "Maybe I should have known that you would always die for Vi and not me, maybe that's why I closed the door before Vi escaped. I never wanted to be death-touched and remain in York working for Father for the rest of my life. I want the stage, America, a future of my own. By choosing Vi, you freed me. I'd say that I am sorry, but what I really mean is thank you. I am glad to be free of the pressure now that I am not Father's heir."

"Then who is?" I ask. She's his daughter, unless he plans to hand the business over to Merle.

"Isn't it obvious?" Bea blinks at me. "*You*, Vi. You became death-touched. Pa was livid when I emerged from the fire exactly as I am, until he found out that it worked on *you*." She bites her lip. "I think I always knew that Edie loved you and I put on a show for my father, and for her, but nothing was ever going to come between you both. It was inevitable, perhaps."

"Inevitable?" I spit, clenching my fists until my nails bite into the skin, drawing blood. "No, you *did* this. Edie is dead because of *you*. You are a murderer, no better than Lottie."

"She had no choice." Mr Spicer himself draws back the curtain and steps into the red rooms. "Forgive her, Viola. I understand your anger, but Beatrice acted on my wishes and mine alone."

We spin to face him. He looks the part of the friendly, eccentric uncle. His hair is as wild as it always is, curled around his ears and peppered with grey and yet I see him utterly unmasked for the first time. He has no real respect for our lives. There was no guarantee that the fire would work. Edie might not have given her life for anyone. The four of us could all have been asphyxiated, but it was a risk he was willing to take.

"This is not how I intended you to find out," he says casually. "Bea has made some silly, selfish choices squandering the soul bottle I gifted her in petty attempts to secure her career and cover her mistakes, but here we are and time is of the essence. You will no longer wed Henry—"

"I never had any intention of marrying Mr Saunders," I say. "But if you mean for me to work for you instead, I refuse."

Any residual warmth in Mr Spicer's stone-grey eyes fades as the smile drops from his lips. "You will do as I say, Viola."

He means it, the bastard. He really thinks he can control me. The Hand were right. Be careful who you trust. "I'm not your daughter."

"You're as good as. I've been more of a parent to you than your father ever has. I've given you books and bones, brought up the witch in you and I am proud of what you've become. I made you death-touched and now you will turn your new-found skills to my advantage. I have plans for you, Viola. This is not a negotiation."

If this man thinks I will simply forgive and forget and then turn my life over to him to do his bidding trapping souls, then he is utterly delusional.

My ears tinge pink as angry heat flushes through me: shame and adrenaline and resentment. Holding my head high, I clench my fists. "Fuck you."

Mr Spicer takes a small obsidian mirror from his pocket, angling it to sweep the room. When he sees Edie, he addresses her.

"I am terribly sorry, Edie. But needs must." Mr Spicer sighs, as if all this is a terrible imposition. "You have your new friends to thank for the soul-shortage crisis, and I have deadlines to meet."

What is he—? He cannot mean to do what I think he does.

A snap of his fingers. Magic flares and a ghost line shimmers into sight along the skirting board, crossing the open doorways to enclose us perfectly. There is no escape for Edie.

"You will not touch her," I threaten, shielding the girl I love.

"That is really not up to you." Mr Spicer holds an empty bottle made of fancy cut glass with a green tinge.

Edie's fear is plain. The last time she was contained in a bottle trap the experience drove her to despair. She disappeared for days. It almost broke her.

A voice I once trusted speaks words that wrench my soul,

trying to drag it out of me. Bea and Merle bare their teeth too, but we are all still alive and he cannot take us. Edie is not safe. I grasp her close as if my touch can save her but she's already flaking apart. My heart is alight with pain, nerves screaming. I don't know what I am saying but I'm babbling, half begging, half cursing Mr Spicer. No matter how hard I cling on, Edie's flesh disintegrates under my touch.

"Uncle, don't do this!" Merle shouts.

For a final, precious moment I have hope. Merle will act, join hands with Bea and fight for us. Coven sisters together. This has gone too far. But she doesn't move and neither does Bea. Bea's eyes gleam with pent-up tears but she doesn't turn away. She always meant for Edie to be the sacrifice, just as I was supposed to be a sacrifice of a different kind. I know what they are thinking: *Better them than us.*

I curse how unprepared I am. I have no witch bottle, nor blade with me. Nothing to damn them with except the vitriol in my heart. My anger is a torch, the antithesis to Tempest's protective flame. My fire will ignite all it touches. The air sours. I need raw magical glyphs to channel my anger and I need fuel, but I have nothing to burn except my own essence, essence that has barely recovered from soul burn.

"Don't!" Edie gasps, her voice stretched thin. "One more theorem will be your last."

She gasps as she shatters into a thousand fragments drawn in a whirlwind into the bottle in Mr Spicer's hands. It happens so quickly and I want to cry but the tears won't come. We shouldn't have come here so unprepared. This is the fault of my explosive anger and my need for revenge. In seeking it, I have condemned Edie to a worse fate.

Mr Spicer corks the soul bottle immediately, keeping Edie's prison firmly in his grasp.

I need the Hand. If I break the disc they gave me, they'll hear me calling and know where I am. As casually as I can, I reach into my pocket. I'm not subtle enough. Striding forward, Mr Spicer grabs my wrist and wrenches my hand up, the clay disc caught between my fingers.

"From your new friends, I presume."

I clench my teeth and try to pull out of his grasp but he's stronger than he looks.

"Let me guess, you break it and they come running?" he sneers. "Well, let's not keep them waiting."

Taking the token, Mr Spicer snaps it clean in two. A rush of power bursts from the small disc. The flare dissipates within seconds.

"Let Edie go," I demand.

"Not until this childish, misplaced independence of yours is tamed." Mr Spicer smiles at me. "If you're good and you work for me, then I will release her. If not, I'll trade her away and you'll never see her again."

33

IMPRESA

"Please, Viola, just do what Father asks." Bea's voice cracks a little but she grits her jaw and I know that she has made up her mind. She will not betray her own family. How long until the Hand arrive? And when they do, will they be able to do anything? I haven't given them enough time to prepare and Mr Spicer obviously has plans for them.

Besides, I don't want a rescue. I want revenge.

But what options do I have? Thoughts of Edie flare brightly in my mind. Her laugh, the curve of her neck, the way her lips taste of strawberries, the glint of the snake brooch on her lapel and what her voice sounds like when she says, "I love you."

I will do anything for her.

Anything.

Including giving up my autonomy, allowing a man to

dictate my future and my life, and throwing away whatever semblance of a moral code I ever possessed. I don't want to trap and hurt innocents, but compared to Edie, they don't matter in the slightest.

I meet Mr Spicer's gaze. "Very well, I will do as you ask."

For now.

His jaw works as he considers me, seemingly composed, but there is sweat on his upper lip. Stalking forward, he comes close enough that I might be able to grab Edie's bottle from his hold, if I can catch him off guard. I try to keep my eyes fixed on his face, but my attention drops to it momentarily and that is enough to give me away.

He grasps my jaw roughly, a spark of anger flaring in his eyes. The air between us turns thin and cold. "Forgive me if I don't merely take you at your word."

Before he can do whatever it is he plans, I take my chance and lunge but he shoves me back harshly, holding me by my neck. I struggle, gasping for air. Mr Spicer is surprisingly strong.

I look at Merle, pleading silently for her to act. She's barely five paces away, she could so easily take the bottle from her uncle and smash it while he's distracted by me. But I'm asking her to go against her own family and Merle has always bowed to Bea's control, ever since we were children. She will not help me; she cannot even meet my eyes.

Tears leak down my cheeks.

"Viola, it doesn't have to be this way." Mr Spicer sounds so genuinely regretful and that only fuels the clash of mixed-up emotions in my heart. "One day you will realize everything I have done for you. Until then…"

The words he speaks next are in Latin, not a language I know well. A sharp sting flares at my wrist and my eyes fly open. The bite of magic instantly fades, replaced by a wave of somnolent warmth that chases the hook of his power. Mr Spicer is suddenly a sun in my vision, blazing and bright and I feel a warm rush of affection for him and a sense of safety. The bone impresa bracelet that he gave me for my protection tingles against my skin.

Meryem's words from only a few hours ago play through my thoughts: *It's not the gift you think it is.*

I'd assumed she meant the book that Mr Saunders gave to me, or perhaps even becoming death-touched in the first place. But I'd touched the impresa bracelet as I awoke, comforted because I thought it was there to protect me from harm. And, yes, there are strong protection theorems written into it, but Mr Spicer has added something darker and more insidious to the spell work that I did not recognize before.

No, he wouldn't hurt me. He is a father to me, loyal, kind. All he has done, he has done to turn me into the best version of myself—

Lies.

Instinctually, I try to rip the bone bracelet off my wrist.

"Behave." The command is simple and quietly spoken. My hand falls limply at my side as my body obeys without hesitation.

My throat tightens with dread. What has he done? I feel

like a moth uselessly flapping its wings against the brightness of a lantern. The urge to serve Rupert Spicer, in whatever way he demands, is irresistible and right now he wants me to be quiet and obedient. But beneath the fake feelings, my true hate and resentment still simmers. That hasn't died; I can still think for myself, but it is an effort requiring conscious focus. I know that if he asks me to do something, I will not be able to stop myself.

More tears slip silently down my cheeks. I am utterly helpless. What's worse is he syphoned from Edie to activate the latent magic in the bracelet. He took from her to control me. It is the ultimate cruelty and I feel something deep inside me shatter.

On the periphery of my vision Bea and Merle do nothing but watch. Only a short time ago the three of us were closer than sisters, sleeping wound together, limb over limb, breathing the same breath, hair tangling as we whispered spells into the night. I would have died for them. I might have killed for them.

I have never felt more alone.

Footsteps sound in the hall and the flat-cap-wearing occultist from a few nights ago enters.

"The trap's set, boss," says Flat Cap. He nods at me. "Ah, I see you have the bait."

Mr Spicer finally releases me. "Viola, how many members of the Hand are in York?"

I don't want to answer, but the truth is dragged from my lips. "F-four."

Rupert has always known more than he let on. He's been manipulating me, playing me like a sacrificial pawn on a chessboard for weeks. Maybe he meant for it to come to this, certainly he's prepared. He did tell me he knew it would come down to a fight in the end.

Him against the Hand, and our coven will be collateral.

"With our reinforcements, we outnumber them," says Flat Cap. "They'll be here soon." I don't know if he means the reinforcements, whoever that may be, or the Hand themselves.

"Bea, get the soul bottles from the safe," Mr Spicer orders. "The time has come to defend what we have built."

Bea obeys without question and I wonder for a brief moment if he is controlling her in the same way he is me. I cannot see any impresa on her, but I cling to the hope that she isn't doing this all on her own. Merle stands stock still against the display of ghost glass and crystal balls, looking completely overwhelmed.

The curtain to the main gallery is pulled aside and Rachel Tussle enters, followed by Henry Saunders. They both hesitate on the threshold, taking in the scene.

"What is the meaning of this?" demands Mr Saunders.

Rachel hisses, "Rupert, have you lost your mind?"

"She was being uncooperative." Mr Spicer is so calm. "I did what I must for the moment, at least until the Hand have been dealt with."

Henry bristles. "This isn't what we agreed."

"You vowed to help me find and neutralize the threat against my business."

Mr Saunders looks at me, his gaze possessive. I want to believe he has my best interests in mind, but I am sure he's only thinking about what he wants. He doesn't want his future bride damaged. "And I will stand with you against the Hand, but only if you leave Viola out of this."

Bea returns from the office with several soul bottles in her arms. Mr Spicer takes two for himself. "For goodness' sake, Henry." Taking a leather bandolier from one of the display cabinets to our left, he belts Edie's bottle and the two others into it. "If you want a witch for a wife, then marry Merle; she has nothing better to do."

"I don't want to get married," Merle protests quietly.

How can Mr Spicer be so callous? My mind screams as I fight back against the theorem threading through my thoughts, but it feels like his hand has reached inside me and wrenched out my heart. I want whatever he wants. I want him to be proud of me.

I hate this.

"Spicer." Rachel's tone is clipped. "Enough. Let Viola go."

"I will not."

Rachel taps her fingers on her own bandolier. She came armed with two soul bottles and the gesture is a clear threat. "Then we are in opposition."

Will Rachel and Mr Saunders truly fight for me? Surely Spicer isn't a match for them both, and hopefully the Hand will be here soon.

"The thing you should remember about me" – Mr Spicer twists his hand and bright, elegant theorems blaze into sight on the walls – "is that I prepare for every eventuality."

Spicer attacks. Tapping the seal of the topmost bottle on his bandolier, he shapes a glyph in the air, draws back and releases. His casting is fast and elegant, magic as I have never seen it before because these are active combat theorems worked with the backing of soul bottles. Rachel defends, falling back as a blast of air strikes her, forcing her away.

Flat Cap has broken the seal on the bottle at his belt and stands in front of me as he throws a raw glyph at Mr Saunders. The spell is visible in the air like writhing snakes and then Henry begins to suffocate, clawing at his throat for air. Drawing on her own reserves, Rachel strikes at Spicer with three glyphs in quick succession.

"Stop!" I scream, because one of the bottles on Mr Spicer's bandolier contains Edie's soul. If Rachel keeps attacking, he'll tap into her essence to fuel his defence.

The building rattles, glass shaking in the panes. Cries of shock fill the room as wards flare to life, blaring alarms. Then the windows shatter, cascading to the floor with a successive popping. A second pulse of power discharges through the air, cracking all the ghost mirrors and crystal balls on display, sending a river of shimmering shards across the floor.

I know from the surprise on everyone's faces that this is not their doing.

Please let it mean that the Hand have arrived. With only Flat Cap on his side, and no sign of his reinforcements, Mr Spicer is heavily outnumbered. This will be over in minutes. I will free Edie. It is going to be well – all will be well.

Red-faced and livid, Mr Spicer grabs for me and I cannot move away from his demands. Blood on his thumb. He presses it to my forehead and my bottom lip, marking me with copper. I want to spit away the taste of him but I can't. A strange, lifting sensation drags on my bones, like I am rising into the air but my feet remain earthbound…

"I'm sorry, Viola. I'll only take a little."

The impresa is giving him access to my phantasmic residua.

"Wait," I gasp as the pain sends me to my knees. Having suffered soul burn recently, I have so little left to give, but he doesn't know that.

"Spicer, no!" Rachel screams. "They'll kill us all in retaliation!"

But it's too late. Magic rips through me. The bandolier across Mr Spicer's chest flares with a complex theorem that I immediately recognize. Cyrillic and Quentenian blend into elegant script. Bea might have worked the magic at the theatre and studio, but she based her workings on her father's style. Equations flare to active power, pulling on my soul. The power ruptures the first soul bottle on Rupert's bandolier, melting the seal at its neck.

Fleshy fragments and swirling dust erupt from within, coalescing into a jawbone, an arm, a leg. With a crack, they break apart again, reforming into a bulbous fleshy mass.

What is happening?

The glyphs glow even brighter, reaching for the next bottle in the bandolier and a second stream of ghostly dust bursts into the room. On the floor, the first soul has become a horror. A pale naked torso, topped by a hideous skull like an upside-down head: elongated jaw, sharp teeth and hollow eyes. Sound hits me as a broken, inhuman wail pours from the ghost. It flexes four crab-like limbs in a horrific jerky movement, and then launches itself at Mr Saunders.

Spicer's intent becomes clear.

As a last-ditch defence he is deliberately corrupting souls into powerful shades he can neither control nor contain, and he will drain my soul to do it.

34

JUST A GIRL

Mr Saunders goes down with a startled, pained cry. I don't see what happens next because a second shade has already formed; spindly and crooked, it has none of the fleshy bulk of the other. It's incredibly tall and slender, its skeleton visible through translucent skin. Blundering forward, it swipes for Rachel.

Cursing Spicer, she pulls bundles of salt from her pocket and throws them, making the monster shriek with anger.

They can fight the shades, and distract them, but there is no simple way to contain them. Only a rhu tasi can. Where's Meryem? The broken glass and crystal… I thought the Hand were here, but I can't see any of them—

And then all I know is acute panic as the magical theorem creating the shades reaches the final bottle in Spicer's bandolier. Edie's bottle.

The wax seal starts to melt.

She's next.

I thought I knew what terror and despair felt like. I've faced it over and over again, seen the girl I love bottled and trapped, felt my own soul violated. But this. This is worse and there is no time to wait for rescue.

I know then what I have to do. Edie sacrificed for me. Now, it's my turn.

She always loved Medusa, aggressor and victim, utterly tragic in her fate and hunted for her power. I remember the myth well. From the drops of the maiden's spilled blood came many monsters.

A drop will not suffice.

Around me are broken remnants of crystal and obsidian mirror. Their edges catch in the low electric lights like the shine on a sharpened blade. I grab a shard before Mr Spicer realizes what is happening and slash into my arms, not caring how deeply the blade bites. Soon, it won't matter. These are not wounds I can heal from. The warm, hot flush of liquid rushes down my skin. Everything feels needle-sharp and precise.

"Stop, Viola." The impresa burns at my wrist as Spicer's command sings through it. My intention wavers and I drop the bloody crystal shard.

But he cannot stop me. My intent is stronger than his will ever be. Closing my eyes, I remember the feel of Edie's lips on mine. I bask in the breadth of our friendship, of our love, and hope for the future unwritten and unravelled. Dancing dust motes. Ash in her hair. Storms in her eyes. I see them, those eyes connecting through the impossible. Trust. Perfect trust and endless love.

No man can touch that love or take it from me.

This will cost more of my soul than I can afford. What do I care? There is nothing I would not give to save Edie from becoming a monstrous shade.

I sink into the remnants of my own essence. It smells of red wine and rusting metal. Rotting apples. Of hot meat on a griddle. Damp fur after a rain and sweet skin. It smells of ritual and bees' wax and sex. It smells of angry vengeance. Of women.

I reclaim myself.

Anger returns, molten and strong. Grabbing it, I rise to my surface, tracing along the theorem tied to the impresa at my wrist. With the ghost of Edie's kiss on my skin and the memory of her taste on my tongue, I wrench the magic through me and spit out a spell, shaping glyphs on the floor in my own blood. It is raw and unanchored, born in sacrifice, syphoned from my soul with such force the agony curls through me like a hot iron on skin.

My theorem hitches on to the bridge made by the impresa at my wrist. If Spicer can take from me, then I can send to him, and my curse flows into the bandolier across his chest. It cuts off his spell, releasing his hold on Edie's ghost.

She is already free of the bottle. Dust and bone and flesh and sinew swirls only a few paces from me. Strands of dark hair, the wool of her fedora, the pink of her lips. Am I too late? Please don't let me be too late. Slowly, she begins to pull herself together.

Spicer's original theorem strains against my control, seeking her. It is designed to corrupt, break a soul's sanity and create horror. It needs a new focus.

"Wait, wait." Mr Spicer stumbles, finally sensing what I intend to do. "You'll die."

He breathes the last word in awe. As if he can't imagine I would do such a thing for another person. I don't expect him to understand. Men like him only know how to sacrifice others on the altar of their need.

It is not enough to merely end his theorem. The magic he has set into motion is a flood that needs direction, so I give it one: turning his glyphs away from Edie, I twist them back on themselves. More of my blood falls, pattering on the ground from my fingertips. If I could carve out my heart and feed it to the earth in exchange for Edie, I would, but I need it to beat, at least long enough to take apart everything and everyone standing in my way. Digging deeper, I tear through my viscera into the dregs of my body, wrenching my thin and twisted soul into my throat.

Whoomph whoomph whoomph in my ears. A heart having to work too hard to keep life flowing. I will not fail.

Spicer begs. He pleads. I do not care.

When I reverse the flow and dig into his phantasmic essence, hauling it into my curse, he cries out and falls to one knee. He tries to stop me with a paltry conjuring as he wrestles for control over the pool of our linked power. I panic and unleash the full wrath of my engorged curse. It rips from me like a blade through entrails and I scream, and scream and scream.

When I am dead, boil the flesh from my bones and etch magic into my remains. Turn me into an impresa. Remember me.

My theorem flays Mr Spicer's skin to ribbons. He bellows, his scream of agony turning choked and bloody and I push and push, forcing the deadly power I wield to slice deeper. Parts of him start to slough off. He gasps, bloody mouth wide as he dies.

The bone and gold impresa breaks, scattering beads into the gore and crystal at my feet followed by the shattered corpse of Rupert Spicer.

35

EDIE

The sob that breaks from me is desperate: part-relief, part-pain.

Rupert Spicer is dead. I killed him. I *killed* someone that I once loved. Maybe I should feel sorry this time, but I don't. I don't *at all*. Still, I can't stop crying. Tears blur my vision and puff my face. I don't know what is happening, only that I am choking on Edie's name and my lungs are a harsh rattle in my chest.

Where is she?

Somehow, I'm still upright on my knees. I wipe my eyes and blood stings them. Salt and sweat. "Edie?"

A weight slams into my chest, sending me painfully backwards with a cry, legs twisting out from under me and I gasp. Hot breath on my cheek. I blink to clear my vision. Vapour claws solidify to deadly points against my stomach as the fragmented mass pinning me down takes on a monstrous shape. Fear, syrup-slick like swamp water, rises to drown me and I cannot defend myself even if I had the strength.

Of course, I think dully. I turned Spicer's theorem back on him. I didn't just kill the man; I made a shade of his ghost. And what a shade. His skin is wax yellow, bulbous and bubbled like melted tallow. The eyes are bloodshot and ravenous, and he seems so much larger than he was in life, back hunched, limbs elongated. Is that a mouth where his sternum should be?

I'm laughing, because soul burn won't have time to kill me. He will and there is a kind of poetry in that end.

Meryem will never forgive me. I've broken all their rules now, I just hope she will take care of Edie when I'm gone and that she can safely contain the shades created tonight and undo my mistakes.

The bright green glow of Tempest's torch suddenly flares through the gallery. Above me, the shade screeches and retreats. Andreas makes this awful shushing noise like I'm a puppy in distress as he grips my shoulders and hauls me roughly to sitting. My fear bleeds away, leaving me shaking with raw emotion: grief, relief, worry, guilt.

"Oh, child, what have you done?" says Tempest sadly, kneeling beside me.

"I needed to save Edie," I whisper. I can't look away from the light of his torch. It hurts my eyes but the wash of it feels like baptism, like some holy fire that can burn the evil right out of me. "She's… I can't exist without her. I can't go on if she's…"

"Save your breath." Andreas has his arms under me, lifting me up.

"I-I saw her before. Is she a shade? Did she—?"

"We don't know. Meryem and Kavita are fighting one of the shades, an occultist is dealing with another, and now we must also track and contain Spicer."

Three, that's three shades. If Edie had become like them, there would be a fourth, so I have hope.

Slowly I become more aware of my surroundings. The room is a disaster. The display cases are crooked and broken, glass and crystal everywhere mingled with blood. Not just mine. What remains of Flat Cap is crumpled against one wall. I don't want to look. Where are Bea and Merle? There's no sign of them here. Are they alive? Have they escaped?

I don't know what to feel.

Andreas sits me on the sofa beside the office. There are deep tears in the upholstery but the furniture feels solid enough. "Tempest, she's lost too much blood."

"Replenishment charm?" says Tempest.

The men merge, a slow flow of skin into skin and glowing silver eyes. The theorem they work stops my bleeding and eases my pain, and soon they are two separate people once again and Andreas is slicing up strips of his shirt to bandage the deep cuts down my arms.

"I have her," says Tempest. "Go and help Meryem and Kavita. They're outnumbered."

Andreas nods and stands, catching Tempest's arm. They don't say anything to one another; they don't need to.

Bringing both hands up to Tempest's face, Andreas kisses him, his gauntlets manifesting over his knuckles. And then Andreas is gone and Tempest is at my side again.

"Please, Edie… I need to—" I gasp, struggling to stand but my muscles are watery. I'm barely clinging to consciousness but I can't fade, not until I know Edie is safe.

Time dilates. I exist in the swell and sway, preparing to sink but not willing. My body clutches to life with desperate hands. Turning me inside out, fingers pressing on the inside of my skin, I would spill slippery seeds and juicy pith. My skin is leather dried and cracking. This is limbo. I don't know how long I am here, and nowhere, hovering between realms.

Tempest tries to soothe me with words I am too exhausted to understand and then, with gargantuan effort, I stand. He hauls one of my arms over his shoulders and we walk. One foot. The other.

The galleries are a ruin. The shades have slashed the paintings, peeling them from their frames and carving deep gashes in the walls. Bea and Merle? I keep looking for their corpses, not sure if I want them dead for their betrayal. In my heart I want Bea to pay for what she has done.

I hear the fight and then it is in front of us. A bulbous shade looms over Rachel, who is splayed on the gallery floor near the front window, her shirt soaked in blood, salt crusted on her hands. Before it can strike, Meryem twists her body out of Kavita's, turning from their battle with the shade that was recently Rupert Spicer, to strike with the sharp point of her manifested stylus. It punctures the shade's flesh, peeling it back as she drags it down, and the thing splits open like a sack of pus.

"Quickly, a rhu tasi," she shouts. "It will reform in seconds."

Tempest lowers me down. I feel hard wood and wax polish under my hands, the stairs at my back. "Go," I breathe. "Help them."

I am alone for mere seconds before delicate hands find mine. Edie, whole and unhurt. Relief balloons in my chest, taking flight amid the ruins of my soul. She takes me in her arms, rolling me so that I'm held against her chest, looking up at her and, for a moment, nothing else seems to matter. She strokes the tears from my cheeks.

"What have you done? Vi, what have you done?"

I'm dying. I've done it before and this is how it feels and I am most definitely fading.

"What I had to," I whisper, cupping her face.

We have been here before, her and I. This time she is not wreathed in smoke and ash, but torn canvas and blood. This time there are monsters. This time she can't do anything to save me, and that is how it has to be.

"I'll stay earthbound, for you," I promise. "I'll stay."

"You are not going to die, Viola—"

I am. Perhaps not this instant, but I can feel how little time I have left. I watch the skin around her eyes tense under the soft brush of my fingers; I trace the curve of her cheek, her mouth, as she shudders out a watery breath. A battle rages around us like a storm and yet it is distant. Here it is calm.

Edie is my world, narrowed to a single focused brushstroke that somehow encompasses all that she is.

"Kiss me," I whisper. "Please."

She does, pulling me up to her and pressing her mouth to mine. I kiss her back with the dregs of strength I still possess. Edie's breathy groan seems to reverberate through my chest. Her tongue is hot, her lips wet, my tears are on her cheeks. I saved her. She isn't a shade. She is safe. She is safe. My heart races, senses filled with only her. It is a desperate kiss, wanting and devouring. I never want to let go. I will die and my ghost will stay earthbound and our souls will spend an eternity together.

A cry cuts the room, tearing Edie and I roughly from the little huddle that we have made of ourselves. We both turn to see the shade that Spicer became sweep his arm up in sudden violence to take root in Kavita's belly. Blood blooms down her body to spatter the floor. Her face is caught in an expression of surprise. The cry that breaks from Meryem is one of pure fury.

"No," I whisper in shock.

Kavita is dead.

Movement resumes. The battle rages on. Tempest and Andreas are a blur of anger and magic as they take out their grief on the shades. First one, then a second, is trapped until it is only Spicer left. Rachel is standing alongside them, exhausted but determined and I wonder if this means the Hand will make an exception for her and not seal her. I don't see Spicer's final moments because light particles start to rise from Kavita's fallen body like a mist that dances in the light, forming and dispersing.

It reminds me of birds on the wing, gathering to flock and fly to far distant places. I watch, transfixed as the fragments coalesce, taking on substance, an opacity replacing the ephemeral until Kavita stands before us as colourful and full of life as I have ever seen a person.

Her corpse lies at her feet, but she smiles at Edie and me. "Take care of Meryem for me," she whispers and then she is disintegrating into the air. Gone.

Shock bleeds into my exhaustion and I can't hold on any longer. Fatigue takes me over and, cradled in Edie's arms, I slip into nothingness.

"I'll be here when you wake up," she promises.

"I love you," I whisper, thinking that if those are the last words I ever say in life, I'll die without regret.

PART 8
SELF

The eighth and final bone is the self, representative of the individual. The asker. The visceral, naked self.

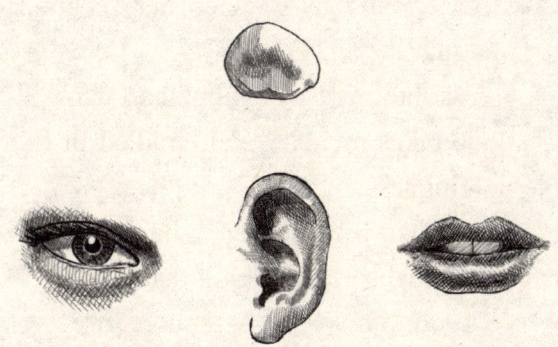

36

BIRCHDAUGHTER

I wake beneath a cobweb net of sustenance theorems, uncertain if I am alive or dead. What does being dead feel like? Then comes pain – every nerve aching and sore – and I know that I'm still with the living, if only for a little while longer. I groan and sit up, Edie's name on my lips. She promised to be here when I woke, and her absence is a knife to my heart.

"Edie?" I whisper again, voice a bare croak in my throat.

A body lies beside me. Kavita Jha is covered in flowers: marigolds strung on strings, fresh roses and sweet-smelling jasmine arranged around her head like a crown. I have been resting beside her corpse. The shock of that is strange. I am used to ghosts, but the body without life is entirely different, perhaps because I know her soul is no longer present. I wonder why Kavita didn't stay earthbound as a ghost.

Perhaps she was tired. I can understand that.

"I wish I'd had the chance to know you better," I whisper, bowing my head as a sign of respect. She died because of my mistakes. I'm not blind to the fact that I made the shade that killed her, and I will have to carry that knowledge into whatever awaits me.

I must find Edie.

The air in the small room smells strange, not rotten or oversweet like death, but complex in a way my senses don't recognize. Onions cooking, cookfire smoke, earth, old stone, wet wool, skin, lye soap, straw strewn with dried herbs. It feels as if it's the air of another century, just like it did in Sarah's necromic cycle, but I don't feel like I'm in danger here.

The walls are stone and brick and there is light from a narrow arrow slit in the curved wall. A tower, then, maybe part of the city walls. I venture down the narrow spiral stairs carefully, entering a room that is the mirror of the space above only this has a fireplace and some basic wooden furniture. There are two arrow slits that send a beam of dull light over the room. It's freezing and the fire is welcome even if the wood smoke makes my lungs tighten.

Tempest and Andreas both look up from their conversation, faces brightening with expectation, but there's sadness and concern there too.

"Welcome back," says Andreas, nodding to the skillet beside the fire. "We saved you some eggs and pancakes. You must be hungry."

As ravenous as I am – and I am starving – I don't care

about anything except the only question that matters. "Where is Edie?" My voice croaks again.

Tempest ladles water into a pewter cup from a little barrel in the corner, offering it to me. I drink deeply, throat soothed by the cool water.

He won't meet my eyes. "You need to ask Meryem."

Panic hits me because that sounds ominous and terrible, like she didn't make it. But, no, that's impossible. Edie and I were wrapped in each other's arms; she was free, unharmed and mine.

"I'm asking *you*." My tone is dark, dangerous. "Tell me where she is."

There is the slightest hesitation before he speaks. "We ... lost her."

The words penetrate slowly – a shard of pain, like being stabbed an inch at a time right through the heart. "L-lost her?" There must be a mistake. "No, that's... She was *free*. I destroyed the soul bottle she was trapped in—"

"We were fighting the shades; Kavita's death shook us and ... we were distracted." Andreas shakes his head sadly. "We think Bea Spicer trapped Edie in a bottle and fled with her cousin while you were unconscious."

WHAT? No!

I'm too exhausted to handle the rage and crushing disappointment. Bea took Edie? My head pulses with pain; my heart aches. It feels like there are ants under my skin that make me want to unfold into something terrible and vengeful. After everything Bea has already put us through, how could she do this to Edie? It doesn't make sense. Ultimately, all Bea really wanted was the chance to leave York and become a movie star.

"You killed her father, Viola," says Tempest softly.

And then it makes sense. Revenge. Always revenge.

A sob wracks me, tearing through my guts and out of my throat. The despair I felt last night crashes down with the weight of ages. This cannot be how it ends. I won't let it. I can't give up. Tempest and Andreas are at my side in a heartbeat, wrapping me in their embrace like we are friends.

To think that I must face today, and the next day, and the next: weeks, months and years without Edie. But, no, I will not live that long. I've burned through my soul by self-syphoning into magic I had no place using. I have very little time left and even if I stay earthbound as a ghost, what can I do to save Edie with no influence over the world? As a ghost, I would have no power in the physical world at all.

I have to leave this place – wherever we are – track Bea and save Edie.

Andreas must see the confusion on my face because he says, "We're at Birchdaughter." He names the desolate, ruined tower on the south side of the old city walls. Situated at the top of a steep bank, it's a squat single-storey semi-abandoned structure that looks nothing like this simple but comfortable space.

"It's not the Birchdaughter you know," says Tempest. "We call this an aperture, a pocket of time and space created using a ghost's memory. Andreas and I made it from the necromic cycle of a ghost who was a guard at this tower several hundred years ago. It's complicated, but all you need to know right now is that we're safe from the reach of occultists or shades."

Trembling, I put the mug on a nearby table. "Where's Meryem?"

Tempest motions to the main door, his schooled expression giving nothing away. "On the battlements. You'll need these." He drapes a heavy woollen jacket over me. It's strangely shaped, a man's jerkin bearing the scars of being reworked as the fashions changed. It smells of smoke and an unfamiliar person. He also hands me thick woollen socks and sturdy boots, and I do need to sit to pull those on.

When I struggle with the boots, Andreas kneels and helps me. "Viola, I know that you were betrayed by the people you trusted most, but you can rely on us. I promise."

He is going to make me cry again if he carries on like this. So I say nothing in return, just leave the tower, forcing exhausted limbs to move until I am squinting in the bright sunshine. The cold hits me at once. I gasp in surprise. Outside, snow blankets York in a deep powder and the day is clear and crisp.

A middle-aged man I don't recognize, attired similarly to myself, gestures to the steps that curve up to the city wall. With a mutter of thanks, I take them carefully, each one a small victory. When I was ten, a friend of Pa's took Theo and I sailing on the river. Walking now feels like being on that little boat in choppy water. I am unbalanced and everything seems to be moving in strange ways. I almost fall but catch myself and reach the flat top of the tower.

Meryem leans on the battlements, looking out across a landscape that doesn't exist any longer. The land beyond the walls feels lower and the banks higher so that the walls themselves feel like a castle. Instead of the urban sprawl outside the city, with omnibuses and rows of Victorian houses, there are open fields dotted with clusters of woodland, smoke rising from farms in the distance. Something about the view feels painted on, like scenery in a play.

What did they call this: an aperture? I have so much still to learn about magic and the spirit world. For a second my heart leaps at the prospect, before I remember the challenges I'm facing and that I will have no opportunity to learn.

Meryem turns as I approach. I didn't think that ghosts could change much, but she looks, not older, but newly burdened.

"I need to find Bea and save Edie before I die," I say by way of greeting, because I don't have time to mess about.

Meryem's lips pinch, the frigid air blowing her silks around her. "Viola, you syphoned from a living soul and murdered with magic. You created a shade. You've broken every single one of our laws."

I swallow, suddenly afraid. Will she seal me here and now? There is very little of my soul left to bind. I'll be dead before I can care and Edie will suffer the consequences.

"I know, and I'm not sorry. I'd kill Mr Spicer again if it meant saving Edie. I love her more than anything in this life and the next. You told me that you work to save souls trapped by occultists. If Bea really does have Edie, then you need to help me save her before it's too late—"

"There's no time."

"But—"

My despair must show on my face because Meryem steps towards me and closes her hands over mine. "You will die today if you remain unmirrored."

I frown, remembering what was said about mirroring, something about the two souls working in symbiosis. "Mirroring can save my life?"

"It stabilizes the soul burn, reversing the damage. I know that you want to join your soul to Edie's, but the seal used in the mirroring process requires a certain amount of phantasmic energy to adhere, and if we wait much longer—"

Hope bursts through me. "What are you saying?"

Meryem closes her hands more tightly over mine. "Mirror with me, today." Her chin trembles and for a moment I glimpse beneath her mask of strength to the core of her grief. "I would never normally re-mirror so soon after losing my symbiotic partner. We prefer to build a bond before any decisions are made; mirroring is for the life of the death-touched, but you don't have the luxury of time."

She's doing this for me, even though I am the reason that Kavita is dead. I don't deserve such kindness or sacrifice on her part. But if I die, I will be abandoning Edie. Bea has her bottled, and I don't know what she intends to do with her.

I bite back tears. This should not matter but it feels like a betrayal of Edie. I promised my life, and afterlife, to her. But without this, I won't even have the chance to save her.

"I lived in Ancient Byzantium, Viola," says Meryem. "I am old and strong. I will make *you* strong again and together we will hunt down the dregs of Spicer's occultist network and find your lost Edie. Surely giving up the chance to mirror with her is worth it to save her, and yourself."

I feel as though I have been flipped over, belly up, the worst parts of me exposed. Edie is all I want. She will always rule my heart. My decisions will be made for her. I do have a choice in this, not much of one, but still, it is a choice. And so I make it.

"It will hurt," Meryem warns, as if that might change my mind. "It will be worse than anything you have ever experienced."

A snowflake catches in her hair. I watch it melt. "Living always does."

Agony I know. Agony I can take.

EPILOGUE

I once rolled the bones for my fate and didn't see death coming.

Today, I roll the bones for the past, chips of painted bone clattering against one another, stirring up secrets and memory. The heat of summer has broken for the early autumn rains. They lash my bedroom window, casting shadows like tears over my bed and the suitcase open on the coverlet. I'm taking very little with me – a few dresses, skirts and blouses, my atomizer, some toiletries, and the well-read copy of *Nightwood*, because it reminds me of time spent with Edie and I can't let it go.

The only other thing I need is the knucklebone set itself. I don't pose a question this time. I've rolled for Edie's fate a thousand times since her disappearance, seeking any clue as to where Bea fled to or where she's keeping the bottle she trapped Edie in. Every time I do, I see Meryem and her heartfelt promise that she will help me. Which means that mirroring with her and joining the Hand is the right path back to the woman I love.

But I am not a patient soul. I want. I crave. I am a desperate, dangerous thing with desire wound around my heart. Leaning over my bed, I close my eyes and think of Edie, pushing my intention into the reading and throw the bones high. Air shifts, magic stirs and the bones strike the coverlet beside my suitcase, rolling into position.

Hive.

Gravestone.

Moth.

The gentle, passive magic washes over me, sending images dancing behind my closed eyelids – Edie in the attic, wrapping quartz stone with enchanted thread. Edie stroking a thumb over the serpent brooch the night I gifted it to her, a gleam of something devilish in her eyes. Edie hunched over her notebook, fingers ink-stained. Edie in the rain, cheeks flushed, lips swollen from kisses. Her cheek under my palm. Her mouth on mine.

Edie's perfume is everywhere, fresh and floral. I can smell her hair, feel its strands on my face and neck, and I breathe her in like an addict. She tastes of strawberries and home. Just before I open my eyes, I remember that summer day on the hill outside the city. Edie in the long grass swatting at the strand I kept sweeping up her bare forearm. A giggle in my throat and on her lips. "Stop that, Vi."

"Me? I'm not doing a thing."

She swats at me again. "You are and you know it."

I flutter my lashes and grin, then tickle her neck with the long grass. She's on me in a second, rolling over, pinning my wrists into the fragrant meadow, her freckled face close enough to feel her breath on my cheek. Something hot and bright sputters to life inside me.

I should have kissed you then.

"You're so much trouble." Her eyes are so bright. "If you keep teasing me, I will push you down this hill."

I laugh. "Not if I push you first."

And then we are rolling, limbs entwined, shrieking with mirth, buttercups and cow parsley pollen in our hair and the quiet drone of bees and the moment is perfect. Perfect and endless and forever.

I cannot go on without you, Edie.

"Viola, I wish you would reconsider."

My eyes snap open, the present crashing down on me as I sit up. Ma stands in the doorway, all a flutter in worn silk and an antique shawl. "Although it is very kind of your employer to offer accommodation, you could easily stay here."

I sigh and collect my knucklebones, storing them carefully in a new silk purse that Theo sent as a late birthday gift last month. "Some independence will do me good and the library will take excellent care of me."

The collection of manuscripts and esoteric items that Mr Spicer left behind is far more extensive than I ever realized. It must be catalogued and safely stored lest budding occultists misuse it. Meryem, Tempest and Andreas have agreed to remain in York long after they would otherwise have moved on, setting up a permanent base here. The affectionately known 'Old Palace' will become our base. A grand building adjacent to the Minster, it is used for the church's archive and local records and houses a necromic cycle that Meryem assures me is the perfect seed for a safe and secure aperture for us to live in. My folks are under the impression that I have secured employment and accommodation at the library to train as an archivist. In reality, I will be working with the Hand, continuing my training and learning about my mirror connection to Meryem.

"You will visit often, won't you?"

"I'm only on the other side of town." I'm surprised to find my throat tight with emotion. "When I'm settled, I'll take you to tea at Betty's."

Ma's smile is thin and I know she's thinking of Henry Saunders and the wedding that will never be. There has been no word of him since that fateful night at Spicer House. I expect he has returned south to his own plans. After all, now that I am mirrored to Meryem, I'm out of his reach, and if he shows his face in York again, Meryem will insist on sealing him.

What surprises me most is that she let Rachel Tussle go for services rendered. That night, Rachel saved Andreas's life and fought on our side, but it doesn't change the fact that as a soul catcher and occultist she is, technically, the enemy. Meryem has made no secret that she doesn't want me to have any contact with Rachel, let alone develop our friendship.

But what she doesn't know won't kill her – again.

Latching my suitcase, I grab my coat, hat and gloves and make for the front door, Ma on my heels. I almost forgot the parcel I left on the sideboard at the top of the stairs, purchased with the last of my savings.

"Will you give that to him when I'm gone?" I ask Ma.

"I'll see he gets it." Her voice is melancholy, as it always is when we talk about Pa.

Before I can leave, the door to the living room creaks open and the man himself stands on the threshold. He seems to have withered since I last caught a glimpse of him a few days ago. His skin is sallow and too thin, showing dark veins in the backs of his hands.

"You off?" he asks.

I nod. "Yes, Pa."

"Well, then…" He clears his throat and falls silent, as if there is little else to say between father and daughter. I look my pa up and down, taking in the bags under his eyes and his unshaven chin and his too-clean fingers when once they were paint-stained and cracking from long hours at the easel. He has not picked up a brush for months.

"Here." Before I can lose my nerve, I shove the brown paper package in his hands.

He accepts the gift with a frown and unwraps it slowly, the string falling away, packaging seconds after and then he's staring down at a fresh sketchbook and new charcoal pencils.

"Oh, lass, I can't…"

"Either you're an artist, or you're not," I say firmly. "What strength of vision could you possibly have if you fold in the face of one setback?"

He shakes his head. "I lost everything."

"*You* lost everything?" I snap. "The girl I love *died*. I lost our family. My best friends. Your affection. I've accepted the blame for a fire that was not my fault while you indulge in pitiful self-pity. Well, it stops today, Pa. You are going to take these charcoals and sketch something, and then take those sketches and put them to canvas and oil paint."

He swallows, glances down at my gift. "But … my best work is gone, it all burned."

Fire. Destructive. Devastating. It scorched through our lives, ravaging and without remorse. Before buying the charcoals, I went back to the site of the studio with Meryem. I think I needed to see it for myself, just once. There is no roof any more. The beams are like a charred animal carcass, a broken ribcage upturned to the skies. The remaining walls are little more than a blackened frame. Nothing survived, not a single canvas.

But in the ruins, I found fresh tufts of green. The intrusion of nature over time offered new life growing in the gaps of what was broken. Standing in our hallway, ready to start my future with the Hand, I finally shrug off the guilt of my past.

"When your world burns, paint with the ashes," I tell my pa simply. Either he will understand, or he will not.

I descend the stairwell and let the front door close behind me with a decisive click. Meryem, Tempest and Andreas slip quietly over from where they have been waiting under a large black umbrella. The magic of my mirror connection to Meryem pulses in my chest.

"We saw the Grey Lady earlier, but she's still managed to escape us." Andreas adjusts his cap against the rain.

"Now that Vi and I are mirrored, Agnes isn't the threat she once was." Meryem's voice is molten gold, but slick as wet leaves and just as cold. "I won't let anything happen to you."

I respond to her promise with a smile. "Let's go home."

A touch of Meryem's hand to my shoulder and the abscondium theorem she prepared unfurls, cloaking me from both the rain and from unwanted attention from the ghosts of York. I link my arm with hers and together we stride side by side up Blossom Street to forge our future.

Home.

I'm not truly home without Edie. I carry her in my soul just as readily as I would if we were joined. She is the fluttering of my pulse and the breath I draw into tired, swollen lungs. She is the fight, the struggle to survive. It all belongs to her. I will find her. And free her. And make this world safe for her, no matter the cost.

It is thanks to Meryem, Tempest and Andreas that I do not have to fight alone. I've lost one family, but I have gained another.

Edie, I love you. I love you.
Wait for me.
I will find you.

ACKNOWLEDGEMENTS

Every story blooms from somewhere different and this one – angry, ungentle and unapologetic – came from the parts of Viola I didn't get to explore in *Twelve Bones*. It always seemed to me that her story of love and loss was an important one to tell, an itch I had to scratch.

A huge thank you to my wonderful editor Polly Lyall Grant and to Lauren Fortune for giving me the opportunity to explore her story. To Wendy Shakespeare, Sarah Dutton, Alice Duggan, Jenny Glencross, my amazing publicist Tina Mories, to Ellen Thomson and Hannah Griffiths, and everyone in the production, sales and rights teams at Scholastic for all your hard work and dedication.

I am lucky to have the best agent in the world, the incredible Maddy Belton at the Madeline Milburn Agency. You have my undying gratitude for putting up with my chaos, random ideas, constant unhinged ramblings and looking after my mental health when I am clearly incapable of doing so myself. Every author should be blessed with a Maddy!

My thanks, appreciation and love to the coven; Kat Delacorte, Ella McLeod and Faith Young. There is no one else I'd rather sacrifice boys with under a blood moon.

To Elisabeth, you talented and phenomenal human! Yes, I know that you hate compliments, but I must tell you how you're truly one of the most impressive people I have ever met and a brilliant writer. I am so proud and grateful to be your friend.

To Lydia, Alison, Pippa, Lisa and Aaron: thanks for body doubling with me and getting me through the editing trenches. You are wonderful!

To all my friends and colleagues at Waterstones, I literally don't know where I'd be without your unending support. Thank you for letting me be part of the magic. To Kurde, the best bookshop manager in the world. I am incredibly proud to be one of your booksellers. To Katie, who bakes the best cake in the world and lets me eat it. The cinnamon deliciousness literally saved my life in the final editing stages of this book!

A special thank you to the staff at Gail's cafe in my home town for dealing with my deadline stress and general chaos and letting me camp in the corner and sob quietly into my laptop with no judgement. You have become friends and I appreciate you all.

My darling Palomi. You never fail to amaze and inspire me. Your friendship is a highlight of my life and I am incredibly grateful for you. Thank you for your support while I wrote this dark and emotional book and for always believing in me.

To Mum and Dad, Helly and Kitty, Richard and Fiona and all my wonderful family, thank you for being my people!

My Ed, thank you for letting me build writing nests made of blankets and pillows, and leave half-drunk cups of tea around our house. I love our little life together. I'm having a wonderful time. I promise I'll dedicate a book to you one day, just not the one about angry, vindictive lesbians.

And lastly, always, to my readers. To everyone who has picked up this book, or any other of my stories, thank you for going on this journey with me and for putting your trust in me as a writer. Everything I write is for you.

Also by Rosie Talbot

SIXTEEN SOULS

Delight in more spooky, swoony YA.
Set in a city filled with spirits and secrets.

"Deliciously dark"
Cynthia Murphy, author of *Signed Sealed Dead*

"Outstanding"
Bex Hogan, author of *Black Heat*

"Delivers fun and frights in equal measure.
A fantastically spooky, thrilling adventure!"
Kat Ellis, author of *Harrow Lake*

TWELVE BONES

The thing about death is … it sneaks up on you.

"Stunning"
Patrice Lawrence

"Spooky and queer, what more do you need?"
Waterstones bookseller

"If you like modern gothic fiction, but also like LGBT+ inclusive books, then this is definitely the book for you"
Ivan, review on *Books Up North* website

PHANTOM HEARTS

A Good Girl's Guide to Murder meets *Heartstopper* with a supernatural murder mystery twist.

"Gripping, gorgeous ... and ghostly"
Ella McNicoll

"*Scooby Doo* meets *Heartstopper* in this stylishly illustrated queer mystery that will keep you guessing with every twist and turn"
The Scotsman

"Be gay, befriend ghosts, fight crime – Rosie Talbot and Sarah Maxwell's *Phantom Hearts* is an engaging, emotional adventure with a twisty mystery at its core. A must-read for fans of queer paranormal fiction."
Jules Arbeaux, author of *Lord of the Empty Isles*

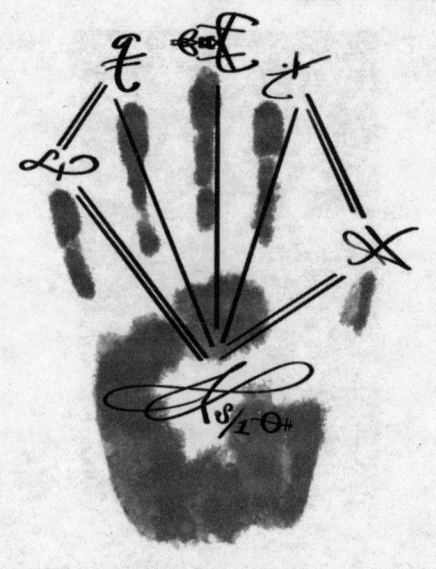